The Many Adventures of

AquaCraft

Spring

Ethan Evans-Ngo

Beaumont, CA 92223
AquaCraft76139@gmail.com

ISBN 979-8-9872785-0-5
Printed in the United States of America

Special Thanks To

Donna Evans, my editor,
and the
AquaCrafters, who gave me the inspiration…

Table Of Contents

Part 1: A Land of Mystery

Part 2: The Eclipse

Part 3: Civil War

Part 1
A Land of Mystery

Prologue

Deep within the world of Minecraft, inside a world of blocks, building, and creativity, is a realm known as AquaCraft. It was named for its vast amount of water, rivers, and oceans. This realm, AquaCraft, is found at the farthest reaches of the known Minecraft world. Few have ever ventured or visited or explored this land in the infinite world of Minecraft. But here, in the land of AquaCraft, begins this saga, a story of the first to live in AquaCraft. And it all starts with Orion...

Orion and ArcticCat were walking side by side along a path that led between their houses. The sun was slowly setting, casting shadows on the path from the trees. The lighting was majestic. They sat down on a bench overlooking a valley that led somewhere. They lived in a realm known as Evenglade, a small realm near the edges of the known world. Orion and his friends lived on the far side of a forest close to the border of the realm. They were not that far from Evenglade's closest government center, the center in charge of each of the provinces of Evenglade. Their province was known as Land's End, though Orion didn't know exactly why it was called that. ArcticCat and Orion looked at the lovely scene in front of them but talked for a long time about entirely different things. They were disturbed about government issues that weighed on them. Their government gave little freedom to its people, and this was the way it was for many realms—stringent laws restricting people significantly. By the time Orion and ArcticCat had finished their conversation, it had begun to grow dark.

Getting up from the bench, they parted ways.

"Don't forget our breakfast with Starpig tomorrow," called ArcticCat over his shoulder.

Orion waved in acknowledgement and entered his house.

Breakfast with Starpig was in a nearby restaurant run by a friend of a friend of theirs. Orion got there a few minutes late and slid onto the bench just as ArcticCat was finishing sharing his experience in Skywars.

"And so, I pushed the last enemy off the edge of the island and was victorious! Now, I haven't played Skywars for very long, so I think that was pretty good for a first run!" he said, his face glowing with pride.

Skywars was a mini-game used in many Minecraft server networks closer to the center of the Minecraft world. The servers were giant cities with arenas that were created specifically for mini-games. Skywars just happened to be one of these mini-games in which the aim of the game was to be the last man standing after battles on floating islands high in the sky. When someone died, they just respawned back in the lobby or in a spectating zone.

Starpig looked up as Orion settled on the bench. "We were talking about servers," he explained.

Orion nodded. "You know, it'd be kind of cool to have a realm of your own," he said thoughtfully, his eyes already somewhere else. "A whole new land to conquer and make your own. Wouldn't that be cool?"

"I guess so; but how would you even find your own realm in the first place? The only realms unconquered are in the unknown regions," Starpig said reasonably. "Besides, we don't even know if there is any land out there. Or if there is, maybe it would be a land of extremes. Hostile to everyone." Starpig was always about facts.

"Still, it might be cool, I don't know," ArcticCat sounded hopeful.

Orion was still thinking out loud. "Yeah, but maybe it will be hospitable, and we could all have our own land instead of renting from a government that controls everything. Just imagine! There may be lands just beyond Evenglade. We are close to the border, after all. A whole new land to explore!" He was getting excited.

"Yeah!" ArcticCat was still hopeful.

"If only," Starpig said, raising his eyebrows.

"You'll see. I'm going to do some research and find information about what is beyond. I will find a realm," Orion argued.

Later that day Orion headed to the local village library but wasn't able to find anything. He shook his head. Maybe he had to go to the local government center. They might have more books. So later that week he traveled by horseback all the way to the provincial library where he then set to work. He searched in the exploration aisles. He read everything that he could find that had anything to do with the unknown regions. Still nothing. Maybe he should look in the realm maps section. *Yeah, maybe something there*, he thought. He moved on, looking through the rows and rows of books. Eventually, something caught his eye. It was at the far corner of the shelf, at the very bottom corner, dusty and unused. Orion picked it up and shook the dust off. The cover read *The Lands Beyond Evenglade.*

"Wait...this is from the last decade...still, maybe it will tell me something," Orion muttered to himself.

He read for a while; the book told of lands that had recently already been explored and conquered. But then, near the end of the book, in the last section, it had a few realms listed that he hadn't heard of. The page read:

The NetherLands. Extremely hostile, giant volcano at the center of the realm. Fire and lava rivers run everywhere. Land mainly of netherrack and obsidian. Very few animals live on it. Only the toughest and fiercest. Thought to be a piece of Nether that came into the overworld. Luckily the realm isn't very large so that it hasn't caused a Nether Invasion yet.

Orion flipped through to the last page.

AquaCraft. Very few have ventured this far. Past the NetherLands Island is a Land of unknown size, and shape. Animals and Monsters unidentified. Hospitality or hostility unknown. Stats unknown. All that is known is that it is unexplored and extremely remote from all other realms.

"Huh, that last one wasn't very helpful," Orion said to himself. He walked over to the librarian and cleared his throat. "Excuse me," he said. "Do you know anything about this realm, AquaCraft? It says here that it is unexplored."

The librarian looked up at him and raised her eyebrows. "I have no clue what or where AquaCraft is. You better ask the mapping expert. Not me." The librarian pointed Orion to the mapping expert's office.

Orion walked patiently over to the office and repeated his question, except this time to the realms expert.

The expert sighed and was silent for a while before speaking. "AquaCraft...AquaCraft, I have heard of that realm somewhere before. Very few people have even heard that name. I'm surprised you found a book that mentioned it. Come over here to the map. As you can see here, Evenglade is on the eastern part of the Minecraft world. Past Evenglade's Land's End province is a giant ocean. Somewhere in the ocean is the NetherLands, which is a Nether outbreak. One or two explorers went past the NetherLands to the land they named AquaCraft, which is in the unknown regions, as you can see here."

The expert pointed to the edge of the map which said unknown regions. "We really don't know what is over there because it has never been mapped. AquaCraft is land, according to these explorers. Again, they may be wrong—there is no way to prove it either way. Anyway, AquaCraft is a land that is said to have beautiful fields and hills and forests with endless rivers flowing through it. But these are just rumors. I may know someone who may be able to tell you more. Sorry I haven't been able to be of more help. but this person will know more. He lives in a village near the giant ocean."

Orion thanked the expert for his time and left the building. Slowly he made his way back home, lost in thought. Now he would have to make another trip, an even longer one.

His new journey took him all the way to the ocean on the edge of Evenglade, and it took him a few days. Eventually, he found the cabin with the retired explorer.

"AquaCraft...now I haven't heard that name in a long time," said the old explorer. "Yes, I have seen it. There was even a local there, though not human. I don't know what they were, but they were human form. I don't know. Anyway, they told us about the endless rivers that eventually came to a deep ocean at the center of AquaCraft. It said that it lived in a jungle forest full of people like it, and that the forest was right next to this ocean, which they called the heart of AquaCraft."

"Incredible. Is it possible to journey to AquaCraft?" Orion asked.

"Yes, though it is a difficult journey." The explorer responded.

Orion said quietly, "Thank you." He thought hard all the way home. Then he made up his mind. AquaCraft, here I come, he thought.

Orion spent the next month or so purchasing materials to make a boat. Then he built it. He crafted it well so that he could sail the long way to AquaCraft, and so that he could sail it alone. If this journey was successful, then he and his friends could be exploring AquaCraft in a few months. But first he would have to try alone. A few days after he finished his boat, he set out.

The journey was tedious and dangerous. Orion almost died many times. There was the time when his boat started sinking, and the time the Nether Monsters attacked him in the Nether outbreak. There was no way to respawn if he died because he wasn't in a specific realm. In order to respawn one must have established and used a respawning center, usually in government buildings. But there was no government in a land that was unexplored and unestablished. So no respawning center. This is why so few people tried to conquer or establish new realms, because of the danger of dying permanently. Orion knew there were dangers before he left. But he didn't expect the journey to be that hard.

Eventually he came to a land full of rivers and trees, grass, and overall, an amazingly hospitable place. And there was so much water here—a rich, endless land that stretched as far as he could see! He steered his boat toward the shore, and stepping out into the shallow water, he stood on the sand by the beach and marveled. He had made it! Orion had finally arrived in AquaCraft after the very, very long journey that had almost cost him his life permanently. He was alive! He had made it! Here he would begin to build.

And build he did. He was all alone, and the work consumed him. For days he assembled materials, chopped down trees, dug up rocks. Then he began to create. But finally, it was finished, done, completed. After weeks of work, the build was finally a reality. Welcome...to The Theater, he whispered to himself as he stood back and looked it over. He was proud of what he had done, and he smiled as he looked upon it. Even then he hoped that this something that had just started as a normal Minecraft project would grow into something bigger, grander. This first build would lay the groundwork for what would become something greater than any Minecrafter alone could achieve. It was the start of the community that would become AquaCraft...

Orion turned from his project and got on a long-distance transmission with a friend.

"Hey Jojo, want to see the new realm I found?" Orion said. "I can give you directions and the indications that chart the way."

"Sure, but is it far?" Jojo was hesitant.

Orion explained briefly.

"I could be there in a few weeks!" Jojo said slowly. "If I start right away..." he sighed.

"Come on! Get yourself started! See you soon! Just make sure you follow the path I charted," instructed Orion as he put down the phone.

Orion had traveled back to Evenglade once to see if he could chart a safer way for his friends to travel through. He had created a clear course, and he thought Jojo would follow it fine. Now he thought about himself and his friend and their differences.

Minecrafters had avatars or "skins," as said in Minecraft terminology. These were mostly square-like because that was how Minecraft was, but the skins were human-shaped forms. Minecrafters have the ability to change these avatars whenever they want, but it doesn't happen very often. Orion currently had a blue skin. He had a red visor on the skin and neon blue on the rest of him. But there were white idents in the skin that made lines all over his avatar. This avatar was known as the Lord of Power. Orion didn't care so much about power, but he liked blue.

Jojo, on the other hand, used a custom-made skin. His avatar had blue hair, a green shirt with a creeper symbol on it, and blue eyes. Since it was custom-made skin, it wasn't named anything, and Jojo liked to be himself—unique, laid back, but hard to stop once he got going.

When Jojo finally arrived, Orion was waiting for him on the beach. He was anxious to show Jojo his new build.

"Observe, the Theater!" Orion exclaimed. "I have been working on it for a long time. Here, let me show you inside!"

"OK, and Orion, you do know that Theater is spelled THEATER, not THEATRE," observed Jojo carelessly as he pointed at the colorful sign above the large, stone theater entrance.

"Oh, I guess I will have to fix that later. Anyway, come on inside!" Orion answered.

The theater entrance was built into a small hill. It was normal-sized, as Minecraft builds go. It was built out of carved stone bricks, with small windows on the front. It was four blocks tall. There were two double iron doors on either side of the middle set of windows. On the far end of both sets of iron doors was another set of windows.

"The middle window here is where you can buy your tickets for a show," Orion explained as they walked through the iron doors. "In here is just the entrance; over there," Orion pointed at the two sets of spruce doors, "that is the entrance inside the lobby and the exit. Once you walk through those doors there is a pressure plate that will trigger redstone that will open the door that takes you inside the lobby. There is another set of doors in the lobby that takes you back here."

"Interesting, where did you learn how to use redstone?" asked Jojo, his eyes drifting across the room.

"Oh well, I have my ways. I mainly just experimented for a while until I figured out how to use them," explained Orion.

"Ah, OK," Jojo nodded. They turned and walked out through the spruce doors.

"Heh, I remember when I first learned redstone was accessible to the public. I can't believe I didn't know that! But either way, I am glad I learned how to get them, because they sure are game changers!" Orion was always into something new.

The two Minecrafters entered the lobby together. It had the same stone architecture, but a much bigger ceiling. Behind them were the spruce doors they had entered, and to their left was another set of doors that would take someone back to the entryway. There were torches on either side of the tall walls, for lanterns weren't added to Minecraft yet. In front of them was a sign that labeled the door at the back of the room and labeled the door on the side of the wall to their right. The sign in the back that labeled that doorway said Minecart Theater, while the other doorway sign said Main Theater. Inside, the lobby was dimly lit so it was hard to see.

Orion gestured with one hand. "Welcome inside the lobby. I will show you the minecart theater another day; today I want to show you the main theater I built."

They went into the main theater and sat down. Orion put on a short film, and they watched in silence. Jojo lay back with his feet stuck out in front of him. Orion sat straight up, his body tight with anticipation. Back in the entryway, Orion turned to Jojo. "Well, what do you think of the theater?"

"It's really cool." Jojo conceded. You've thought of everything!".

"Hey, do you want to do a castle battle?" asked Orion. "We can each build a fort or castle and then battle it out?"

"Sure," replied Jojo, "But you know I will win, right?" He gave a slow grin as he looked over at Orion.

"Not if I can help it!" exclaimed Orion.

Together they moved off to select their building materials and fighting weapons.

. . .

"Well, that was fun, I told you I would beat you." Jojo stated with a grin.

"Hey, if you didn't think to bring potions, then you would have burned in my lava defense," Orion argued, "It's a good thing we set up a respawn center first!"

"Definitely," Jojo replied.

They had set up a makeshift respawn area to use until they could build something more permanent.

Orion hesitated, "You know, Jojo, I always thought of this place as a community place"

"What do you mean?" Jojo asked.

"Well, right now you know it's just you and me, right?"

"Yeah," Jojo turned to look at him.

"Well, I mean that I have sort of thought about making this realm into a community, with the theater at its center." Orion explained, "Anyone could come to the city at any time they wanted to. We could all build things and play mini-games and just have fun. You know, like that server HermitCraft?"

"No, what's HermitCraft?" asked Jojo.

"You haven't heard of HermitCraft?" Orion said surprised, "Oh well, I will show it to you later; it is this community realm some video filmers play on. Anyway, making this realm a community probably never would happen; it's not like I can start a server. I am just a random Minecrafter...anyway, who would even join? We would only have like five people at most."

"Well, you never know, anything can happen," Jojo replied, looking totally unworried as though anything was possible.

"Maybe..." Orion agreed. "Might as well invite everyone over. Anything can happen."

And so, from one small idea, came something so much greater. Orion had yet to see it, but he would soon find out. The idea for the realm of their own became a reality. The settling of AquaCraft became a reality. And the AquaCraft realm would grow into something bigger than Orion had ever imagined.

Chapter 1: The Start of Everything

Friday was the beginning of the season. The season of Spring in the realm of AquaCraft. The spring season would actually become known as the first season of AquaCraft history. On this very Friday, the soon-to-be original AquaCrafters arrived in AquaCraft. To begin with, the original AquaCrafters would only settle on a small portion of AquaCraft, and they had yet to know where its boundaries were. They came together on the edge of the realm, on a part of the land that became known as the Spring territories.

ArcticCat, Starpig, Jojo, Cicer, and Fution arrived first. They met Orion on a tiny floating island near Orion's theater. Small floating islands weren't impossible to be found—-just very rare unless man-made, and Orion had taken over this one. He was sitting underneath a small oak tree when the group had gathered around.

ArcticCat had a blue knight skin for an avatar. Starpig and Cicer both had similar avatars, but with small differences. Both of them changed their skins often, but in this certain circumstance they were using an adventuring pig/human skin. Fution's skin was a mysterious figure, mostly blue and purple.

"Welcome to AquaCraft," Orion exclaimed with excitement once everyone had gathered around. "I know it isn't much, but here we can build amazing things! We can make bases, shops, mini-games, and host events! AquaCraft seems to be very large land, so there is plenty of room for us all. As you can see, I have already built The Theater, which will be the center of this place. This could be our first adventure in AquaCraft! Our first of many! The very start of our time here in AquaCraft... Well, that is if this community idea actually works."

"Cool," Jojo replied, settling himself comfortably on the ground under the tree.

"I'm sure we will have a great time here!" ArcticCat spoke up helpfully. He looked around at the others, "But we'll need to work carefully, keep things safe for all of us."

"What should we do first?" Fution asked.

"How about we start by each of us building a base?" Starpig suggested, "It's what usually happens in HermitCraft.

Orion answered, "Great idea! I think I will start by building a secret base; of course, we'll see if you guys ever find it!" He smiled a challenging smile.

"Hey Starpig, wanna make a house over there?" Cicer asked, pointing behind the theater over to the bottom of a large hill that had a cliff face on it. Cicer wasn't one to be patient.

Starpig looked where Cicer had pointed. "Sure, I will be right over," Starpig replied, then turned to the others and said, "See you guys later!" The two moved off toward the cliff.

"OK, see you later, Starpig, and Cicer!" ArcticCat called after them, surprised that they had left so quickly. ArcticCat turned to Orion. "Hey, do you want me to help with your secret base? We could find a really cool spot, past where you and Jojo built forts that time."

Orion replied, "Sure! We could share it! Definitely some redstone for the entry door. Maybe we could find a cliff like the one Cicer is going to use."

"Hey, Orion, can you show me your theater?" Fution asked.

Orion frowned and hesitated. "Um, Jojo, could you possibly show Fution the theater? I kind of want to go find a cool place for my base with ArcticCat." Orion was anxious to start his own base, but he tried to be polite.

"Yeah, I can do that." Jojo responded casually, still sitting under the oak tree and in no hurry at all.

"Thanks then, JoJo. I will see you guys later! Have fun!" Orion motioned to ArcticCat, and they went off together.

Later that day, Orion and ArcticCat were walking side by side past Jojo's castle fort. They were looking around at the hills, trying to find a good place for a secret base. It was growing dark, so they needed to find a place for the base before night when the monsters came out.

"Over there is where Jojo started building his fort, but he ran out of time to finish, so he really has only just built a wall," Orion was explaining to ArcticCat about Orion's and Jojo's awesome 1v1 building and fighting competition.

"Nice, so who won the fight?" ArcticCat asked, sounding interested.

"Oh well, we don't talk about that." Orion responded sheepishly.

"Ah ha! So Jojo won." ArcticCat laughed.

"How did you know?" Orion asked, surprised.

"Come on Orion, we know each other too well not to know when one of us is not telling the full truth," answered ArcticCat.

"Well, it wasn't exactly lying, but anyway yes, Jojo won," explained Orion. "But technically, if he didn't use brewing, he wouldn't have respawned after going through my lava defense."

"OK then," ArcticCat said as he looked over at the surrounding hillside. "Hey, how about over there for the base?"

Orion looked, then shook his head. "No, I want more of a steep mountain, not a sloping hill."

"If you say so," ArcticCat said.

The sun had started to set as they walked past the fort and onwards through the land. To their left were sharp mountains with steep cliffs, while on their right were gentle rolling hills. Time flew by as they walked through the beautiful landscape, admiring nature and the peace in the moment. They hiked through a small grove emerging on the other side, neither one of them speaking, as if afraid to break the silence. They looked around at the area they had entered. Orion slowed down for a second, peering at a part of a tree. He turned around to see ArcticCat looking up at the sunset sky.

"WATCH OUT!" Orion shouted, pulling ArcticCat back just in the nick of time.

ArcticCat responded, "Oh wow! A huge ravine! Thanks, I almost..."

Just then a skeleton fired an arrow from its bow from a few blocks away and hit ArcticCat in the back, not hard enough to badly harm him, but just enough to make him lose his balance, which then caused him to fall over the edge of the ravine.

"ARCTICCAT!" Orion shouted in shock. He turned around just in time for a zombie to smack him in the face. Orion saw everything grow dark as he went unconscious. Then he, too, fell into the dark abyss of the ravine.

Chapter 2: The Ravine

"Orion! Orion! Are you OK? Orion, wake up!" A voice echoed urgently in Orion's head.

"Wha? Where am I?" Orion responded sleepily.

"OK, good, you didn't have to respawn. I know how painful it can be if you have to respawn when you die," said ArcticCat, feeling relieved.

"What happened?" Orion asked, his mind starting to clear.

"Well, after those monsters knocked us off, I was unconscious for only a minute or so, as were you, but we were lucky. If we hadn't hit this ledge, we would have fallen all the way down there." ArcticCat pointed down into the dark below.

Orion looked around and up. The sky was growing darker and darker.

"We shouldn't be out at night because all the monsters are out right now, but it can't be helped now. We should probably get out of this ravine, make camp, and call it a night," Orion suggested.

"It's one thing to say we are going to leave this ravine; it is another to actually do it. You realize that we have no blocks to bridge up—we didn't bring anything with us on our exploration," ArcticCat pointed out.

"Hey, wait a minute; how come it became dark so early? We left early this morning; it can't have been more than a few hours since we left the others." Orion's mind was racing. How was it possible that this could happen? Time couldn't just speed up. Or could it?

"You're right! There are only a few things that can speed up time. But I wouldn't think that this place could have one." ArcticCat paused, then slowly turned to look at Orion. "Orion..."

Orion responded quickly, "Yes, I know what you're thinking; we'd better look around. That thing doesn't just turn itself on. There must be someone else who turned it on."

"Man, I wish we had brought some tools with us, or something, at least something!" ArcticCat complained angrily.

But Orion had already started walking away from ArcticCat. He walked over toward the edge of the ravine. Maybe he wanted to climb out of the ravine where it wasn't as high to climb. But either way, whatever he was thinking didn't matter, because right then and there Orion spotted some cobblestone.

"ArcticCat, come over here and look at this," said Orion quietly.

"Cobblestone! Wait, cobblestone doesn't naturally spawn, it has to be placed by a person." ArcticCat looked worried.

"Keep your voice down! If there is another person nearby, we don't know if they are friendly or not. Either way, maybe they had something to do with the time thing, you know..." Orion snapped.

"But they're so rare; why would this person have one?" ArcticCat asked.

"I don't know; come on we need to check this out!" Orion replied.

They headed across the cobblestone bridge that crossed from one side of the ravine to the other. This part of the ravine couldn't be longer than 20 or 30 blocks, so it wasn't that far across. A few torches lit the way across the cobblestone bridge where it came to a path on the other side of the ravine. It was a little past dusk now, so the ravine was dimly lit. They could see to the one end of the ravine, where earlier Orion had been heading to escape the ravine. But they couldn't see toward the other end where the ravine widened. There were indents in the rock where ore had been mined out. Underneath the bridge was almost pitch black, so they could only see that it went 70 blocks down but couldn't see what was down there. They eventually came across a cave entrance to their right.

"A cave! This may be where the person is staying," ArcticCat whispered.

"Indeed. I will check out the cave; how about you stay here at the entrance to let me know if someone comes," Orion suggested.

Orion followed the row of torches that went deeper into the cave. It wound back and forth for a little while until the cave came to a dead end. This dead end seemed like a safe place for someone to sleep and stay while monsters roamed outside. The room was silent, except for the torches burning. Torches wouldn't be on unless someone was still staying here. And sure enough, Orion found a chest on one side and a furnace on the other. At the back of the cave was a small bed. He had just passed by a doorway that would stop any monsters from entering the room unless they broke down the door. Orion went over to the chest and opened it.

"I don't believe it! ArcticCat!" Orion exclaimed as he ran back to where ArcticCat was guarding at the entrance of the cave.

ArcticCat joined him in the cave, and Orion showed him what was inside the chest.

"No way!" ArcticCat exclaimed. Only seconds later they heard a sound coming from the cave entrance.

A tense silence hung over Orion and ArcticCat. Then a sigh of relief came from both of them. It was only the wind blowing, but it just echoed around because of the edges of the small cave.

Then they stared back into the chest. Inside the chest was a clock, but it was not an ordinary clock. From the weird glare of light that came from it, both Orion and ArcticCat knew that it was enchanted.

"Wait, I thought only command blocks could enchant a clock to create a TimeClock?" ArcticCat asked as he looked over at Orion, puzzled.

"That means that there must be a Command Block somewhere in AquaCraft," Orion replied.

They both knew Command Blocks were very, very rare—there were only 64 Command Blocks in existence. But usually only very powerful Minecrafters or the creators of Minecraft themselves had one. For one to be in AquaCraft, and to add to that, that it might belong to the person who owned the TimeClock in the chest meant they were dealing with someone very dangerous and powerful, or that this person knew where to find a stray Command Block, owned by no person. But they had no time to ponder their thoughts; at that very moment footsteps approached the cave entrance.

"Someone's coming! Quick! Grab one of these swords," Orion exclaimed pointing at the two swords that were lying in the chest next to the timeclock.

Both Orion and ArcticCat drew swords to be ready to defend themselves against this possible threat. The figure came slowly walking towards them, holding a torch in their hand.

"Who goes there?" It was a firm, female voice.

"We know who you are, TimeKeeper; you have a timeclock," ArcticCat stated bravely and very politely.

"TimeKeeper? Are you confusing me with someone else?" laughed the figure standing there.

As the figure came into the light, they saw that it was wearing a purple cloak on its avatar.

"What are you doing in AquaCraft?" asked Orion quietly.

"Is that what this place is called? Well, I am just visiting here; I mean you no harm, but what are you doing in my cave? asked the figure.

"Your cave? If you're traveling, then you aren't originally from here, right? Besides, this is our land; we are the first people to arrive at AquaCraft. Or are we mistaken?" Orion returned.

"Oh well, I only just got here a few hours ago, so if you're the first ones to claim this land, AquaCraft, then yes you are the Original AquaCrafters," answered the stranger cheerfully.

"Who are you and what do you want?" ArcticCat spoke firmly, but cautiously.

"No need to sound so agitated! My name is PurpleTimeRift, and that timeclock was a gift from the Order of the Time Rifters. I did them a big favor, and they gave me the enchanted clock so that if anything bad happened, I would be able to undo it just in time," the stranger answered.

"Were you the one that made the day pass so quickly?" Orion asked.

PurpleTimeRift shrugged and gave a half smile. "Oh, well my

timeclock has been a little iffy lately; here I can fix it if you hand me the clock."

Orin and ArcticCat hesitated.

PurpleTimeRift sighed, "Oh come on. I mean you no harm. If I wanted to harm you, I would have already attacked you."

Reluctantly Orion went over and handed PurpleTimeRift the TimeClock.

"Just need to turn the dial over here and reset it here..." PurpleTimeRift shifted the dial and made a few adjustments to the clock. "There, next time you go outside things should be back to normal. Anyway, I'd better be going, I only meant to stay an hour, but I got distracted by the abundant resources."

"Do you want to join us AquaCrafters?" Orion asked politely.

"Orion should you be..." ArcticCat started.

PurpleTimeRift interrupted. "No, it's alright; I have places to go outside of AquaCraft...Now, I am just curious, but what are your plans for AquaCraft?"

Orion went on to explain what they had in mind for AquaCraft and how they got to the ravine.

"AquaCraft is supposed to be a realm like no other. One that actually values its people and gives them freedom to build, craft, mine, and explore without restrictions. A community where the community makes the decisions, not oppressive leaders," Orion explained.

"Well I can tell people about you guys and what you are doing if you'd like, you know, spread the word?" PurpleTimeRift offered.

"Yes, I would appreciate that!" answered Orion.

They parted ways, and PurpleTimeRift packed up her stuff. As she was leaving, she said, "You can go ahead and keep some of my supplies because I cannot take all of it on my travels; it should help you get out of the ravine."

"Thanks a lot, PurpleTimeRift! I hope we meet again someday," Orion said gratefully.

ArcticCat dipped his head and PurpleTimeRift gave him a half wave as she went out the door.

They exited the ravine only to find that it was the middle of the day once more. Time had been reset. Orion and ArcticCat headed back on the way back to meet with the others...

Chapter 3: Base Builds

It was evening by the time they arrived back at The Theater, truly evening, unlike the time rift earlier that day. Jojo, Starpig, Fution, and Cicer were gathered around a campfire. They were sitting on some logs when Orion and ArcticCat came to join the group of original AquaCrafters.

"Yeah, so we were able to complete the main frame of the base. Still need some more materials to actually start building the entire house/cliff." Seeing Orion and ArcticCat were back, Cicer was explaining what they had been doing that day

"Hey! You're back! We were just telling Jojo and Fution how Cicer's base is going!" Starpig said enthusiastically.

"Yeah, we had quite the adventure," ArcticCat responded somewhat ruefully. "Isn't that right, Orion?"

Orion nodded. "Indeed, we'll tell you about it soon. But first let's hear what you guys have been doing today."

"Well, after I showed Fution your Theater, I went off exploring. I hoped to find a village. The villagers usually have good trades, and I wanted to get some pretty awesome items!" Jojo said to Orion.

"And I was mining for diamonds. See here?" Fution showed the group the chest he had next to him. Inside it were six shining blue diamonds. "Do you think I should use them for armor or tools?" he asked the AquaCrafters.

"Up to you," Starpig answered. "But that's a great find. You can do so many things with them." He sounded a bit envious. He turned to Orion. "Well, what did you and ArcticCat do today?"

And so ArcticCat and Orion took turns explaining the crazy events of the ravine, including the TimeClock and the meeting with PurpleTimeRift.

"Wow! I wish I could meet this PurpleTimeRift person. She sounds like an interesting Minecrafter," Fution commented.

"Hey, can you show me this ravine? I think it could be a cool place to make a base. Well, as long as we monster-proof it, that is," Jojo added.

"Sure," Orion said to Jojo before turning to Fution. "I don't know where PurpleTimeRift is; as I already said, we split up, and she said she was only staying in AquaCraft for a short time."

"Well, that's too bad." Fution returned.

"Oh, Orion, ArcticCat, make sure you stop by the mine tomorrow morning. Next time you should be properly equipped with armor and tools so no monsters should give you any trouble. Fution found diamonds there, so who knows? You might get lucky!" Starpig recommended wisely.

"OK then," Orion said, "That settles it. Tomorrow we will go mining and then show Jojo the ravine."

The next morning Orion found enough iron for almost a full set of iron armor. He also found two diamonds—enough to craft a diamond sword. He even found some redstone, which could be used for the secret base entrance Orion wanted to build. ArcticCat wasn't available in AquaCraft that day, so Orion and Jojo went by themselves towards the ravine.

"Wow! I can see why you almost fell in," Jojo commented to Orion, his eyes wide.

They were standing near the place where ArcticCat and Orion had fallen in. The ravine was almost invisible from their approach; you wouldn't see it until you stood right above it. It could easily take someone who wasn't paying attention. But this time Orion was prepared, and so was Jojo. They made sure to watch for monsters before using ladders to slowly traverse the ravine downwards.

"This could work. This could really work! I could have a house at the top of the ravine and another floor below it that hung into it. I can use stone supports there and there. And I could have a special mining exit there, to access the ores at the bottom of the ravine." Jojo was explaining and pointing out different ideas for his base.

"Yeah, you could even make a business out of this. Whenever

someone wanted to mine in the ravine, you could charge a fee from the amount that they had mined," suggested Orion, "Anyway, while you get started with that, I am going to find a place for my base. There are some really cool mountain-like hills not far from here."

"Ok, good luck! Make sure you don't let a zombie knock you out again," Jojo joked, laughing.

"Hey, this time I am properly prepared. Anyway...see you!" Orion replied, also laughing.

Orion left the ravine and headed north from the ravine to the mountain-like hills. They weren't quite as big as a mountain, but not as flat as a hill—just more rocky.

I wish ArcticCat was here; he could have helped find a good place for something secretive, Orion thought. Oh well, this way I can surprise him! He will be so surprised when the side of the cliff just opens up in front to reveal a door.

Orion had always been the better one at redstone. Redstone could be used like circuitry, connecting a button to say a piston that could push or pull blocks out of the way. That was what Orion wanted to build. A stone button would blend in with a stone cliffside and pushing it could activate pistons that could move a part of the cliff out of the way and reveal a secret entrance. Now Orion just had to find a good cliff to use. This is why he wanted mountain-hills, not flat hills for a base.

Just then Orion reached the base of one of these mountain-hills. It was not that far from the ravine. The mountain-like hills were around 50-70 blocks tall. At the base of it were a few oak trees. The hill went up gently at first before going up at a vertical angle, creating a steep cliff. The cliff was made of generic stone. Just what Orion needed.

"Why, this is perfect!" Orion muttered to himself. I could put a stone button on the right side of the cliff, close enough from where I would build the door in the middle of the cliff, but far enough not to arouse suspicion, Orion thought. All I have to do is dig into the cliff and hollow out a decent amount of the hill, and I will have enough space for a secret starter base!

And so Orion got to work; he dug out a space for some pistons and redstone for the entrance. He hollowed out the hill yet left enough support so that the ceiling wouldn't collapse. He used torches to see what he was doing and placed signs to label what section was to be what. After he did that, he built the secret door. He placed six pistons, two to pull back the part of the cliff wall, and four other pistons to retract the two pistons and the rock they pulled out of the way to form a walkway. He connected the redstone to the button he had placed and connected it to the pistons.

Time to give it a test. Orion thought. Just push the button and click! The cliff face went inside itself as the sound of pistons working could be heard. Then silence.

Well, it pulled itself back. But the other four pistons didn't move the two pistons and rock out of the way. Orion was thinking quickly...If I move this here, and add some redstone there...

He pushed the button again and it worked! A flat cliff face became a walkway into the secret base. The only problem was that he had to add redstone on some parts of the walkway. But doing so made it look weird. Redstone was to be hidden away, functional and not used as decoration.

"Well, at least it works. Functionality is better than looks. I guess I can live with redstone on the walkway," Orion muttered to himself, then sighed, "Oh well, better than nothing."

Orion added another button on the inside to open and close it there too. He would add some iron blocks later as extra security in case any intruders found the base. Orion would have to wait to go mining again to get some iron, though.

He also wanted to decorate the interior with quartz, but quartz in Minecraft could only be found in the Nether, another dimension outside the overworld. Some said the Nether was underneath the Overworld, near the center of the Earth. Others thought that was foolish; it was just another dimension somewhere unknown. Those who thought the Nether was beneath the overworld also thought the mysterious dimension, The End, was above the overworld, near space. But then, The End could also just be a myth, about endermen serving their master, the great Ender Dragon. Orion knew endermen were real because he had seen and heard about them, and he also believed the Ender Dragon existed, just so high up in the sky that you had to use a portal to reach The End. But he doubted that the endermen served the Ender Dragon. The reason he believed in the Ender Dragon was because he knew people who said they had fought it.

Anyway, he was getting off topic, he thought to himself. He would have to just get quartz another day. Just finish what he could and remember the coordinates on the map for where he was so he could return to the base.

Orion finished what he could before heading back to see what the others were doing.

. . .

It was the middle of the afternoon when Orion arrived at Cicer's house, near the Theater.

"Starpig! Cicer! How is your base building going?" Orion yelled.

"Come see!" Cicer yelled back, not turning to look at Orion. Cicer wasn't much into conversation.

Orion jogged over to them. The house looked nearly finished. There was a beautiful path going from the house (that looked like it was inside the hill) to halfway towards The Theater. Orion hiked up the path; it went up the hill and looped to the left and arrived at the house. There were two cliff faces on either side of the house that seemed wedged between them. Starpig and Cicer had done a great job decorating, adding plants and details to the wooden, mountain-like house. Orion went inside the house through the oak door and into what looked from the outside like a relatively small house, but actually it was bigger on the inside. Starpig and Cicer had probably inserted the house into the cliff face, into the hill, which gave the interior more space. Or at least that is what Orion thought.

"Wow! this is quite the place you have here!" Orion commented in awe, "You sure have made it look nice in the little time you have been building it!"

"Yeah, we will add some carpet on the wood floor to make it a little more homey," Starpig explained.

"We are also thinking of connecting our bases!" Cicer added enthusiastically, turning around to look at Orion.

"Wait, have you already built your base?" Orion asked.

"No, not yet. Well kind of. You see, I am planning on making three bases. A starter house that would connect to Cicer's, A large luxurious quartz base. And finally, I have already built a sky base, though it is a little hard to get to," Starpig explained.

"Well, if you had those ender elytra wings, you could easily fly up into your base," Orion suggested. "Speaking of sky bases, now I want to make a sky base, too!"

"You're right! If we get elytra, we could easily get to the sky bases! But they are only found inside an End City. And even then, only in the floating ships! (Gravity is less strong there) But we would have to defeat the Ender Dragon if we wanted to go into the outer floating End Islands," Starpig reasoned.

"Well, I have already been to the End once, but the Ender Dragon in that realm was already slain. And all the End cities were already looted," Orion complained.

"Well, I mean this realm's End probably hasn't been attacked or looted yet..." Starpig returned.

"Are you thinking what I think you're thinking? Orion questioned.

"Yes, I think we should go give The End a visit," Starpig answered.

"What's this about going to The End?" Cicer asked.

"I am going to gather everyone. ArcticCat and Fution should be online soon. I think it is time we had a meeting about going to The End."

Orion forced himself to be calm, but inside he was already boiling with plans and ideas.

And that is how Orion and his friends started their journey to The End dimension.

Chapter 4: A Long Journey

..."And so if we can defeat the Ender Dragon, we could access the outer End Islands. In one of the cities, we are bound to find elytra. As long as we are properly equipped, then together we should be able to defeat the dragon and fetch the elytra wings." Orion was explaining his plan to all of the original AquaCrafters, who had gathered together to hear about his plan.

"Just one problem, how exactly are we supposed to get properly equipped? If we want to get to The End before anyone else does, we have to have an easy way to get resources. Not only that, but we also need to go to the Nether to get Ender Eyes to open the portal," ArcticCat reasoned.

"Well, I mean...there are loads of resources in the ravine. I have already gotten the main part of my base done, so we can all gather all the resources we need for the journey without having to worry about monsters. It is mostly mob proofed," Jojo suggested. He lay comfortably on the ground while the others sat around in a circle.

"That could work. While four of us can go gather resources, the others can go hunt endermen to get ender pearls. You know, to make Ender Eyes." Orion looked thoughtful. "As for blaze rods—which we also need—we can get those from the Nether on the way to the stronghold."

"Hey, can we possibly stop by the library in the stronghold? I heard it has loads of books. Maybe it even has some enchantments. It wouldn't be out of the way, since the portal is in the stronghold," Starpig asked excitedly.

"Well, now I think that is settled," said ArcticCat ending the discussion, "Unless there is anything else you want to add, Fution and Cicer?"

Fution said no, and Cicer shook his head. So, the group split up to get ready for the journey. Cicer and Fution hunted down some endermen while Orion, ArcticCat, Jojo, and Starpig went mining in the ravine, which was much safer now that it was monster proofed. In order to monster proof a place, you must keep it well lit. Monsters can only spawn in low light conditions.

Once everyone had gotten all the resources needed as well as the ender pearls, they set out for the Nether. They were fully equipped with iron armor and tools, with some diamond gear scattered around as well. They also made sure to get a bow and arrows to take out the End Crystals, which will be mentioned later. Since Jojo was the best at combat, he was given the diamond sword. And since it was Orion's idea for this expedition, he was put in charge of the expedition. ArcticCat and Fution were given the bow and arrows, since they had the best aim. Starpig and Cicer would be in charge of mapping and charting the expedition so that they could return home when they succeeded or failed.

Needing obsidian to make a portal to enter the nether, they went into a deep cave at the bottom of the ravine.

"OK, so who has the flint and steel?" Orion asked. They needed to start a fire to light the portal to the nether.

Cicer stepped out from the back of the group and held up the flint and steel, exclaiming, "It's right here!"

"OK, can someone place some torches on the walls so we can see where we are going?" Orion was directing the action.

"Here, I can do the torch holding and placing," offered ArcticCat, thoughtful as usual.

They were far enough down the cave that no sunlight could reach them. They ventured onwards and downwards, deeper still into the cave. ArcticCat continued placing torches until they reached a dungeon.

"Careful, it's a dungeon. There are usually monster spawners in them. Here, let me go first." Jojo jumped into the dungeon dimly lit by ArcticCat's torches.

"YAH!" Jojo yelled as he swung at the giant spiders.

"It's a spider spawner apparently. Maybe we could make bows and arrows for all of us from the drops." Starpig looked at Orion hopefully.

"WATCH OUT, CREEPER!" Fution shouted in alarm.

Everyone leaped for safety as a hissing sound came from the direction of the creeper. And then BOOM! The creeper, a green human- like figure with four feet and no arms, exploded, making a huge hole in the dungeon. Since Jojo was closest to the creeper, he was knocked all the way to the dungeon wall, landing on it with a thud. Meanwhile, the spiders all died, and even the monster spawner was destroyed. Luckily, the chests on the other side of the dungeon were unharmed. Orion and Fution were also knocked back, but not as far. They landed outside of the dungeon but were lucky not to take much damage. Starpig, Cicer, and ArcticCat were unharmed.

"Jojo! Are you alright?" Orion asked as he got up, looking around. Meanwhile everyone else was recovering from the blast.

"Argh..." A groaning sound came from the direction where Jojo had landed.

Orion ran over to Jojo with the others close behind him. "Are you OK, Jojo?"

Jojo was lying on the ground against the wall. His armor was badly damaged, but otherwise he wasn't too badly hurt.

"I...I think so..." Jojo replied with some effort.

"Here eat this; it should allow you to recover faster." ArcticCat offered Jojo a golden apple of healing.

"No, save it for when we need it. My armor kept me from taking too much damage. I will be fine, was lucky to have it. Otherwise, I would have to respawn." Jojo argued, and slowly got up.

"You're lucky indeed; without your armor you probably wouldn't have escaped unscathed," Orion commented quietly before raising his voice. "Well now, let this be a lesson to us. We need shields!"

"I have some iron," Starpig offered helpfully.

"And I have wood," added Cicer. "I'll craft a crafting table."

"Do we have enough iron for all of us?" Fution asked cautiously.

"I think so, but we may have to use all of it," ArcticCat answered calmly, after a swift calculation.

"Well, it's better than being blown up by a creeper!" Orion said sarcastically.

"Hey, guys, cool. There may be more loot in the dungeon chests," Jojo reminded.

"Oh, I completely forgot about them in the action!" Orion replied. "Well, the good news is the creeper also took out all the spiders with it!"

Orion, Jojo, and ArcticCat went over to the chests while everyone else was crafting shields. They each went over to a separate chest. They were lucky, because dungeons usually only had one to two chests, not three. Orion opened his chest; inside were some rotten flesh, a golden apple, and some cobwebs.

"Ugh, all that is in mine is a golden apple and a bunch of cobwebs," Orion complained with disgust.

"Oh hey! I found some diamonds and iron in mine!" ArcticCat called from the other side of the room.

"And I have chainmail horse armor, as well as an ender pearl! Jojo said triumphantly, "And another ender pearl to add the collection!"

"Well, I guess you guys got luckier than me. ArcticCat, can you use those diamonds and iron to replace Jojo's armor? And well, that was very lucky to get another ender pearl!" Orion said. He looked around at his friends. "Well, we better get going again."

They walked over to the others, who had crafted brand new shields.

"Here you go, Orion, Jojo," spoke Starpig, handing them each a shield. They were well-made shields. Starpig smiled as they took them.

And then they were off again. About an hour later they had come very deep into the cave. ArcticCat, who was leading the procession with the torches, warned, "Watch out!"

"Lava! We could use this to make obsidian. Does anyone have a water bucket?" Orion exclaimed.

Cicer held one up.

"Ok, now be very careful. I will pour the lava, you pour the water. Now be very careful and quick. One wrong move and it could ruin everything. Too slow and the lava or water will go all over the place," Orion explained.

They made slow progress, but after a while they had done it. They had created a portal frame. Cicer lit the portal, and flames turned into purple swirls before becoming the faint image of a portal. Eventually it grew brighter until it lit up the dimly lit room with purple light.

"Well, everyone. Here we go. Make sure you have your weapons ready and your shields up. We are about to enter the Nether," warned Orion. "Is everyone ready?"

Everyone said they were. Slowly, one by one, they entered the portal. As they came to the other side of the portal, the world turned from the dimly lit, cramped cave into a huge vast hot place, bright with red and orange light throughout the environment. They had entered the Nether Wastes. Underneath their boots was netherrack. Behind them was an identical obsidian portal. Above them was netherrack. Behind the portal was netherrack. To their right and left was netherrack. It was an eyesore, dark red netherrack. Very hot to touch. In front of them, the underground dimension opened up into a huge, vast space; at its bottom was lava; from the ceiling was more lava flowing downwards. Not a place you would want to live.

The only creatures that lived in this terrible place were weird monster creatures such as pig-like human tribes, and large hoglins that were like giant orange warthogs. And there were striders who walked on two feet that stood in lava; on these legs was a giant mass of a cube. They had hair coming out like an old man might. Very ugly, yet their young were very cute because they piled up and stood on top of each other. Sometimes they were even as tall as an adult on the bottom, and three smaller versions of it on top. There were also ghasts, who were giant floating cubes with leg-like things coming out of them. Ghasts shot fireballs out of their mouths. Even endermen could be found in the Nether.

Many more monsters, or creatures that are called mobs in Minecraft terminology, existed in the Nether. But the only other one to mention in this story is the blaze—a single floating head or skull of yellow, with fiery blaze rods floating around the skull. Killing one would drop these rods, which are used with ender pearls to craft an ender eye. These eyes are used in an end portal frame to open a portal to the end.

The original AquaCrafters needed to find a Nether fortress. These fortresses were large structures that were built over the lava lakes and oceans. They were made primarily of Netherrack bricks. Huge pillars of this supported bridges that went every which way. Connected to these bridges and inside these bridges were large netherrack brick rooms. Inside these rooms could be loot chests, or monster spawners. One of these spawners could be a blaze spawner. This is what the group was looking for. That is the only place blazes spawn naturally. And so the group left the portal to find a Nether Fortress.

"Hey, make sure you map where this is. We want to come back, you know. Also, maybe block off the portal so no one or no monster can go through it. We don't want them to be in the overworld," ArcticCat suggested, always the careful one.

"Good idea; when you are done with that, we'd better get going. I don't like being in this horrible place any longer than I have to." Orion looked agitated.

"Well, this a good start; we are in the Nether Wastes biome, which is the only biome Nether Fortresses spawn," Fution said thoughtfully, "If we look around, it shouldn't take too long to find one. Just as long as we don't find a Crimson Forest; that place is swarming with piglins and hoglins."

"OK, done; we are ready to go." Starpig put down the map and rolled it up and packed it into his inventory pack.

They went back to the search for a Nether Fortress. They didn't encounter much on their journey to the Nether Fortress. Well, except for netherrack, lava, netherrack, some lava over there, oh and can't forget more netherrack. But that doesn't mean it wasn't a hard journey, It was very hot, and they were all sweating after traveling so far. And as you can probably guess, they did eventually find a Nether Fortress.

"How much...so hot...how much farther?" Cicer panted.

"I don't...I don't know..." ArcticCat panted back, "I am used to much colder environments than…"

"Hey, look, there it is!" Orion interrupted urgently.

"Phew, I don't think I could have made it much farther…" replied Starpig.

Orion grunted a reply. He wondered. *They had come far, but they still had to deal with the dangers of the fortress. Plus, he didn't know how far the stronghold would be from there. It wouldn't be easy, and he knew that. He just hadn't expected they would actually go on this journey. The elytra had better be worth the trouble they are to get,* he thought.

They entered the fortress from one of the many bridges. They had only come a few blocks when EEEEK. Swoosh! A ghast was making its weird high-pitched noises, opening its mouth wide before bwoosh! A giant ball of fire was launched towards them.

"Shields up!" Jojo yelled.

They raised their shields just in time as the fireball landed against Jojo and Starpig's shields. Crash! The shields were on fire and their armor was damaged as they fell onto the bridge floor. ArcticCat and Fution both raised their bows and shot in the direction of the ghast. Twang went their bows. ArcticCat's arrow nearly missed. But Fution's struck the ghast straight into the mouth. The ghast screeched horribly as it fell into the lava below. Jojo and Starpig picked themselves off the bridge floor and checked themselves for serious damage. Starpig shook his head and looked over at Jojo. Jojo grinned, his face dirty and gray. They had survived for now.

"Good job everyone! We showed that ghast who's boss! Now come on! Let's find these blazes before they find us!" Orion encouraged before running on the bridge towards the cube netherrack building ahead.

They were moving quickly now so as not to be seen by any more monsters or be blasted to bits by fire in one way or another. The quicker they were at getting the blaze rods, the better. The Nether isn't a nice place. And very unsafe.

They reached the closest building, only to find an empty basin where lava was usually stored. The next building had some loot chests, but still no blazes. Finally, in the third building, after many twists, turns, and a few wither skeleton encounters, they finally found a blaze spawner.

When they entered, the blazes turned around and just floated there for a second making hollow groaning sounds. Then spurt, flame, swoosh! Dozens of small fire orbs launched by the blazes hurled themselves at the original AquaCrafters. They all lifted their shields automatically; then Jojo and Orion charged at the blazes. They took out a few, but then they caught themselves on fire from the orbs. When they retreated behind the shields, they only stopped the swarm of fire for a second before a shield broke with a SNAP. Then another. They had to end this quickly before using up too much more energy and resources.

"Hey, Starpig, you and I will hold up our shields while ArcticCat and Fution shoot down the monsters with their bows," Orion ordered.

"Copy that," Starpig confirmed.

They came out of the corner that they were hiding behind. Orion and Starpig came out with their shields in front of them, making a wall. Behind them ArcticCat and Fution drew their bows at the ready. Cicer waited with Jojo so that he could recover from their last attack. As the AquaCrafters came out of the corner behind a netherrack brick pillar, blazes lit them up with another swarm of fireballs. They hit the shields with a thang, thwack, and sizzle. ArcticCat and Fution came out from either side of the shield wall, and let go of the arrows, and the arrows went flying towards the blazes. Then they both reloaded and fired again. They repeated the process until most of the blazes had perished. But before they could do anything more, the shield wall broke with a snap, the shields fell to the ground, useless. Jojo and Cicer charged from the back, slicing at the blazes, while ArcticCat and Fution gave them cover fire.

"Argh..." Jojo groaned as a blaze hit him with fire.

"Hot, hot, hot, hot!!!" Cicer yelled for he caught fire from one of the blazes' many fireballs.

Orion ran in to help, drawing his sword. He killed one blaze and Jojo was able to stab the other one. Starpig ran in and lit up the spawner with torches, allowing no more blazes to spawn. The room was emptied of blazes; they had won.

"Phew!" Cicer sighed with relief as the fire died down.

"Sorry about that, Cicer, but water evaporates instantly in the Nether," Orion said apologetically while pointing out the scorch marks on Cicer's armor.

"I'm fine, it's Jojo who got the worst of it," Cicer replied, gesturing towards Jojo.

Jojo coughed. He looked exhausted. His armor had burns all over it. He limped over to the others.

"Do we...cough...do we have enough blaze rods?" Jojo grunted.

"Starpig? Do we have enough?" Orion asked before turning back to Jojo.

"Starpig says we have enough; are you alright?" Orion looked concerned.

"Yeah, just...tired, and well, battered," Jojo responded heavily.

"You'd better take it easy from now on. Now, we'd better get going. Can you walk?" ArcticCat said, coming over to them and looking Jojo over carefully.

"Yes." Jojo sounded sure.

"Good, then let's go. The sooner we are out of this place, the better." Orion turned and walked back to the entrance of the room.

Starpig had gathered all the blaze rods into his and Cicer's inventories, splitting them among them. The original AquaCrafters exited the Nether Fortress, careful not to attract attention from the monsters.

"Should we head back to the portal? Or make a new one?" Fution asked as they exited the fortress.

"We should probably head back to the portal; we don't have enough obsidian to make a new one." Orion responded.

They went back to the portal, only to find it in ruins. A ghast or a person must have destroyed it.

"What do we do now?" Fution asked, his face troubled. He turned around to face the group.

"I'm not sure," Orion responded slowly.

"If this was a Minecrafter's work, then we may have a griefer on our hands," ArcticCat commented.

"I don't think this is a Minecrafter's work; see here? A Minecrafter would have removed all of the obsidian. They would not leave a dismantled portal frame. I'd gather it's a ghasts' doing." Starpig turned to ArcticCat.

"Well, what do we do? I don't want to be stuck in this terrible place much longer!" Cicer said urgently.

"We must stay calm," Orion responded gravely, "We have two choices that I see. One, we try to find obsidian close by to open the portal. Two, we scout for another Nether Portal, hopefully nearby."

"How about we find a place to camp for the night?" Cicer suggested.

"No, it's too hot here to get any sleep," ArcticCat remarked.

"Plus, there is no night or day in the Nether; we cannot sleep in this dimension," Starpig added.

Jojo spoke quietly. "I think we should go with Orion's option two..."

"Right, I don't think there is any obsidian nearby," Fution agreed, "unless someone has seen any?"

Everyone said they hadn't.

"Then it's settled. We go to find another Nether Portal." Orion insisted.

"But we may be traveling for days here trying to find a Nether Portal," Cicer complained, scowling.

"True, but I don't see any other options," Orion reasoned calmly.

And so the group left the ruined portal in search of another one that wasn't ruined, so that they might get to the overworld once more. They traveled on for a few hours. They had passed the Nether Fortress, crossed a lava lake, and finally reached a Warped Forest. In this weird biome, there were tree-like fungi that grew everywhere. There were tree-sized, blueish, greenish-colored tree-like fungi. The netherrack ground was even covered in similar fungi. Vines grew down from the tall tree fungi. This biome was known to have many endermen but was otherwise abandoned. All that could be heard were the eerie sounds that echoed around the forest.

They were plodding along, weary from the heat and the long journey they were on. At least it wasn't as hot as the Nether Wastes biome, in which lava was much more common. Not that lava wasn't common in the forest, but there was just less of it, which made the forest dimmer and creepier, yet also cooler.

"How much farther is it?" Fution asked.

"I don't know," Orion answered.

"I don't like the feel of this place," Cicer whispered, "It's kind of creepy." He looked around himself and fingered his sword.

"Well, at least it is cooler than the Nether Wastes," ArcticCat pointed out.

"Everyone quiet!" Orion whispered hoarsely, "I hear something..."

The group froze. Off in the distance, through rows of trees came the sound of footsteps. Someone was heading their way.

"Weapons at the ready." Orion ordered.

The footsteps grew louder...and then they stopped.

"Hello? Is someone there?" A mysterious voice said.

Jojo drew his sword.

"Hey, that sounds like..." ArcticCat began.

Orion interrupted, "PurpleTimeRift, is that you?"

"Orion? Is ArcticCat with you?" PurpleTimeRift stepped out from behind a tree.

"What are you doing here PurpleTimeRift?" ArcticCat questioned, "I thought you said you were leaving AquaCraft."

"Hey, is this the same person you told us about from your first encounter at the ravine?" Jojo asked, turning to Orion.

"Yes," Orion responded quietly.

"Well, I was leaving AquaCraft, but the truth is that I wanted to join the AquaCrafters, if that is OK," PurpleTimeRift hesitated. "You see, I finished my business at the place I was journeying to, and now that I am finished, I thought I might come and see if I could join you guys."

"Sure, we'd be glad to have you!" Orion replied, and then hesitated. "You don't happen to have a Nether Portal nearby, do you?"

"Yeah, there is one only a dozen blocks back the way I came," PurpleTimeRift seemed confused. "I am using the Nether to traverse to AquaCraft more quickly. Why do you ask?"

And so Orion went on to explain their mission and why they needed a Nether Portal.

"Ah, that makes sense. Well, don't let me keep you waiting; come on, it's this way!" PurpleTimeRift said sympathetically.

The group seemed to gain new strength as they now had a way to escape the Nether's wretched environment.

"Speaking of your journey, you wouldn't mind if I tagged along? I have beaten the Ender Dragon with a group similar size to this one once before. I may be of some assistance," PurpleTimeRift suggested.

"Of course! Is that OK with everyone?" Orion turned to the others.

They all nodded. They seemed to have taken a liking to PurpleTimeRift as soon as she gave them a way to escape the Nether. Besides, she had a quirky kind of energy that lightened their hearts. The AquaCrafters arrived at the Nether Portal, and again, one by one they all eagerly jumped through. From there, they journeyed on as quickly as they could, occasionally camping along the way to get some rest.

Chapter 5: The Ender Dragon

The AquaCrafters were camped near a riverbank. The Nether Portal was a day's trip behind them. Starpig and Cicer had crafted the Ender Pearls and Blaze Rods into Ender Eyes, which would not only open the portal, but also lead them to the stronghold in which the portal was located. It was dawn by now, and the group was well rested and had renewed strength after two nights of rest.

"Well, we are pretty much ready to head out," Jojo reported to Orion.

"Good, we will soon be on our way then," Orion responded enthusiastically. He was in a good mood now that they were getting closer to the stronghold.

Once they were packed, they began to start moving again.

"OK, so go ahead through the Ender Eye; let's see where it leads us now," Orion decided.

ArcticCat threw an Ender Eye, for each of them had one. The eye floated straight ahead before dropping down to the ground. ArcticCat picked it up, and the AquaCrafters trotted along, following the river, for that was the direction the eye headed. Fution threw the next eye; instead of going straight ahead, it veered to the right leading away from the river and across the grassy plain. They were in a savanna biome at that point. They continued the process for about an hour before the eye suddenly stopped.

"Hey, why won't it work?" Starpig asked. The eye refused to float and instead fell down into the grass.

PurpleTimeRift came over; "Here, let me give it a try."

She threw the eye into the air and it fell right into the ground.

"This is good news; if it falls into the ground, that means the stronghold should be right below us!" She explained in triumph.

"It is good news indeed! Well, time to get digging!" ArcticCat responded excitedly.

And so they each got out their shovels and started digging.

"I've hit stone!" Cicer called out, resting on his pickaxe.

"Let me see." Orion came over to where Cicer was digging. "That isn't ordinary stone; that is carved stone. We have hit a structure!"

Orion took out his pickaxe and started hacking at the stone. Eventually it broke, revealing what was below. Underneath him was an open room surrounded by the same carved stone material. It was similar to how the dungeon had looked earlier in their journey, but it was much better lit by torches and much more decorated.

"It's the stronghold!" Fution commented.

Jojo came over to look. "It looks easy enough to jump down; it isn't that far."

"Wait, make sure you..." Orion started, but Jojo was already leaping down the hole.

"Well, I guess we are jumping in!" Starpig grinned at Orion, also jumping down into the hole.

Orion shrugged and joined them in the stronghold. The AquaCrafters ended up all jumping down into the stronghold.

Once everyone was in, Fution asked, "Where to now?"

To that Orion answered, "I don't know."

"How about we split up? One group head that way, and the other group goes the other way," PurpleTimeRift suggested, pointing at the two different hallways that went in opposite directions from where they were standing.

"Well, the stronghold can't be too big. If we find the portal, we will send someone to get the other group," Starpig agreed.

"OK then, ArcticCat, how about you lead a group that way, and I will lead on this way," Orion suggested.

Starpig, Cicer, and PurpleTimeRift went with Orion while Jojo and Fution joined ArcticCat as they headed in the opposite direction.

"Remember, I want to stop by the library, if this stronghold has one,"

Starpig reminded, then added, "Most strongholds have them. They have great enchanting books that could strengthen our tools and armor."

"Well, if we see one, we will stop by." Orion answered evenly.

As they walked and looked around, they passed by stone architecture. Iron bars and iron doors sometimes blocked their way so that they had to change directions. The stronghold was like a maze, hallways going every which way, rooms here and there. They even passed a few loot chests, which had some pretty good loot, though not a lot that would help them to defeat the Ender Dragon. Much of the stone architecture was cracked or had vines and moss growing on it. No one knew who built the strongholds, but they all had portals that led to The End dimension.

They turned a corner and passed through some broken iron bars. Past the bars, on both sides, were stone basins full of lava. In front of them were stone stairs leading up to the dark green, white, yellow End Frame.

"We found it!" PurpleTimeRift exclaimed.

"Watch out—silverfish!" Cicer warned, pointing his sword at the small silver-looking fish that would slither across the ground.

Though they were called fish, they were only on land, evil little monsters that attacked whoever bothered them. They were often found burrowed into stone. They infested it and made their nests there. If you broke the block of stone, all the silverfish around would instantly attack whoever broke the block.

Inside the stairs was a monster spawner that the silverfish spawned from. Whole hordes of them caught sight of the AquaCrafters and started slithering towards them. They started snapping their mouths, eating whatever got in their way. (At least almost anything).

Everyone who had not already drawn their swords drew them. They swung at the silverfish, killing some, injuring others. But oftentimes their swords just swung and missed, for the silverfish were as small as rats.

"Ack!" Starpig cried in pain; a silverfish had bitten him on the foot.

Orion sliced the silverfish in half, freeing Starpig from its bite. Then he turned to Cicer and ordered, "Cicer, go and find the others! Let them know we found the portal frame!"

Cicer turned and ran down the tunnel back towards where ArcticCat's group had gone. Meanwhile, Orion, Starpig, and PurpleTimeRift slowly pushed the tide of silverfish backwards, inch by inch, each swing killing one or wounding another. There were so many silverfish now it was impossible to miss. Eventually PurpleTimeRift leaped onto the monster spawner and broke it with her pickaxe. Orion and Starpig defeated the remaining silverfish before joining her on the portal staircase.

"Well, that was intense!" Orion commented laughing.

"It sure was!" Starpig agreed.

"Should we remove this lava here?" PurpleTimeRift said, pointing at the lava below the rows of portal frames.

They turned and looked where she was pointing. The portal frame included four sides of three portal frame blocks. These blocks were invincible to any material yet to be found; the only other block that was invincible was bedrock, which was found near the bottom of the overworld.

"It would probably make it safer," Starpig responded, looking thoughtful.

And so Starpig and PurpleTimeRift covered the lava with cobblestone so that no one would fall into it. Orion didn't come to help because he had turned around to see Cicer running breathlessly back.

"Wow! You were quick, Cicer!" Orion praised, looking impressed.

"They, they were already heading this way...when I, when I found them." Cicer said as he caught his breath.

Jojo came into the room with ArcticCat and Fution close behind.

ArcticCat walked over to Starpig, and said, "Hey, Starpig, I found these in this stronghold's abandoned library!" He handed Starpig a few books that shone with an unnatural gleam.

"Oh wow! Three enchantment books!" Starpig exclaimed excitedly. "Let's see here...We have some protection II, sharpness I, and unbreaking IV!

What a find! We can use these on our armor and a sword."

Across the room, Jojo was chatting with Orion before calling everyone over for a group meeting.

"It's time to discuss plans for defeating the Ender Dragon!" Jojo said, as everyone gathered around.

"Jojo and I think we should split into groups, each with their own tasks," Orion explained.

PurpleTimeRift got up. "Remember, we need to take out all the End Crystals first. Otherwise, the dragon will just regenerate its health."

"Good point; anyway, we could split into three groups. One group would take out the main crystals with their bows. Another group would take care of the crystals with iron bar protection. And a final group would keep the dragon distracted," ArcticCat explained evenly.

"That's a great idea!" Cicer replied.

"Yeah, Fution and ArcticCat have the bows, so they should shoot down the crystals. Starpig and Cicer can take out the protected End Crystals. I will keep the dragon distracted with..." Orion looked over at the group.

"I can help keep the dragon distracted with you!" Jojo volunteered lazily, as if it were no big deal.

"And I have a bow, so I can join the bow group." PurpleTimeRift added.

"Great!" Orion exclaimed.

They continued discussing the logistics of the mission and what to do if something went wrong. The AquaCrafters also exchanged gear and prepared for battle. When they were ready, they gathered around the portal, and each of them took turns walking up the stairs to place their Eye of Ender in each of the End Portal Frames. Orion came up last and gently placed his Ender Eye into the small hole in the frame. As soon as he let go of the eye, the portal shivered, and the air inside the portal frame started swirling and bending. There was a loud swish, and then a bright light as the portal activated. Inside the portal frames, where it used to be transparent, there was now a black, starry night appearance. Small star-like particles emitted from the portal like torch flames, but more starry.

Orion turned around to look at his AquaCrafters. Then he spoke, "Well...here we are; once we pass through this portal, there is no coming back. The only way out of The End is to either die and respawn, or defeat the Ender Dragon, and a new portal will spawn that leads back to the overworld," Orion explained carefully, looking at each person to be sure they understood. "I can't ask you to come if you don't want to. So, who is with me?"

"We have come this far with you; we will see it to the end," Starpig replied quietly.

Everyone murmured their agreement.

Jojo joked, "Seriously, The End! We will see it to The End."

Orion laughed, then everyone climbed up to the top of the staircase, and then paused.

"When we go in, we go in together." Orion said, "On the count of three."

One, two, three. Orion walked into the portal falling downwards into the black starry darkness. Starpig, and ArcticCat followed, and then everyone else slowly joined them.

Orion opened his eyes, blinking twice. Though it wasn't visible, his skin had a visor, making it impossible to see his eyes. He looked around. Around them were endstone blocks which had a yellow cheese look to them, but they were very rough and pointy to touch. Endstone was the main substance that made up the Ender Islands, which was a space rock that got caught in orbit. Below him was an obsidian platform, purple and black and one of the hardest blocks in Minecraft, excluding bedrock. The air was very musty, unnatural-like, but then again, they were in another dimension. He looked around to see the AquaCrafters slowly stirring from the disorienting experience of going through the portal.

"Argh, I will never get used to the experience of going through portals," ArcticCat complained.

"Well, the Ender Portal is more disorienting than a Nether Portal," PurpleTimeRift explained, for she had been to The End recently.

"Is everyone alright?" Orion asked quietly.

"You mean other than the throbbing in my head?" ArcticCat replied. "Yeah, we are fine."

"Good, the throbbing should go away soon," Orion commented calmly, then turned to PurpleTimeRift. "Can you give us a description of what to expect above us?"

"Well, apparently we spawned inside the space rock island," PurpleTimeRift explained. "There we will see the large obsidian towers. On top of each tower will be an Ender Crystal. Each tower differs in height, and some are protected, as you know, by iron bars. The towers surround a bedrock podium at the center. Inside that basin is where the portal will spawn if we defeat the dragon. The Ender Dragon will be flying around in the sky but will always stay on the main Ender Island. Only if we can defeat the dragon, can we go to the other islands or go back to the overworld."

"Well, there's no going back now..." Orion said thoughtfully. "OK, we'd better get to work. Let's split into groups!"

The AquaCrafters split into the three groups that they had decided upon. They took out their pickaxes and started hacking away at the dimly lit space. They hacked at the walls made of endstone, making a small passageway upwards. They took turns at the front of the tunnel, each mining upwards and forwards. The people behind the front person would widen the tunnel so that they could more easily fit. Eventually they reached the surface and emerged one by one.

Above them the sky was dark, with stars scattered across it. It was dark, yet unnatural light existed so that they could see in the dark. A few dozen blocks forward were large obsidian towers coming out from the endstone ground. In the distance was a faint outline of the bedrock podium. The Ender Dragon was flying somewhere above, diving down towards the podium.

Behind them, around 10 blocks back, the End Island ended. Past it was a void that they couldn't see the bottom of. Probably the overworld was below it. There were a few scattered pieces of endstone that floated not far from the main Island.

Orion turned to face the AquaCrafters and spoke quietly but confidently. "You all know your role in this fight. Remember, don't engage the dragon one on one, or you will surely die. And we all know dying isn't fun. If the dragon is flying your way, get out of there and the rest of us will try and distract him. Stick with your group."

"Oh wait, I forgot to mention, once we destroy the crystals, the dragon will probably roost on the center bedrock podium, so that is where we should attack once we have destroyed the Ender Crystals," PurpleTimeRift added.

Starpig froze, and whispered, "What about the endermen? If we stare at their eyes, they will be aggravated and attack us!"

The group turned and faced in the direction that Starpig was looking. There stood an enderman, and they were staring the enderman straight in the eye. The enderman shrieked and vanished as it teleported. Orion and Jojo drew their swords just as the enderman appeared behind them. Before they could react, PurpleTimeRift threw a trident at the enderman, killing it instantly. The trident flew back to PurpleTimeRift.

"I didn't know you had an enchanted loyalty trident?" Orion exclaimed, surprised.

"You really should try one," PurpleTimeRift's smile was gleeful. "They are really helpful because you can use them for melee and ranged attacks!"

"We can't waste time; more endermen could spot us! We need to split up and attack!" Fution interrupted, drawing his diamond sword.

"Fution's right; we must attack now!" ArcticCat agreed.

"Then go! ArcticCat, you go that way, Starpig, you and Cicer head towards those lower towers with the iron bar cages. Jojo, follow me!" Orion ran off towards the bedrock podium without waiting to see if his orders were followed.

ArcticCat, Fution, and PurpleTimeRift headed towards the large towers, drawing their bows. Starpig and Cicer got out blocks to scale the towers with, while Orion and Jojo ran towards the Great Ender Dragon, which was roosting on the bedrock podium. Orion and Jojo's job was to distract the dragon, but as they drew near the podium, a monstrous roar from the great dragon echoed around them. It had caught sight of them and flew towards them.

It was a huge black dragon with purple eyes, and when it opened its mouth, it breathed out purple flames. It was fast, and out of the abdomen of the beast came a large bone skeletal structure that supported the black wings behind them. The Ender Dragon's large legs had sharp, pointy claws big enough to throw a Minecrafter off the Island.

The Great Dragon opened its mouth and shot a massive Ender-fireball, making a purple trail behind it. The Ender-fireball barreled towards Orion and Jojo with a whoosh. They brought out their shields to make a wall similar to the one they had used back in the Nether Fortress. The Ender-fireball hit the shields with a large cracking sound, and the shields broke, instantly destroyed. Both of the AquaCrafters were thrown back and hit the ground with a thud. They groaned as they slowly got up just soon enough to see the dragon land only a few feet in front of them. It opened its mouth and charged up huge amounts of Ender Energy to blast at its enemies. Orion stabbed at the dragon's mouth with his sword, hitting it in the top of the mouth. It bellowed in pain, then swung around and wacked its huge pointy tail and hit Orion before he could duck. He was knocked out from the impact.

"Orion!" Jojo exclaimed in shock.

Jojo furiously attacked the Great Dragon with all his might, slicing the dragon on its side; the dragon pushed Jojo away so that it could get away and retreated to one of the obsidian towers to heal in the beam of an Ender Crystal. Greatly relieved, Jojo dragged Orion over to the side of a tower where he wouldn't be attacked by anything else. Jojo leaned against the tower and drew deep gulps of air into his starving lungs. Slowly he recovered his strength.

Meanwhile, ArcticCat and his group of AquaCrafters had started shooting down the Ender Crystals. Fution snipped a crystal down from the end stone ground. PurpleTimeRift destroyed the next one, while ArcticCat slew an enderman trying to stop them. They continued the process; sometimes it took ages to destroy a crystal. Other times they hit it with one shot.

Starpig and Cicer were by another tower while this was going on, climbing the tower, using blocks and ladders as support. Quickly they reached the top of a tower. Cicer broke a crystal with one quick swipe, but the explosion of the crystal threw him off the tower. He fell around 70 blocks to the ground. At the last moment, just before he hit the ground, Cicer brought out his water bucket and used its contents to reduce the damage of his fall.

"Cicer! Are you alright?" Starpig shouted out in concern as Cicer reached the ground.

"Yeah, I think so...just very sore." Cicer smiled slightly, looking over at Starpig from where he was lying on the ground.

Starpig held out his arm. Cicer grabbed it, and Starpig pulled him up from the ground.

Starpig commented, "That was a close one!"

"Yea! Did you see that water placement?" Cicer agreed triumphantly, "If I hadn't had a water bucket, I would have been splat! I would have been all over the ground and had to respawn,"

They laughed, then Starpig responded, "Well I am glad you didn't. But we better get going; the others will need our help."

Over by the podium, Orion stirred. "What...what happened?"

"You took a direct hit from the dragon," Jojo explained.

"We need...we need to distract the dragon," Orion started.

Jojo interrupted, "You still need some time to recover; can you take care of yourself? I will keep the dragon distracted for a while."

Orion nodded, so Jojo ran off towards the dragon. Orion looked over to see ArcticCat trotting towards him.

"ArcticCat, where are the others? Shouldn't you be finishing off the rest of the crystals?" Orion asked, confused.

"PurpleTimeRift and Fution are taking care of the rest of them. I wasn't that good with a bow anyway. Besides, I wanted to see if you needed help with that dragon," ArcticCat responded, trying to sound casual.

ROAAAR!!! They looked over to see Jojo sprinting towards them with the Ender Dragon close behind him. He turned around to give the dragon a swipe, but they knew he wouldn't be able to hold it off for long.

"Jojo needs help! Stay here." ArcticCat exclaimed.

He ran off, drawing his iron sword. He had his shield in the left hand and his sword in the right. He bravely leaped onto the dragon, which was about to shoot Ender Fire at Jojo. ArcticCat pushed his shield forward just as the dragon breathed out large amounts of bright purple flames. The shield shattered, then ArcticCat counter-attacked by swinging his sword on to the dragon's head. Unfortunately, he only angered the dragon more. The dragon then instantly healed himself by coming close to the last remaining Ender Crystal that was protected with an iron bar cage. The dragon bit ArcticCat, and then flung him against one of the obsidian towers. ArcticCat's armor broke with a snap! He flew through the air and hit the tower with a force no one could ever survive. He fell down onto the ground in a crumpled heap. Jojo was wide-eyed with shock. ArcticCat's body jolted, then vanished as the items from his inventory exploded around the site where he had died.

Chapter 6: Elytra

"ARCTICCAT! NO!" Orion shouted as he got up.

Orion ran over with Jojo not far behind him. As they reached ArcticCat's site of death, Orion fell to the ground, defeated.

"Orion! We have no time to wait! He will respawn. we have bigger problems to deal with," Jojo said urgently. He pulled on Orion's shoulder.

Orion turned around to see the dragon leaping towards them with loud thuds. Orion looked up, and his visor shone from the dragon's fire. He charged at the dragon, blinded with fury. Jojo joined him; stroke by stroke they used their swords, swipe by swipe, slowly overwhelming the dragon. Then the ground shook, and the Great Dragon's wings flapped twice. Taking to the air, it flew up into the sky, circling the towers. But this time it didn't heal, for Starpig and Cicer emerged from the top of the last tower. They had destroyed the last remaining Ender Crystal! The Ender Dragon flew towards them, bellowing with fury. But before it could attack them, it was driven off by two arrows; one of the arrows was a flame arrow, and it hit the dragon in the neck with a thwack, while the other hit its belly. The dragon flew over and sagged down on the center bedrock podium. From the direction in which the arrows had emerged, Fution and PurpleTimeRift appeared. The AquaCrafters gathered around, though it took a moment before they reached each other.

"ArcticCat will respawn, but we must win this battle for him!" Orion said once they had gathered. He seemed to have regrouped and was surprisingly calm after what had just happened.

"For ArcticCat!" he exclaimed, raising his sword.

The group followed him.

Fution spoke up. "The dragon is weak on the bottom of the head."

"And how do you know this?" Starpig asked.

"Oh, well I learned it from..." Fution began.

Jojo interrupted, "Come on, the dragon is resting! Now is our chance!"

They turned and drew their weapons, charging at the dragon from different sides. Confused, the dragon attacked one AquaCrafter only to find another AquaCrafter stabbing or shooting it in the backside. They all attacked from different sides, keeping the dragon distracted so that one of them could attack the bottom of its head. Roaring in frustration, it shot Ender-Fire in all directions before taking to the sky. PurpleTimeRift and Fution shot arrows at the dragon, hitting it with everything they had. The dragon's wings were torn so it was forced to land, close enough for Jojo, Orion, Cicer, and Starpig to attack it. Starpig made a critical hit, and the dragon limped away, now in retreat. It shot a fireball, knocking Cicer and Starpig back, but Jojo and Orion persisted. The dragon broke Orion's sword. It attacked Jojo, desperately attempting the same move it used to kill ArcticCat. Luckily, it wasn't able to kill him. Orion now was the only one close to the dragon, but he was weaponless. The dragon growled.

"Orion! Here take this!" PurpleTimeRift shouted as she ran and threw her trident towards Orion.

He caught it, jumping into the air to catch it. Then he leapt upon the weak dragon, stabbing the trident directly into the Great Ender Dragon's weak spot. The Dragon Roared in anguish. It floated into the sky, light shining from first one side, then another. It was a spectacular show. Bright light emitted from its abdomen, like it was cracking open to reveal light. Then it exploded into a huge show of light. Orbs of greenish, whitish light fell from where it died; these orbs fell upon the AquaCrafters, healing them and strengthening them. Orion picked up the trident that he had used to kill the dragon, walked over to PurpleTimeRift and spoke,

"Here take it, it's yours," said Orion.

"Thanks," she said and smiled. "We did it!"

Everyone cheered! Each of them had their part; without one another, they would never have succeeded. This was the first great victory the AquaCrafters had experienced. They did not know then about the fierce battles that lay before them, but they felt changed, a battle-hardened group of warriors.

"Well, what now?" PurpleTimeRift asked, once they had slowly limped over together.

"Now, we go find some elytra," Starpig said confidently. "Isn't that right Orion?"

"Indeed," Orion answered, sighing with relief. "Well, I can't believe we did it. But we must get going again. We have to find an End City soon. We don't want to keep ArcticCat waiting too long back at home."

"Well, the fastest way to get to the End City is going through the side portal on the edge of the main island. It is much faster than bridging slowly to an outer island," PurpleTimeRift explained.

"Yeah, but elytra isn't the only thing found in the End City. I heard that you can also find shulkers there. You can use their shulker shells to make shulker boxes. Very helpful for storing a large number of items on the go," Fution added.

"I've heard about that, too. Apparently, you can get shulker boxes from these weird creatures that live in the End City. We have to be careful, though, because these creatures look exactly like the blocks that the End City is made out of. They have a similar skull-like feature to what those blazes have, but inside they have a purple shell," Starpig warned.

"Well, if they are anything like blazes, they shouldn't be too hard to defeat as long as we can make more shields." Orion looked thoughtful.

Fution replied, "Well, except that they shoot bullet orbs that can levitate you. If hit, you rise into the air and then fall back to the ground when the effect ends; that is how shulkers try to kill you."

"I have extra wood to make shields, just no iron." Cicer offered.

Jojo looked around slowly, then drawled. "I have some iron, Cicer. Here, we can go make some while everyone else is exchanging facts about shulkers."

Orion sighed then laughed. "We are done, Jojo, and you're right; it is time to get going again."

"Good, 'cause if you want to get multiple elytra, we will need to visit multiple End Cities," Jojo approved.

Jojo and Cicer went over to craft some shields while everyone else started repairing what they could of their armor. They also needed to hurry if they wanted to get multiple elytra, and each End City usually had only one elytra in it, for it was a rare artifact.

Once they had recuperated, they headed over towards the edge of the floating island so that they could find this outer island portal. It didn't take that long before they were able to find it. It was an identical portal to a normal Ender Portal, but it was floating in the sky, with bedrock that encased it on two sides. Since they couldn't break bedrock, they had to use some of their remaining ender pearls to pass through the portal, because ender pearls allowed them to teleport anywhere they threw it. So, by throwing the pearl into the portal, they in turn traveled through the portal to the other side. They all threw their pearls and teleported onto another similar island like the main island. Behind them was an identical portal that led back to the main island, which had the portal to the overworld.

"At least this time it isn't disorienting," Orion commented.

To that Starpig replied, "I think that is because we only have to travel to another ender island, not traveling interdimensionally."

"That makes sense," Orion said before looking around at their new surroundings.

This end island was similar to the main island, for it was made out of endstone. But this one didn't have any obsidian towers and wasn't as big. Instead, purple plants came out of the ground, growing in random directions but always going upwards.

"Hey, look! Chorus fruit! It can be eaten raw or cooked. Eating it raw makes you teleport randomly in a 10-block radius or so. Useful if you want to travel through a wall," PurpleTimeRift pointed out.

"What about the cooked version?" Cicer asked curiously.

"Eh, nothing much when cooked, but it sure tastes a lot better then," PurpleTimeRift chuckled.

"Might as well harvest some," Orion commented.

They journeyed on and left the chorus fruit island and bridged to another nearby island. A hazy form of a building was in the distance of this much larger island.

"Hey, could that be it?" Jojo wondered, waving a hand vaguely in the direction of the island.

"It could be!" Starpig replied.

"Come on, let's go see if it is an End City!" Orion ordered.

They drew nearer, and sure enough, a huge End City appeared as they came closed in. The city looked like the building version of chorus fruit. It started at its base like a small house and then extended upwards and outwards until it made a huge city. The only reason why the building didn't collapse was because the End had much less gravity than the overworld. The city was made of end stone bricks, as well as purpur blocks of many different designs. The purpur blocks made up the pillars and edges of the buildings, while the end stone bricks made up the main structure.

"Careful! Endermen ahead!" Fution warned, pointing at the base of the city.

The AquaCrafters ducked down behind an end stone rock. Endermen were all black-looking creatures, but super tall, with very skinny long legs and arms. An enderman had purple eyes and teleported often. It was the only mob (which refers to both monsters and animals in Minecraft terminology) found in all dimensions. The only other inhabitants of the End Cities were, of course, shulkers. The AquaCrafters crept over towards the city, careful not to attract unwanted attention from the endermen and shulkers. They eventually reached the door into the bottom of the End City's lowest room. They went inside, and found mainly an empty room, with carved purpur floors and ceiling and endstone brick walls. On the opposite side of the door were stairs leading upwards; underneath the stairs was a chest.

Cicer broke the silence by saying, "I will go open that chest and meet you upstairs."

To that Orion frowned, then replied, "OK, but don't take long." The thought of not being together was a bit worrisome.

The next floor was almost identical, except that it had no chest and had small windows on three sides of the square building. The AquaCrafters continued up two more floors. They reached a spiral staircase in a huge atrium room of the same design as the other rooms.

One of the purpur blocks cracked open like a shell, and a face peered out. With a woosh, a bullet orb shot out of its skull and floated over towards the AquaCrafters.

"Shulker bullet!" PurpleTimeRift exclaimed with alarm just as the bullet hit her on the side.

The purpur block wasn't a purpur block, it was a shulker! PurpleTimeRift took damage and started floating upwards, like air was pushing her upwards with a swoosh. Orion grabbed her leg to try to stop her from floating upwards. Instead of helping, he also started floating upwards in the large room. More shulkers revealed themselves from the purpur blocks, shooting out more shulker bullet orbs! Everyone brought out their shields and frantically tried to dodge and block the orbs that cascaded upon them.

"There are too many bullets!" Starpig exclaimed.

Just then Jojo was hit as well and started floating. Orion was hit next, but PurpleTimeRift stopped floating, and this time PurpleTimeRift was holding onto Orion's leg. She drew her sword, swiping against the orbs. She hit her target and the orb exploded with a little burst.

"We can slice the orbs! Draw your swords!" PurpleTimeRift shouted, letting go of Orion and destroying orbs that were all over the place.

Fution blocked a bullet, and then attacked an open-shelled shulker, killing it with one swipe, "Attack the shulkers when they open their shells!" He shouted.

Jojo took heed of this advice, for he killed another shulker.

Meanwhile, everyone else continued blocking and stabbing or slicing at the shulkers. Orion stabbed at a shulker higher in the room, only for the shulker to close its shell at the last moment.

"Argh!" Orion cried with frustration.

"Here, let me help." Starpig spoke as he stabbed the shulker just as it opened its shell to shoot another bullet. But instead, the shulker was stabbed in the back.

"Thanks!" Orion managed to say, before continuing up the stairs.

The AquaCrafters finally got past the shulkers and climbed to the top of the tower that they were in. Now they needed to find the floating ship in the End City. The top of the tower opened up on two sides. On one end a purpur bridge led to other towers; the other side was almost identical, but instead of leading to towers, the bridge just jutted upwards before ending abruptly at an arch.

"Hey, that looks like the entrance to an End Ship!" Cicer pointed out.

"You go ahead. We will continue to check out the towers to see if we can get more shulker shells and loot from chests," Orion responded.

"No more shulkers for me!" PurpleTimeRift exclaimed. "I have had enough of them! I would like to go with Cicer if that is OK?"

"Sure, just meet us at the bottom of the city." Orion waved her away.

While Cicer and PurpleTimeRift went off to go get the first elytra, everyone else headed up to the tower. After collecting some more shulker shells and whatever loot they could find, the AquaCrafters returned to the bottom of the city. Cicer and PurpleTimeRift flew down with their new elytra wings, which surprised Orion, who thought they would take the stairs.

PurpleTimeRift said, "Who wants to take the stairs anyway?"

All the AquaCrafters headed out to find another End City so that they might get more elytra. Not long after, on a nearby island, they were lucky enough to find an End City. They snuck into the tower, and this time instead of confronting the shulkers, they scaled the tower on the outside so that they wouldn't have to deal with the shulkers' levitation bullets. They used ladders and blocks to get to the top of the tower. This End City was much bigger, so they weren't able to explore the entire city. Instead, they headed towards the floating purpur End Ship in the sky. Orion and Starpig headed over to the ship this time, while the other AquaCrafters looted the nearby tower. Orion and Starpig bridged over to the floating End Ship and jumped on board.

"Shulker bullet! Look out!" Starpig warned as he destroyed the bullet with his sword.

Together they were able to defeat all shulkers on board the ship. They headed down into the cabin of the ship. It was mostly empty except for end rods that lit up the cabin with bright white light. Past a center support beam was a chest at the back of the cabin. On either side of the chest were gray, gleaming elytra wings that hung on the wall of the purpur cabin.

Orion exclaimed excitedly, "Elytra!"

They went over to the wings, and each claimed their own elytra wings. Then they opened the chest. Unfortunately, the chest was empty.

"Huh, weird! I haven't usually had chests empty before," Starpig said, confused.

"Well, maybe someone took the items from the chest already," Orion suggested.

Starpig countered, "But then why didn't they take the wings?"

"I don't know. I guess we may never know," Orion responded, equally confused.

They left the city, using the elytra to fly down. All the AquaCrafters were waiting for them near the center tower. Once they gathered around, they started discussing plans.

"Just one more End City should do it and we all will have elytra!" Jojo said.

"How do we even know that one more End City will even have two elytra? Or even have elytra at all?" Fution reasoned.

Orion added, "Besides, ArcticCat should have some elytra, too. Speaking of which, ArciticCat may be wondering if we are alright while he is at home. I don't want to keep him waiting too long."

"Well, if Orion goes back to the overworld, then the rest of us can continue to the next End City and get more elytra for all of us," Cicer suggested.

"Yeah, that could work." PurpleTimeRift looked at Orion questioningly. "But I would like to go with Orion because I have been traveling for ages!"

Orion said, "Sure you can come! Though I am not sure if we have extra lodgings for you to stay at."

"I can always pitch a tent until I can build a house. The overworld is much safer than the End," PurpleTimeRift reasoned.

"OK, if everyone agrees, then I see no reason not to go with this plan," Starpig said.

They all agreed, and it was settled. Orion and PurpleTimeRift journeyed back to the portal while the rest of the AquaCrafters continued to more End Cities.

Chapter 7: The Dragon Egg

Orion and PurpleTimeRift had finally reached the main ender island. The AquaCrafters had agreed to meet back in the overworld near the theater in one day. Orion and PurpleTimeRift wanted to get back to the overworld to spend the night instead of in this bleak, alien environment. Right now, they were on the edge of the island; the portal to the outer islands wasn't far behind them. Ahead of them were the large obsidian towers, but this time without crystals atop them.

"You go ahead, I will catch up. I want to build a platform under the portal to the outer islands," PurpleTimeRift began. "You know, it isn't very safe below the portal. You could easily fall into the void below."

"Ok, sure; that is a good idea." Orion agreed. He turned and began to hike towards the center of the main island. He soon reached the bedrock podium, only this time, instead of an empty basin below the podium, there was an identical Ender Portal to the one that they had used to enter the end with. As Orion looked up, upon the top of the podium was a large black and purple egg.

Huh, I wonder how we missed that? Orion thought. He climbed onto the podium and carefully picked up the egg. It was surprisingly heavy. Orion reached the ground and put the egg into his inventory. His mind was churning, although he showed nothing on the outside. *He had heard it somewhere, what was it?...Oh yeah, Orion had heard that an ender dragon egg spawned upon the bedrock podium a while after you defeated the great dragon of the end. And he had also heard that this egg was the source of great power. What a marvelous find this was! But...*

"I'm back!" PurpleTimeRift huffed, as she hiked towards where Orion stood.

Orion looked up furtively. "Oh, you're back."

"You OK?" PurpleTimeRift asked with concern in her eyes.

Orion stammered, "No, yes, I'm fine. You just surprised me."

"Whatever, let's just go back to the overworld." PurpleTimeRift responded.

They started off, but Orion kept thinking about the dragon egg he had in his inventory. Could he tell anyone he had it? Was it a dangerous thing?

On the journey back to the overworld, the Ender Portal can take you wherever you want in the realm below. So, when Orion and PurpleTimeRift entered the portal, instead of taking them to the stronghold, it instantly took them back to the entrance of the Theater.

It seemed like forever, but it was really a second later when Orion opened his eyes. They were back in the overworld of AquaCraft. ArcticCat would be waiting for him, Orion realized with a glad feeling. Unaccustomed to the bright light of the overworld compared to The End, Orion had to squint before he could get used to it.

"Orion!" said a voice.

Orion turned and exclaimed excitedly, "ArcticCat!"

PurpleTimeRift slowly walked over. She nodded to ArcticCat.

"Well, tell me, were we successful?" ArcticCat asked eagerly.

"Yeah! Look at these!" Orion opened his inventory and showed ArcticCat his elytra wings.

"Awesome!" exclaimed ArcticCat, taking the wings and examining them. "Oh also, there is someone here that said they wanted to join us AquaCrafters! I met them shortly after I respawned."

"Oh really? Also, sorry, you had to respawn," PurpleTimeRift commented thoughtfully.

ArcticCat said, "It's fine. Anyway, come on! They are staying at Orion's hotel."

Orion had started constructing a hotel before they left for the End. People who were journeying and visiting AquaCraft could stay, and for the AquaCrafters who hadn't finished their bases. He had only finished the lobby and the first floor so far. Orion, ArcticCat, and PurpleTimeRift walked over to the hotel where this new person was staying. They entered the lobby of the hotel. A figure stood up from one of the small tables on one side of the lobby.

"PurpleTimeRift, good to see you again!" The figure came over and shook hands with PurpleTimeRift.

PurpleTimeRift replied, "Gestroyer!" She turned to the other. "Meet Gestroyer; he was one of the few people I told about your AquaCraft endeavor. I met him while I was doing the business that I spoke of."

"Gestroyer," Orion said shaking hands with the newcomer.

ArcticCat smiled. "Gestroyer mentioned that he wanted to help you build districts for where our shops and bases and mini-games can go. He also said he may have some ideas for mini-game events we could do."

"Oh really? Well, I would be happy to work with Gestroyer on that," Orion replied, sounding interested. He continued to look Gestroyer over.

Gestroyer wore a black suit and white tie, and he had black hair and brown eyes. Very professional looking.

"Great! And ArcticCat mentioned there were more of you guys?" Gestroyer asked politely.

"Yeah, where are the others?" ArcticCat added.

Orion replied, "Oh, well, everyone else wanted to get more elytra, but PurpleTimeRift and I wanted to head back to the overworld, so we split up."

Gestroyer seemed satisfied with that answer. PurpleTimeRift walked over and began a conversation with Gestroyer; they were catching up with recent events. Meanwhile, Orion led ArcticCat up to the second floor into a room.

Orion turned to ArcticCat and said quietly, "Elytra wasn't the only thing I was able to acquire in the End."

"Oh?" ArcticCat said curiously.

"Now don't tell anyone about this..." Orion began.

ArcticCat promised he wouldn't. Orion pulled out the dragon egg from his inventory.

"Is that..." ArcticCat said in wonder.

Orion replied, "It is."

"Ender dragon eggs are said to contain great power. Power beyond anything we can comprehend," ArcticCat whispered.

"I know. That is why I want you to safeguard it," Orion explained.

"No, I couldn't..." ArcticCat began.

Orion interrupted, "Listen to me, I want you to hide it where no one but you can find it. If a time of great need arises, then we may need to use it. But in the wrong hands it could do great evil. Will you do this?"

"OK, I mean yes. I will do what you ask. Of course I will." ArcticCat responded, his mind already searching for a place that would be safe and secret.

"Thank you," Orion said with appreciation. "Thank you for being someone I can trust."

ArcticCat picked up the egg and put it into his inventory. They left the room, and ArcticCat went outside and saddled his horse in a pen near the hotel. Orion watched as ArcticCat rode away. Then he turned and walked over to the others.

ArcticCat rode all afternoon. It was dark by the time he reached his destination. Tomorrow morning the other AquaCrafters would arrive from The End. He needed to hide the egg where no one could find it–Orion had been very clear about that. ArcticCat also needed to get back by morning before anyone wondered where he had gone. He had reached a large mountain. After an hour's worth of climbing, he came to a large waterfall. He had been here before. When Orion and ArcticCat had first explored AquaCraft, they had found this place. It was remote, far away from where anyone might explore or build anything. ArcticCat had brought a torch so that he might see in dark places. Now he felt around and found it, took it out and held it up. He went through a small crevice that led behind the waterfall. Behind the waterfall was a medium sized cave. In the middle of the round cave was a part of the rock that jutted up. Upon it, ArcticCat placed the egg. Satisfied, he left the cave and journeyed back to the hotel. He would have to come back to add protection devices, but for now it would have to do.

It was late in the night when ArcticCat finally arrived at the hotel. But despite the time, Orion met ArcticCat at the door. It was raining gently. ArcticCat came in; he was damp all over.

"Is it hidden?" Orion asked quietly.

ArcticCat nodded. "But I will have to return in a few days to add more protection."

Orion replied, "For now it will have to do."

They went inside and up the stairs to their rooms.

The next morning Orion awoke in his bed inside the hotel he had built. He got up and then remembered the events that had recently passed. The AquaCrafters would all return today. The egg was safe for now. ArcticCat would protect it soon. What power did the egg possess? When might they need it? Orion sure wanted to add two more floors to his hotel, maybe even a rooftop pool. All these thoughts came to Orion and many more. Orion wondered many things about what the future of AquaCraft would hold. He knew nothing about what misfortunes would come from the Dragon Egg. He knew nothing about what epic, terrible battles that lay ahead. And he knew nothing about who would enter AquaCraft and join the AquaCrafters, expanding the community into something greater than he or any Original AquaCrafter had ever imagined. But AquaCraft had a great destiny ahead of it, and that was something Orion would eventually learn.

Orion came downstairs to see ArcticCat getting some food from the dining area. They saw each other and nodded, acknowledging what had happened the night before. PurpleTimeRift came down the stairs.

"Good morning!" She said cheerfully.

Before either of them could respond, they heard footsteps from outside. It was a bright sunny day, not a cloud in the sky. The door opened and standing at its opening was Cicer.

"Cicer! You're back!" ArcticCat exclaimed.

Cicer looked at ArcticCat and smiled. "Yeah! The others will be here soon! I'm glad you're back."

Starpig and Fution were walking and chatting as they followed Cicer inside. Jojo came in from the back of the group.

"Welcome back, everyone!" Orion exclaimed, "So, how was your Ender City expedition?"

Starpig replied, "Well...after you and PurpleTimeRift went back to the overworld, we continued on to another End City. Unfortunately, it was a while before we arrived at one. So, we had to call it a night, even though it is permanently night in The End. Once we had awakened, we explored the city, only to find it didn't have a ship, so no elytra. That is why it took us so long to get back."

"We did find two more Ender Cities later though, before heading home," Fution pointed out.

"True. Oh also, ArcticCat, we got you some elytra too!" Starpig said.

ArcticCat looked surprised, "Really? Awesome!"

"Well, we wouldn't forget about you!" Orion said, turning to ArcticCat.

Gestroyer walked in just then from the entrance of the hotel. He explained that he had been tending to the horses. Once he was introduced to all of the AquaCrafters, they sat down and chatted about their knowledge of Minecraft. Occasionally, an AquaCrafter would ask Gestroyer questions like why he came to AquaCraft and how he heard of it.

Later that day the AquaCrafters all gathered around outside under a tent, which was situated on the hill that the theater was built on. The tent was strategically placed looking down at the valley so that one might be able to see everything. The AquaCrafters gathered inside the tent. They were looking around and creating plans for the city and its different districts. The shopping district would be west of The Theater. They would put the mini-game district south of The Theater, past the ridge. Further along the hill where The Theater was situated, they would have event booths to sign up for events. Near the entrance of The Theater, below the hill, they would place a large quartz podium with beacons that would mark the center of the AquaCraft city. They would have paths connecting each of the districts. They continued planning the logistics and discussing how and where to put what. It was also decided that people could build their base anywhere, as long as it was not inside a district, but also not too far from a road or path of AquaCraft so that they might arrive and find each other's bases. That is, except for secret bases. AquaCrafters would be required to have one normal base that wasn't secret so it could be easily found. With their new elytra, they could now build in the sky. In Minecraft, the physics allowed them to build floating structures under certain circumstances. And so began the construction of the city...

Chapter 8: City Building

"The plans are complete! You know Orion, I never thought we would have a realm of our own to explore. If you had told me that this was possible even a year ago, I wouldn't have believed you! I thought all realms had already been explored. Apparently not!" ArcticCat stated, while admiring the plans.

Orion stifled a laugh. "You would have said I was crazy!"

"Yeah, well we have come a long way from one year ago," ArcticCat said.

"Indeed, we have," Starpig contributed as he came into the tent, for he had overheard part of the conversation. "And Orion, Fution and I have been discussing the shopping district."

"What about it?" Orion was confused.

"Well," Starpig began, "We think that we should make a shop that sells building materials for cheap prices so that we all could get the materials needed to build the city and its districts. Like your hotel, for example; you could finish the top floors. And everyone could just stock the shop with materials whenever they had some. The diamonds or whatever you want to use as currency could be paid to the person who provided the materials. What do you think?"

Orion thought about it. "Seems like a good idea, but you and Fution will need to figure out a way to keep track of who gets paid for what."

"Does that mean we can get started building?" Starpig asked.

"You don't need my permission! I'm not the leader of AquaCraft or anything; you just need to let me know if it is something big so we can all discuss it." Orion explained.

"Well, you were the one who found AquaCraft," Starpig countered.

Orion shrugged. "I mean, technically I am not the one who found it; just the one who settled it. Anyway, you had better get started; there is a lot to do."

Starpig said, "OK," and then walked out of the tent.

ArcticCat was staring at Orion.

Orion stared back, "Um, yes, ArcticCat? Hello? Why are you staring?" Orion was confused.

"Sorry, I was just thinking, you would be a good leader of AquaCraft. I don't think any of us would say no to that. I was wondering if I should bring it up with everyone," ArcticCat explained.

Orion was surprised. "Me? Really? I mean...I could be the leader, as long as everyone is OK with that."

"Just a thought." ArcticCat said.

A few days later, Starpig and Fution, with Cicer's help, were able to finish the shop for materials so that the AquaCrafters could get started on the rest of the city. They had begun designing and plotting the layout of the city, using temporary blocks to show where what would go where. At this rate, they would be able to finish most of the city and the districts in a month or two. They were going to build a minecart train station near the center of the city that would have a track to each of the districts. One minecart track would go to the shopping district, another to the mini-game district, while a third track would go to the mountains. For the center of the city, they wanted a colored beacon podium that was built on a nether quartz platform. That meant someone needed to go to the nether to get quartz and a fire star to make a beacon. But they would do that later. In the meantime, the AquaCrafters gathered together at Orion's hotel for a special meeting.

"Welcome, AquaCrafters. This evening we have gathered around to discuss an important topic," ArcticCat was saying to the group who were sitting around in the hotel lounge. "We must vote for a leader, someone who will lead us AquaCrafters. Until now we have mainly just made decisions as a group, and I don't want that to change, but it might be helpful to have someone to lead us and organize things. The leader could be elected now and then re-elected or replaced as needed. The people would still stay in control mostly, so that we don't end up like those other realms. Anyway, I would like to propose that we elect as our leader the person who found and then settled AquaCraft in the first place; without him we wouldn't be AquaCrafters or have access to AquaCraft. I propose we elect Orion as leader of the AquaCrafters."

The AquaCrafters broke into murmurs and whispers as they discussed what they thought of the proposal. After a minute or so, they were all nodding in agreement.

Jojo stood up looking around, "I think we are all in agreement. Orion, do you accept the position as leader of the AquaCrafters?"

"I...thank you, yes, I accept," Orion started. "I never thought that this would be possible—a group of Minecrafters gathered around to form a community. I always hoped to be part of a group like that, but never thought it would happen. I promise I will try my hardest to be a leader who will listen to all of you and will put AquaCraft above myself."

Once everyone stopped clapping, Orion said, "As my first act as leader, I proclaim this," Orion pointed to everyone, "I present The Council of AquaCraft. The council shall gather whenever there is something of vital importance to take care of. The council will make the most important decisions, while I, the leader, will organize and make the everyday decisions. That way all of us can have input on the important things so that the community has power as well. I will also be a part of the council, but while we are together as a council, we are all equals."

PurpleTimeRift spoke up. "What will happen when more Minecrafters come to AquaCraft?"

"I hadn't thought of that," Orion said, open to ideas.

"Maybe only we get to be part of the council. New AquaCrafters have to earn it." Fution suggested.

"You know, I will let the council elect their own members, so when more people come, then the council gets to decide if they want more members on the council." Orion said.

"Well, now that we are all a part of the AquaCraft council, we will need a council building. Like a headquarters?" Cicer pointed out.

ArcticCat replied, "Good point. We should build a HQ building sometime."

"I mean, we are the only Minecrafters here right now, so I don't think we need a HQ building right away," Gestroyer was thinking out loud.

Orion nodded. "You're probably right. Well, I think that's everything. Unless there is anything vitally important to discuss, I think it is time to call this meeting to a close."

"Good night then!" ArcticCat said as he got up from a chair and walked to the stairs that led to the hotel rooms.

The meeting ended, and everyone said goodnight as they went their separate ways.

In the following weeks, the AquaCrafters built up the minecart train station and the tracks. Other than that, the AquaCrafters were mainly building bases or houses of their own to live in. Orion had started construction of his secret base in the hill-like mountain near Jojo's ravine. Orion had built a small bedroom, a main hallway to connect different parts of the base, and a small sitting area. He had journeyed to the Nether with Jojo, Starpig, and Gestroyer to get nether materials. Orion mainly mined quartz, which he used as the interior of his base. Orion had just finished a storage room to hold all of his extra materials. He had sent a message to ArcticCat to meet him on top of the low mountain that Orion's base was in. He wanted to discuss something with ArcticCat that the other AquaCrafters couldn't know.

. . .

ArcticCat got out of the minecart; he had taken the minecart track system which took him all the way to Jojo's ravine. From there ArcticCat had hiked up toward the hill and climbed to the top. He wondered what Orion wanted to discuss. ArcticCat stopped to catch his breath.

"You ready to see something cool?" said a voice.

"Orion! You surprised me!" ArcticCat exclaimed.

Orion walked over. "Sorry. Anyway, I have been trying to get this right all day! OK, stand there; no two steps to your right. Too far! OK, perfect. Ready to be amazed?"

"I think so," ArcticCat said, raising his eyebrows a bit doubtfully.

They were standing on a small stone plateau at the top of the hill. Orion reached down to press a stone button that blended in almost perfectly with the stone surface. A few seconds after Orion pushed the button, pistons sounded, and a second later the blocks ArcticCat was standing on suddenly sank down into the stone surface! Where there used to be a flat stone surface, suddenly there was a hole. Orion hopped down the hole to find ArcticCat staring wide-eyed in surprise. The floor had brought ArcticCat into a quartz hallway.

Orion laughed, then said, "Observe the secret entrance into my secret base!" He smiled with satisfaction.

"Impressive!" ArcticCat said, looking around him.

Orion was full of enthusiasm. "Come on, let me show you around."

As they walked off of the stone platform, pistons pushed it back up into the ceiling from where it had come, making the hole disappear.

"On your right—that hallway leads to the sleeping areas. On your left it goes to storage. Ahead of us will be my other entrance into the base," Orion began. "But I didn't bring you here to show you my base. We have things to discuss. Follow me."

Orion led them through a door into a small sitting room.

"Well? Why have you asked me to come here? We could have talked anywhere else." ArcticCat was confused.

Orion's tone became serious, "I wanted to come somewhere private, somewhere no one would find us or overhear us."

ArcticCat found a chair and sat down, looking over to hear what Orion had to say.

"I need you to do something." Orion paused, "And you're the only one who knows where it is. I need you to go to the dragon egg."

ArcticCat asked, "Why?"

"The Ender Dragon egg is said to hold mysterious power," Orion said.

ArcticCat lost his patience. "Just spit it out!" he growled.

"I didn't just learn where AquaCraft was from that old explorer in Evenglade. He also told me about an item called the Heart of the Sea. It holds the power of AquaCraft itself. But it is unobtainable. Yet the Ender Dragon egg grants one wish, and we could wish for the Heart of the Sea. With the Heart of the Sea, we could make AquaCraft into whatever we wanted."

ArcticCat was stunned. "Shouldn't we discuss this with the others?"

"I can't trust this power to anyone else," Orion stated. "We can't have just any Minecrafter use it. I mean, maybe I will tell Jojo or Starpig, but I don't feel like I can trust anyone else with its power."

"And you want me to use the egg to wish for the Heart of the Sea?" ArcticCat asked. "Why don't you just do it yourself?"

"I have to organize the building of the city." Orion was silent for a minute, then he looked over at ArcticCat directly. "Plus, I don't know where it is," he said flatly.

ArcticCat wasn't totally convinced. "OK then, so do I just go to the egg and say I wish for the Heart of the Sea?"

Orion shrugged. "I'm not sure; you're better with mystic objects than I am. I bet you can figure it out."

"Wait, when were you expecting me to leave?" ArcticCat asked.

"As soon as possible. I will cover for you in case anyone asks."

"OK, fine." ArcticCat said slowly and reluctantly.

"Thank you." Orion looked relieved.

The very next day ArcticCat set off on his assignment. After traveling for a time, he neared the mountain where he had hidden the egg. He began climbing the mountain to the waterfall. By this time the sun had started to set. He looked around carefully, then entered the cave behind the waterfall. He could see a purple ender-ish (similar to obsidian) dim light being emitted from the egg, and the egg was exactly where ArcticCat had left it. ArcticCat moved carefully forward, step by step. He neared the egg. Then he stopped. He stood in front of the egg.

He slowly reached out and spoke: "I wish for the Heart of the Sea," he said clearly, and he touched the egg.

Nothing happened. ArcticCat pulled his arm back, and then reached out a second time and said, "Ender Dragon Egg of power, grant me the Heart of the Sea." Again, he waited, and again nothing happened. He reached out a third time, but this time he didn't speak. Instead, as he touched the egg, he pictured the Heart of the Sea. And as he stood touching the egg, it glowed a brighter purple ender light. There was a big swoosh, and it flashed and then it was gone, leaving behind only purple particles in the air. But in the midst of the particles glowed something blue. Just exactly where the egg had been, now, there lay the Heart of the Sea!

Chapter 9: The Heart of The Sea

Lying there on the stone podium was a real Heart of the Sea! As the purple particles cleared, ArcticCat saw clearly the spherical shape of the aqua and dark blue Heart of the Sea. ArcticCat hesitated. *It actually worked!* he thought. A Heart of the Sea right here in front of me. The Ender Dragon egg brought a Heart *here to* AquaCraft. Though the item was most powerful in AquaCraft, it did exist and have power in other realms as well. But a Heart of the Sea was still very rare.

ArcticCat slowly reached down and slowly lifted it up. The Heart shimmered as if it were alive. Like an ocean, the orb changed from dark to lighter blue. ArcticCat wondered what power he held in his hands. He hadn't believed that Orion was right, that it was possible to get this magical power. ArcticCat walked to the edge of the cave where the waterfall was flowing. He lifted the Heart of the Sea towards the water; it glowed bright blue. The water that was falling stopped, and the water started flowing upwards! It started flowing uphill against gravity. As ArcticCat lowered the Heart of the Sea, it stopped glowing, and the water resumed its usual falling down to the river below.

ArcticCat looked back at the Heart; the power of this orb was enormous, for this was only a small portion of its power. ArcticCat thought, *If this orb got into the wrong hands, the damage would be significant. No wonder Orion didn't want to tell anyone else!* Now what to do with the orb... bring it to Orion? Or should he hide it here in the cave. Probably best to leave it here where no one could find it. ArcticCat placed the orb back on the stone pedestal and started his journey back to the city to tell Orion what had just happened.

Meanwhile, in the nether, the Ender Dragon egg appeared in a bastion, purple particles emitting from it. The bastion was a run-down structure in the nether made of blackstone. It was the home of piglin tribes, possibly even more dangerous than the nether fortress.

Unbeknownst to Orion and ArcticCat, when you wish something from the Ender Dragon egg, it couldn't just give you what you wished for; it also needed to create something that was opposite of your wish, so that the balance of the world would stay the same. Because of this, the egg flashed, and in the place where it vanished appeared a star. A Nether Star. The Nether Star was the opposite of the Heart of the Sea, but equal in power. It held the power of fire, lava, and the nether.

The star was only accessible from withers, which were powerful monsters that were almost as strong as the Ender Dragon. If killed, the wither would drop a Nether Star.

Since ArcticCat had possession of the Heart of the Sea, the Nether Star needed someone to have possession of it as well. So, the star floated up, and with its power, it created something. Using the materials in the bastion, it fused armor together with lava and fire, and infused its power inside the figure. The figure's eyes flashed, and it became alive. It grabbed the Nether Star, which was floating in the air, and placed it inside its armor. It would not take long for the figure to find out about AquaCraft and ArcticCat. He would figure out how he was created, and he would seek to destroy AquaCraft and remake it into NetherCraft. He was fueled by rage and anger from the fire within him. But before any of that might happen, he would have to begin plotting his appearance in AquaCraft and how he might destroy that realm.

And in this way, one decision made in the desire for power created a dangerous threat that might mean the end of AquaCraft. All the lives of the AquaCrafters would hang in the balance. Though Orion didn't know it yet, creating a Heart of the Sea from nothing could cause a war so great, it might bring the end to the realm.

Part 2
The Eclipse

Chapter 10: Demise

Starpig and Cicer were busy finishing up the building of their shops. Cicer wanted to give out starter kits almost free of price for the AquaCrafters if they needed new tools and armor. A kit could also be given to a new AquaCrafter if they had just arrived. Cicer would start out with iron armor kits before eventually replacing them with diamond armor kits once he had mined enough diamonds. Starpig, on the other hand, was planning on selling miscellaneous items that you wouldn't really find in an ordinary shop. Starpig and Cicer's shops were built just across from each other on the hill near Orion's theater. The shops weren't big, partly because the shopping district wasn't finished yet and had only had a few unfinished buildings dotted around.

"You know, we should really find a village," Cicer said to Starpig thoughtfully. "Sometimes villagers trade really random items which might help you stock up your shop."

Starpig looked up from what he was doing. "Good idea."

"I should also start mining for diamonds. I'm not sure iron armor kits will sell as much as diamond ones," Cicer continued. "Say, did you hear about Gestroyer's pet shop? He has been gathering cats, dogs, birds, and other animals for the last few days."

"Oh really? It might be nice to have a dog to help out on adventures," Starpig mused.

"Mhm," Cicer agreed.

PurpleTimeRift and Jojo were walking up the hill towards Starpig and Cicer. As they drew near, PurpleTimeRift walked over to Cicer and said, "Hey Cicer, do you happen to have any of those starter kits available? I just broke my pickaxe mining, and it wouldn't hurt to have some spare tools and armor as well."

"Sure; my shop isn't open yet, but I think I can spare a starter kit; come on over." Cicer led the way over to his stock of kits.

As they walked away, Jojo spoke to Starpig. "Nice shop; what might you be selling?"

"Eh, just miscellaneous items," Starpig replied.

"Have you seen ArcticCat around at all? He promised to have a duel against me." Jojo pulled a pretend sword and slashed it in empty air, then grinned.

"Not since he went off with Orion yesterday; he hasn't returned yet. I did see Orion working on his sky base; maybe he knows where ArcticCat is," Starpig answered.

"Thanks, well, see you around," Jojo said, as he flew off with his elytra up towards Orion's base.

Orion was carefully placing glass blocks, extending the glass floor of his sky base when he looked up and saw Jojo land on the roof of his base.

"Jojo! Good to see you," Orion said as he climbed up to the roof of the base.

"Your base seems a bit precarious right now; I feel like this glass might break, and the base might just fall apart in midair!" Jojo commented, carefully testing each step as he walked over to Orion.

Orion laughed. "True, true. It won't be that way for much longer once it has been reinforced and the walls are finished. I have to finish the main shape and structure of the base before I can do anything else. I tried to design it to look like a snowflake from the ground."

"Yeah, I can see that. Anyway, have you seen ArcticCat lately? I wanted to duel him," Jojo responded.

Jojo thought he saw a flash of fear–or was it suspicion–in Orion's eyes behind his visor, but maybe it was Jojo's imagination.

Orion hesitated, and then spoke. "ArcticCat is on a trip right now, but he should be back by this evening."

"Oh, OK," Jojo said carelessly.

"I can finish this later; I have another base to stay in for now. Come on, I had an idea for an event I want to host, but let's discuss it with Starpig first." Orion put down his tools and stretched, then came down from the roof.

The two of them flew down and met with Starpig in a hut similar to the one that was used to plan out the city. Orion explained his plans for the event that he wanted to host. The event was called Demise. The event idea was simple: don't die. If you were forced to respawn, then you wouldn't be able to win. (They had already built a small respawn center so that they could respawn in AquaCraft.) Once you died and had to respawn, then you were out of the game. But even though you were out of the game, you had a new goal: to build traps to try and get all the AquaCrafters who weren't out yet to die and have to respawn. The last person to not die and respawn would win a large cash prize of diamonds.

"And how exactly will this be safe?" Jojo asked.

"As long as the respawn center is protected, then it is completely safe," Orion answered.

Starpig thought about it. "It could be fun, as long as we can keep our bases from getting blown up or something. We will have to make rules about what traps are allowed. And hey, Orion, did you get this idea from HermitCraft?

"Yeah, they did something similar. Anyway, do you think we could do it?" Orion asked, moving around excitedly.

"If we can get enough people to participate in the event, then I see no reason not to," Jojo responded.

"Then I will call a meeting and see who wants to participate. Demise is on!" Then Orion grinned and added "Oh, and I'm going to win!"

"Ha! We'll see about that!" Jojo replied enthusiastically.

That evening the AquaCrafters gathered around in the theater, and Orion showed them the event idea. ArcticCat showed up and brought with him two new Minecrafters who wanted to join AquaCraft. One of them was called TactifulBelt, while the other was called Archan.

Once Orion finished explaining, Gestroyer stood up. "Hey, what if those who have demised (died and respawned) have their own HQ or something. I have space above my castle where I built a giant dragon head building. The demised could use it as a base until the event is over. You know, a spooky theme; it would fit the demise style."

"I won't question why you have a giant dragon head looming above your base, but sure, that works," Orion replied. Then he turned to everyone else. "If you want to participate, there is a sign-up stand in the shopping district. If you don't sign up, then you won't get trapped by the demised. Oh, and traps must not destroy the buildings or bases that the traps are in."

"Can we use TNT?" TactifulBelt asked.

"Well, that's a good question. As long as you fix the person's base afterwards. And this only applies to those who are demised," Orion answered. "No one else can set traps."

Since there were no more questions, the meeting broke up and everyone went to their bases, houses, or the hotel for the night. The next day Orion and Starpig gathered diamonds for the prize from all who planned to participate.

And so the Demise event began. For the next few weeks, all the AquaCrafters were extremely careful not to die. Since no one had died during that time, Orion wanted to speed up the event and maybe earn a profit in the process. He came up with something called demise challenges and built a booth where people could come and see if they wanted to attempt the challenge. He charged five diamonds to attempt a challenge, and if you successfully completed the challenge, then you would win double the amount. These challenges consisted of life-endangering tasks. One was jumping and then saving yourself with a water bucket before hitting the ground. Another was facing off against dozens of mobs in an arena battle. You would think no one would attempt a challenge, but many of the AquaCrafters did actually attempt a challenge!

The first contestant to attempt a challenge was Jojo. He chose to attempt the mob battle challenge in the arena. As he entered the arena, Orion noticed that in the sky dark clouds threatened to rain and thunder. An interesting coincidence, that it would rain during Jojo's challenge. Orion then brought his attention back to Jojo.

"You think you are up to this challenge?" Orion asked.

"Oh definitely; combat is my strong point," Jojo responded instantly.

"OK then, good luck!" Orion said. He flicked the lever which opened the gate that kept the zombies, skeletons, spiders, and creepers back. (Creepers were green monsters that exploded as they grew near.)

Jojo was clad in full iron armor with a shield and a diamond sword. He also had a crossbow and some arrows. Jojo first brought out the crossbow and unleashed a barrage of arrows, taking out the first few zombies. But once the mobs got close enough, Jojo had to take out his shield to stop the onslaught of monsters. He drew his sword and slashed at the monsters. Jojo was skilled with the blade, so it didn't take him long to deal with the zombies. But then the skeletons unleashed their arrows. Jojo brought his shield up just in time to block an arrow flying towards him. Spiders leapt on him, biting at his armor. Jojo threw them off and slew them quickly. At this point Jojo was starting to get tired, but there were still more mobs approaching. He took out his crossbow and shot all his remaining arrows, taking out the skeletons. Now all that remained were the creepers. A few creepers approached, hissed and then exploded! Jojo's shield shattered from the impact, rendering it useless. Jojo and the two remaining creepers were facing off, Jojo had his sword out in front of him, ready for an attack. As the creepers leapt at him, he slashed one of them open but wasn't able to stop the other one from exploding, which knocked him to the far side of the arena.

"Jojo!" Orion shouted as he ran into the arena.

Jojo slowly got up, and said, "Told you I'd beat them!"

"Let's get you some rest; oh, and here are your 10 diamonds. You did well!" Orion said admiringly, handing over ten shiny gems.

The next day, ArcticCat came to the booth, wanting to attempt a challenge.

"I want to try the water bucket challenge," ArcticCat said. "I could use some diamonds."

Orion and ArcticCat walked up a hill to a small cliff. Orion handed ArcticCat a water bucket and pointed where ArcticCat had to land.

"Wow! it's kind of windy up here," ArcticCat commented.

"Good luck!" Orion said, trying to encourage him.

ArcticCat murmured his thanks before leaping off the cliff. He flew through the air and placed the water bucket inches from the ground. But it was a moment too late! ArcticCat hit the ground with a splat, and respawned.

When Orion and ArcticCat met up again, Orion said, "You seem to have a knack for dying!"

"Yeah, I guess I am demised. Hmph, I'm telling you it's that wind," ArcticCat said unhappily.

A few days later, PurpleTimeRift was building in the taiga forest. She was working on building cabins for her real estate. She already had a few AquaCrafters interested in buying. Nearby, she had built her own house. She walked over to her house and went inside. As she walked into the house, she suddenly caught fire. Someone had placed some magma blocks under her carpet! Panicking, she tried to go outside the house, but a shulker bullet caught her, forcing her to respawn. One of her buyers, ArcticCat, had trapped her house! So far, ArcticCat and PurpleTimeRift had demised. Then Starpig also demised from one of Orion's demise challenges, and Gestroyer demised from an ingenious trap placed by TactifulBelt, who had demised not long before!

It happened like this. TactifulBelt's demise wasn't very creative. Someone had just lured a bunch of monsters to his base, so when he returned to his base, he was unable to withstand the horde of monsters. Then TactifulBelt decided to go after Gestroyer. TactifulBelt's base and Gestroyer's bases weren't far from each other. Therefore, it was easy for TactifulBelt to make his way near Gestroyer's base and get out before Gestroyer noticed. TactifulBelt extended the passageway that led out of Gestroyer's castle wall. He placed TNT underneath the passageway and hid pressure plates on top of the stone hallway. The pressure plates would ignite the TNT and blow up anyone who walked through the passageway before they could react. So when Gestroyer exited his base one morning, he had a nasty surprise.

The remaining AquaCrafters who hadn't demised were building base defenses while staying away from everyone else. They did not trust anyone! It was an exciting and challenging time.

. . .

Orion had just arrived in the shopping district. It was a normal day, and he was heading to meet with Cicer to form an anti-demised group. But as he was walking over to Cicer's cottage, Jojo came running towards him.

Before even catching his breath, Jojo spoke frantically, "We have a problem...Archan, one of the...newer AquaCrafters..."

"Hold on, catch your breath. What's going on?" Orion asked, confused.

"Archan is dead! Gone..." Jojo blurted out.

"Demised? Well, that's another one gone," Orion replied, still confused about what the fuss was all about.

"You don't understand. Not demised, Archan didn't respawn! The respawn center has been infiltrated!" Jojo exclaimed.

Orion stared at him, "WHAT?"

"Come on, let me show you! I have already called ArcticCat to meet us there." Jojo replied.

Together they hurried across the terrain and arrived at the respawn center, location confidential. Only Orion, Jojo, Starpig, and ArcticCat knew exactly where the respawn center was. Everyone else just took an underground railroad system back to the main parts of AquaCraft after respawning.

ArcticCat was waiting for them when they walked inside. The doors were broken down, and all the security systems were down. As they went down into the respawn chambers, they saw nothing was left except a crumbled mess of a building. It was completely destroyed, blown up, gone.

Orion spoke gravely as he issued some orders. “Demise is over. Jojo, notify Starpig and shut down the event. ArcticCat, come with me. We must gather everyone together as soon as possible.”

All the AquaCrafters were gathered inside the theater. It was put in lockdown mode, all doors locked. Everyone was sitting or standing, shocked about the news of what had just happened.

Fution broke the silence. “So, what now?” He was looking straight at Orion.

“Well, this is a terrible event. First of all, let me make it clear. No one leaves this place, no one! Not until we are sure that it wasn’t any of us who broke into the respawn center,” Orion said quietly.

Gestroyer said, “If only Orion, Starpig, ArcticCat and Jojo know where the respawn center was, then there is a high chance it was one of them!

“Hold on,” Starpig began.

The AquaCrafters began arguing among themselves, unable to agree whether Gestroyer was right, or that there was no way that one of them destroyed the respawn center. It became so out of control that ArcticCat had to quiet everyone.

“The AquaCraft council will deal with this. We shall interrogate all AquaCrafters to find out what they know until we find out what is going on,” ArcticCat said. “For now, everyone stay calm!”

Chapter 11: Darkness Rising

Days earlier, the mysterious figure bearing a Nether Star had arrived in the overworld of AquaCraft. The figure would later be known as Flamecat. Flamecat had found out about the AquaCrafters months earlier, but he had only been observing them for the last few weeks. He had begun plotting against the AquaCrafters. He wanted to find the Heart of the Sea, so he could use it to control AquaCraft and eventually turn it into nether. For now, he needed to find it. He knew ArcticCat was the one who had it, but he couldn't get close enough to force ArcticCat to tell him, because he was always with another AquaCrafter. So Flamecat decided to see if another AquaCrafter knew anything about the Heart of the Sea. He went after the easiest target for him to get to. That target was Archan.

Finally, an AquaCrafter by themselves, thought Flamecat. *Maybe this one will know something useful. Otherwise, I will just have to kill them.* Archan was fishing in the river which flowed from the main part of the city to where they were now. Flamecat took a fire charge from his inventory and lifted it into the air. With the power of the Nether Star, the fire charge filled up with intense energy. Flamecat threw it in the direction of Archan. It flew with the power of a ghast fireball and hit Archan with a boom! Archan fell, temporarily knocked out from the impact. Flamecat came out from behind the tree where he had been hiding and walked down to the riverbank, each step charring the moist ground. As he reached down, he accidentally touched the river with one of his legs. His leg hissed, and Flamecat leaped back with surprise. He reached out to touch the water with his hand, and it too hissed. When Flamecat touched the water, his armor and skin burned from the water the same way you might burn in lava, for water was Flamecat's weakness. Flamecat reached down again and dragged Archan up the bank, careful not to touch any puddles on the rocky beach. Then he set out to find a cave.

Flamecat had reached a cave not far from the river when Archan began to awaken. Archan took one look at Flamecat and reached for his sword. Archan swung the sword fiercely at Flamecat, but Flamecat just grabbed the sword blade and tossed the sword away. Flamecat's armor prevented him from being hurt by any unenchanted sword. He walked menacingly over to Archan, "Where is the Heart of the Sea?" he demanded in a harsh voice.

"The what?" Archan flinched.

"Don't pretend you don't know! Where is it? One of you must know where ArcticCat or Orion has it!" Flamecat roared.

"Listen, I will help you however I can! Please, Sir, I don't know where the Heart of the Sea is," Archan replied quietly.

"Then what do you know?" Flamecat said in a low voice.

"Well, I, um, I followed one of the Original AquaCrafters, Jojo. He didn't see me, but I followed him to their respawn center. I was just curious. I didn't mean to find it; I know only some AquaCraft members know where it is. By chance, are you one of the AquaCraft enforcers of the rules? Because I didn't mean to break a rule!"

Flamecat glared at Archan in frustration. This AquaCrafter wasn't helping him at all! Then he got an idea.

"Lead me to the respawn center, then," he ordered

They set out for the center, and by the time they arrived, the sun had begun to set. Once they drew near, Archan exclaimed, "Look there is Jojo! He must be just leaving."

They entered the building, and eventually found their way into the respawn chamber.

"Are all the AquaCrafters hooked up to this specific respawn center?" Flamecat asked.

"I think so. Why are you asking? Is this about the demise event?" Archan replied.

Flamecat stayed silent. *Destroying the respawn center would be a great way to put a dent into the AquaCrafters event. Once the AquaCrafters killed each other, he would swoop in during the chaos and steal the Heart of the Sea.*

Even if the AquaCrafters did find out that the center was destroyed, they wouldn't know who destroyed it and would probably blame each other since they didn't know about him. Flamecat was considering all these ideas when he realized Archan was no longer there. He looked around swiftly, then hurried outside. There was Archan walking up to Jojo, who was returning to the center!

"Oh hi, Jojo! I just met one of your enforcers. They were asking a lot of questions about AquaCraft, as if it were their first day on their job. Anyway, I think they were fiddling with the re-"

Jojo interrupted, "Enforcers? We don't have enforcers to enforce the rules. That's not how our system works."

"You don't? Then who was..." Archan began.

Flamecat heard it all. He would not allow one AquaCrafter to stand in his way, so he took out his lava-infused crossbow. It was made from crimson wood, which is fireproof. He took aim and fired without hesitation. A second later Archan fell to the ground, dead. The flaming arrow had hit Archan right in the heart. Flamecat then turned and disappeared inside the respawn center. Jojo just stood there horrified. He unsheathed his sword and glanced around rapidly, wondering where the shot was fired from.

Flamecat returned to the respawn chamber room to find Archan respawning. He walked up to Archan.

Archan looked at Flamecat wide eyed, and spoke, "Who, who shot me? Wait, was it. No, it was you! You shot me!"

Archan was defenseless, having lost all his items when he died. Flamecat continued to approach Archan, who was slowly backing up. Flamecat leaped at Archan and knocked him across to the opposite side of the room. Then Flamecat placed a dozen or more TNT blocks haphazardly around the room. Without even glancing at Archan, Flamecat walked out of the room, turned around and lifted up his arm. He summoned pure nether energy from the Nether Star, charging up an orb of fire and destruction. Archan ran towards the door.

"WAIT!" Archan shouted.

Flamecat threw all the charged-up energy into the room, igniting the TNT and blowing up everything. Orange nether energy also was emitted, making a huge flash of light. Flamecat left the respawn center.

Outside, Jojo saw a painfully bright-orange flash of light emanating from the respawn center. Then he heard an ear-splitting explosion. He put his hands up to his ears and shut his eyes for a moment, and so missed seeing the figure sneaking out of the center. Jojo stood there for a moment, stunned. Then he remembered Archan. He sprinted inside, and what he saw told him enough. He could see that the respawn center had exploded, and that Archan had died. He didn't know what had caused the explosion. But he did not hesitate. He ran as fast as he could to the train track that led to the districts of the city.

. . .

Now, in the theater, the AquaCrafters gathered in small groups, discussing among themselves what they thought about who had killed Archan and who had destroyed the respawn center. Orion and Jojo had begun to interrogate AquaCrafters individually to find out what they knew.

"Still nothing! Well, Gestroyer doesn't seem to know anything. He has an alibi, too. He was with PurpleTimeRift and Cicer. This gets us nowhere," Orion said frustrated.

"Patience, Orion. This process may take time," ArcticCat responded calmly.

Starpig approached them, walking at a brisk pace. He said urgently, "Orion, you need to hear this."

"What is it?" Orion asked. "Hold on, let me get Jojo."

"No, just you. Listen, this is too urgent to wait. I spoke with Jojo the other day. He said he needed to go to the respawn center to check up on something," Starpig began.

"Wait, when exactly was this?" ArcticCat asked.

"About two days ago. Jojo may have been the last person at the respawn center before it was destroyed. He might know something," Starpig explained.

"How come he hasn't told us?" Orion wondered out loud.

"Come on, let's go ask. You should come too, Starpig." ArcticCat said.

They met with Jojo near the stage. Orion asked what Jojo knew, and why he didn't tell them earlier.

Jojo hesitated. "I went to the respawn center yesterday. I was going to tell you, but I didn't have a chance and I didn't want anyone else to overhear."

"Please elaborate," ArcticCat said gravely.

"Well, it was just a normal checkup. I wanted to implement Cicer's starter kits for those who demised," Jojo started.

"Jojo?" Orion said.

"Sorry. I'm still here. I don't know how to put this, but I saw Archan die. I saw the respawn center explode," Jojo replied. "I met Archan outside the center when I returned because I had forgotten something. Archan ran up to me and started ranting nonsense about a so-called enforcer who had met him and was asking about AquaCraft. As soon as I asked him to explain, he was shot in the back with an arrow! A flaming arrow that is. After he died, the respawn center blew up and there was a bright orange light. I ran inside to find everything in ruins! After that I came to tell you, Orion."

Orion and Starpig exchanged glances. ArcticCat then went to gather everyone for an AquaCraft council meeting. The council members gathered in a separate section of the theater away from the rest of the AquaCrafters. At this point, more Minecrafters had joined AquaCraft, though they won't all be mentioned because many come and go. The council members at this point were all the Original AquaCrafters, as well as PurpleTimeRift and Gestroyer.

"We really need to make an actual AquaCraft Council building. A place we can hold meetings instead of this makeshift set up here in the theater,"

Cicer complained to Orion as they entered the extension of the theater.

"Good idea; we will have to do it soon," Orion replied.

Once all the council members had taken their seats around the table, Orion began. "Welcome, AquaCraft Council Members. We have gathered together because we have found important information about the murder and the destruction of the respawn center. Jojo, please explain what you saw."

Jojo stood up and explained what he had witnessed. The council members glanced around, a few of them whispering something to the one sitting next to them.

PurpleTimeRift was the first to speak. "It seems to me that the flaming arrow didn't come from an AquaCrafter. Who has a flame bow? Very few of us have enchanted much yet. We have all been focused on building, not fighting."

"Excellent point!" ArcticCat commented.

Starpig nodded. "I suggest that we send a group of AquaCrafters to the respawn center to investigate. Jojo was distracted by what was going on, so maybe he missed something."

"Agreed," Orion replied.

"It seems as if I owe an apology to you, Orion, Jojo, and ArcticCat. I guess it wasn't a AquaCrafter after all," Gestroyer said.

"It's all good. I would have probably said the same in your place," Jojo responded.

"Well, we can't just sit around! We should act now! The culprit can't be more than a day or two away from the respawn center," Fution exclaimed.

"Right," Orion nodded to Fution. "Since we all seem to be in agreement, I don't think the AquaCrafters need to stay in the theater any longer. Jojo, you will lead a patrol of AquaCrafters to the respawn center. Choose who you'd like to take, and..."

"We should also advise the AquaCrafters to be on the lookout for a suspicious figure that has enchanted gear," ArcticCat said soberly.

"Good idea. Jojo, go now; we can't waste any time. Starpig and Cicer, come with me. I need you to help me build some defenses in the city," Orion said urgently.

Thc meeting ended, and all the AquaCrafters left the theater. Jojo set out with his patrol, which included Fution, TactifulBelt, Gestroyer, and a few others. Meanwhile, Orion, Starpig, and Cicer set out to build defenses.

Jojo's patrol arrived at the ruins of the respawn center. It was early in the morning, and they had traveled in the night to get here. They were exhausted but resolute. They entered the building with caution, leaving two AquaCrafters to guard the entrance. All the lights had been destroyed in the explosion, so the patrol had to hold torches or lanterns up so that they could see. The dim lighting created creepy shadows everywhere. They passed the hallway that led to the rails, which had now been buried by the rubble that had given way after Jojo left. This was the reason why the AquaCrafters had only been able to use the rails part way to get there. The rest of the way they had to go around.

They reached the respawn chamber. Jojo ordered everyone to spread out and search for clues. ArcticCat examined the ground in the middle of the room. He looked closely at the unusual scorch marks on the shattered quartz that hadn't been completely destroyed in the blast.

"Hey Fution, come over here. I want you to take a look at this," ArcticCat said puzzled.

Fution came over, and ArcticCat pointed out his find, "Look here; Jojo said that it was TNT that blew up the respawn center."

"You're right! The explosion would have shattered the quartz, but those scorch marks are unlike anything I have ever seen. They aren't from a normal explosion. This isn't an ender explosion either; let me get Jojo," Fution said.

Fution left, and ArcticCat reached down to touch the scorch marks. As soon as he did, he flinched backwards. His hand burned from the touch. That's weird, ArcticCat thought; it isn't hot anymore, so why did it burn me?

Before ArcticCat could ponder what it meant, Jojo and Fution approached him.

"So, what's this you have found?" Jojo asked curiously.

"These scorch marks aren't from the explosion, and they aren't from any normal fire. I would know if they were" Fution explained.

"Hey um, Fution, could you touch the marks for me please?" ArcticCat asked awkwardly.

"OK? I guess so," Fution replied as he touched the marks.

Nothing happened. The quartz just crumbled. Fution looked at ArcticCat confused. Jojo was also staring at ArcticCat curiously.

"Nothing, I um, never mind. All I can say is something happened here more than just an explosion." ArcticCat didn't say anything else, but his very acute mind was reprocessing all the contradictory evidence.

Jojo and Fution didn't seem satisfied with that answer, but they didn't push ArcticCat to explain. After a while, Jojo called everyone together to share what they had found.

"What we can probably infer is that Archan had just respawned when the blast occurred, which means the blast is probably what killed Archan permanently. Maybe Archan had just a few seconds to see who triggered the blast," Gestroyer explained.

"We also found some footprints that led away from the respawn chamber room. They led outside of the respawn center via the emergency exit. The person who made those footprints had dirty feet, as if they walked through netherrack or something," TactifulBelt added.

"This means you must have just missed the killer, Jojo," Fution noted.

Jojo replied gravely, "That is not very settling. Well, I don't think there is anything else to find here. The person who did this is probably long gone by now."

"How do you know that?" TactifulBelt asked curiously.

"Because don't you think that the person who did this wouldn't just let us see this unless they were sure we wouldn't find anything? Someone doesn't just kill people permanently. It is a crime of the highest order. Especially not in an explosion like this. No sane person could do such a thing," Jojo reasoned.

"Let us hope that you are right, that they are long gone," Gestroyer replied.

Then the patrol journeyed back to the city, arriving around mid-day. Starpig, Cicer, and Orion had finished the defenses around the most important parts of the city. ArcticCat admired their handiwork. The iron golems were a great addition to the city. They were made from iron and were normally found in villages which the golems protected. The iron golems in the city would wander around, keeping a lookout for any trouble. They were like police robots, yet not robots.

"I think that will do for now," Starpig was saying, "The police station foundations are being built by PurpleTimeRift and her builders."

"Good, I...Oh ArcticCat, you're back!" Orion said.

Jojo made his way tiredly to the front of his patrol. "We should talk," he said as he approached Orion. "Somewhere more private."

They both stepped away from the others. Jojo explained what they had found, while his patrol dispersed and went back to their bases or houses to rest after a long night and day. ArcticCat alone stood to one side and waited. After Jojo left, he came to Orion and also asked to talk privately. Orion was puzzled but moved even further from the builders and all the activity. Then ArcticCat explained his weird occurrence with the scorch marks.

"That is strange that only you burned from it. But I am not sure how this is relevant," Orion mused.

"Don't you see? This was a special fire, lava, burns—oh, what's the word?" ArcticCat paused, frustrated, then resumed. "The nether, that's it! Nether is the opposite of Aqua. I was the only one to touch the Heart of the Sea! Maybe the person who is behind this has, like...touched something opposite. I don't know. Maybe if you and I head to the ruins, we might find something. There were footprints that led outwards; maybe we could track down the culprit? Or find out if my theory is correct?"

"ArcticCat, I doubt that there will be anything else to find. But if you really want to go then I guess we can. I need to organize the defenses being built."

"Sorry, I just got caught up with my ideas," ArcticCat started.

Orion interrupted, "But maybe we could go in two days."

ArcticCat replied, "Great! Thank you, Orion. You won't regret this."

Chapter 12: Nether Orion

Two days later, ArcticCat and Orion headed out in the direction of the ruins of the respawn center. They arrived at the site around midday.

"Wow!" Orion stared at the pile of rubble. "You and Jojo were right when you said that the whole place was completely in ruins. Not an understatement."

They paused for a moment to stare, then headed inside.

Side by side, Orion and ArcticCat walked and talked about the recent events and who might be the culprit. They also talked about the future of AquaCraft and what they might do in the future to prevent events like this. ArcticCat led Orion past the corner, turning left into the respawn chamber room. Sunlight peeped through the cracks of the ceiling, casting shadows of mystery and gloom. Orion examined the marks from the explosion. He inspected each rock and piece of rubble. For an hour and a half Orion and ArcticCat looked around the room for clues. Wanting to show Orion the weird scorch marks that ArcticCat had reacted with, Arctic Cat moved carefully around the area, but no luck; the marks were gone.

"They were right here! I remember! I don't know where they could have gone!" ArcticCat said frustrated.

"Hey, don't beat yourself up. Maybe we'll find more clues in other rooms. I will head over to the chest room. You meet me there when you're done here," Orion replied sympathetically.

After Orion left, ArcticCat saw something. He flipped over a piece of rubble, and sure enough there were the scorch marks. The rubble must have been moved when they had searched there the other day. ArcticCat looked around for Orion and called out his name. Orion didn't respond, so ArcticCat walked out towards the chest room. He left the respawn chamber ruins and walked through the half-destroyed hallways. He made his way to the chest room, taking a right and entering the small room. It was more like a large closet than anything else. This room was still intact, ArcticCat thought, but where was Orion? Orion wasn't in the chest room so where could he be? He had said they would meet there. ArcticCat looked around confused.

Moments before, Orion had been in the chest room examining the chests. The chests seemed to be partly looted. *Weird*, Orion thought. *Who would blow up the respawn center and loot the chests? Or were they different incidents?* Just then Orion was distracted by a sound outside the room, but he couldn't make out what the sound was. He left the room in the opposite direction of the respawn chamber ruins.

"ArcticCat, are you there? I said to meet me at the chest room, not the train tracks," Orion said.

Then he heard the sound of someone moving ahead of him. It was too dark to see what was at the end of the hallway because the torches were put out or destroyed. Orion looked carefully; *he could have sworn he saw someone! In fact, he decided, he did see someone back there in the shadows. But who was it?* Orion approached with caution.

"ArcticCat, is that you?" Orion asked, starting to feel a dark sensation around him. It was like a subtle shiver before feeling extremely warm.

Orion drew his sword. He was starting to think that whoever this was, it wasn't ArcticCat.

"Is anyone out there? Show yourself!" Orion exclaimed. He stooped and pulled a torch from his pack. Taking time to be careful, he lit it.

Sword in one hand, torch in the other, Orion turned around swiftly. A dark figure took form in front of him. This certainly wasn't ArcticCat, who was lightly colored. This figure was the opposite—dark, with lava flowing through its armor.

"I have been waiting a long time for this. Finally, I meet the legendary Orion!" said the figure, eyes flashing, taunting, daring Orion to strike. Its eyes were fiery, unlike anything Orion had seen before.

"Who, who are you? Orion asked, backing up slowly, hesitantly.

Instead of replying, the figure lifted up an enchanted sword, similar to a stone sword, but much, much darker. The figure swung its sword at Orion. Orion blocked it with his enchanted diamond sword in his right hand. Orion felt the power of this figure as soon as their blades touched. He pulled away quickly, extinguished his torch, and ran down the almost pitch-black hallway towards the tracks. Taking advantage of the darkness, he drew his bow and shot an arrow.

The flaming figure sliced the arrow out of the air with ease, as though it were a fly.

"You really think an arrow can kill me? You will have to try harder than that!" The figure laughed an evil laugh.

Orion did not answer. He shot three more arrows, and each time the figure sliced them out of the air. Orion thought swiftly. Since the arrows didn't seem to do anything, Orion would try a new tactic. He took out a potion from his inventory and threw it at the figure. The figure winced, turning his head. When he looked back, he saw a blue flash coming down upon him. The figure staggered from the blow of Orion's sword. Orion didn't stop. He continued to swing his sword down with all his might, aiming for any possible vulnerable place in the figure's defenses. This time the figure fought back, but it was on the defensive, not the offensive. They exchanged blows.

"What did you hit me with? Weakness? Not bad; but if you think that is going to stop me, you are mistaken." The figure brought down its sword with the force of a Wither.

Orion blocked the blow with his sword, but he couldn't stop the force of the flame. His sword flew from his hand and clattered on the floor. Orion stepped back, stunned, then sank to one knee.

"You asked me who I was. I am Flamecat, the darkness that shall consume AquaCraft. And you are going to help me." Flamecat was looking down at his opponent now. His expression was triumphant. He reached into his chest and brought out the Nether Star. He pointed it at Orion, who had staggered to his feet, numb from the impact of the strike.

"You shall now be known as Nether Orion! You shall be the one who consumes AquaCraft in a fire that shall transform it into a Nether, my Nether! You, the founder of AquaCraft, will be the one who destroys it!" Flamecat spoke ominously.

The Nether Star's power shot out and grabbed Orion, lifting up the blue figure into the air. Orion groaned, then screamed. The full power of the Nether empowered and consumed him. His blue figure became consumed with orange and red. His red visor turned blue, and his whole figure turned into the opposite of who he used to be. Orion landed on the ground, now Nether Orion, empowered and strengthened by the Nether Star.

Flamecat picked up Nether Orion's sword, and with the power of netherite, upgraded it into a more suitable weapon for the bringer of fire. He handed it to Orion, er, Nether Orion, who grabbed it and examined it.

"Impressive," Nether Orion commented.

"We have work to do. Go now, find the Heart of the Sea and bring it to me. You will know where to find me." Flamecat stalked away towards the tracks.

Meanwhile, ArcticCat had left the chest room and gone in the direction where Nether Orion now was. ArcticCat walked onwards, looking around at the destruction of the hallway.

"Orion! Where have you been? You said to meet in the chest room, but you weren't there." ArcticCat looked at Orion first with relief, but then with horror.

He saw the new Orion and took a step back.

Orion drew his netherite sword, and growled, "Give me the Heart of the Sea."

"I'm sorry? Orion...what happened, are you alright?" ArcticCat drew his sword nervously. "Stop right there! Do not take a step farther! Please explain yourself. Why have you drawn your sword?"

"Hand me the Heart of the Sea before I make you," Orion said in a low voice.

"I don't have it with me. I left it at the place, you know, I told you.

Can you put down your sword?" ArcticCat said even more confused.

"Where is this place, where is the Heart of the Sea?" Nether Orion growled.

"I can show you after you put down your sword. What happened to you?" ArcticCat narrowed his eyes suspiciously, beginning to wonder if this really was Orion.

Nether Orion leaped at ArcticCat bringing down a strike of enormous power. ArcticCat dodged it, then lunged with his own sword, striking Nether Orion's arm.

"Listen, I don't want to hurt you, Orion. Please stop this madness!" ArcticCat shouted.

Nether Orion swung around and launched a series of furious strikes. ArcticCat blocked most of them, his armor blocking the rest. He stabbed Nether Orion, but Nether Orion just continued to fight as if nothing had happened. ArcticCat's sword flew from his hand, and he retreated, running towards the entrance of the ruined respawn center. Nether Orion was in hot pursuit. ArcticCat stopped, turned around, and pulled out the Heart of the Sea.

I didn't want to use this; I only brought it to see if it would react with those scorch marks, but now I don't have a choice, ArcticCat thought. He held it up and pointed it to the ceiling. Water like light emitted from the Heart, hitting the ceiling with a loud bang. The ceiling collapsed in front of Nether Orion, blocking his path.

ArcticCat ran out of the building to where his horse was waiting. He rode swiftly back to the city through the oak forest.

. . .

Starpig was finishing the construction of one of the defensive towers near the border of the city. He had placed a few snow golems at the top of the tower to shoot snowballs at any intruder that was unwelcome in the city.

Starpig had also installed a state-of-the-art alarm system. The police station was almost complete at this point. It would be the center of defense for AquaCraft. Orion had been in charge of the defenses so far, but the AquaCraft Council would elect a chief of police to be in charge of defending AquaCraft from any threats as well as to keep the peace. Starpig finished his checks and stood back, mentally checking over what he had done. He felt good about all of it. He was a careful, inventive builder, and using his skills on defense felt good at this point in time. Turning, he left to go to the council meeting that was set for tonight.

Ten minutes later, Starpig arrived at the police station, where the council was holding its meeting that day. So far, Cicer, PurpleTimeRift, and Fution had already arrived.

"Hi everyone," Starpig said cheerfully

PurpleTimeRift looked over at him and airily waved a hand. "Greetings!"

"We were just talking about who we thought would be a good fit for the chief of police, and about all this curiously-crazy stuff that's happening now," Cicer explained.

"Ah." Starpig looked around. "I see Orion and ArcticCat have not arrived yet."

"I don't know where they are, but here come Jojo and Gestroyer now," Fution replied, pointing in the direction of the tracks.

The minecart tracks went through all the districts; this specific track came from the main station to the police station.

"It's getting late; we'd better start the meeting soon," Cicer stated a bit impatiently.

"Yea, if Orion and ArcticCat don't show up soon, we may have to start without them," Fution said.

"Weird, Orion and ArcticCat aren't usually late to these kinds of things," PurpleTimeRift commented, her eyebrows rising in question marks.

The evening air was cool. Stars were beginning to wink in the sky.

Crickets were making sounds in the grass nearby. The trees near the tracks were swaying gently from the wind. It was a peaceful night. The AquaCrafters gathered inside the main part of the police station. The police station had a central tower coming up from the center of the building. Jail cells were on one side of the building, while the other side was used for offices. The police station was close to a forest where the tracks were, while on the other side was a small ravine that opened up to a large grassy plain.

"We had better start, but I don't know where Orion and ArcticCat are," Jojo said, looking around. "As you all know, the recent events have caused the council to look into a defense for AquaCraft. We all know the candidates for chief of police, myself as one of them. We will vote soon, but first, does anyone have anything of importance to bring up?"

Starpig stood up. "I have finished the construction of many defensive towers on the outskirts of the city. They can be used as a way to alert us of any upcoming threats. They can also be used as turrets to launch projectiles at enemies."

Just then, the main door of the police station opened, and a figure slowly walked in. Starpig peered at the newcomer; all the AquaCrafters focused their attention on the figure.

"Sorry I am late, but there was a matter of importance that must be addressed immediately!" said the figure, who stood nobly, but seeming weary as if he had traveled for a long time.

"ArcticCat! You made it just in time for the meeting," Jojo said lightly.

Starpig asked, "Where is Orion?"

"It's just that. Orion." ArcticCat began.

"Wait, has something happened to him?" Gestroyer blurted out.

"Orion and I set out this morning to the ruins of the respawn center. Once there, I wanted to show him something, but we got separated, and then when we met again, he attacked me! And he started demanding for me to give him something. He looked different, as if he had been consumed by fire, anger, and…" ArcticCat shrugged, at a loss to explain.

"Wait, wait, wait, back up. WHAT?" Starpig exclaimed.

"He…seems to be bewitched by something. This is all my fault, I shouldn't have…" ArcticCat said.

"Where is Orion now?" Jojo spoke calmly, staring directly at ArcticCat.

"I don't know. I barely escaped. He fought so fiercely, as if strengthened by something," ArcticCat responded gravely.

"Then he could be dangerous to us and himself. If something could have happened to someone like Orion, then there must still be a threat out there. Mysterious things have been happening lately," Fution reasoned.

"No one must leave the city! We must be on the lookout for Orion and this mysterious threat," Jojo stated firmly.

"But shouldn't we send a patrol to look for him or something?" ArcticCat asked, "We need to deal with this threat before it harms any more of us!"

"Agreed, but maybe we should find out more information first," Starpig said.

"The first thing that should be done is to organize a defense effort and prepare patrols. Meanwhile a few of us can try to find out more about what has happened. For starters, why did you and Orion go alone to the ruins of the respawn center?" PurpleTimeRift was in action mode now.

"It's sort of a long story," ArcticCat looked at the ground.

"Well, we can't waste any time, I vote for Jojo as the chief of police. We need leaders to help us through these dark times. I fear a battle is approaching, and we must be ready." Starpig suggested. He looked around at the others, and they nodded.

The AquaCrafters voted Jojo as chief of police. Jojo then organized volunteers for patrols, defenses, and overall order. Starpig was put in charge of the first patrol to search for Orion. Jojo, PurpleTimeRift, and Fution gathered in private with ArcticCat to find out as much information as they could.

Back in a private office, ArcticCat was telling the story of the Heart of the Sea and how Orion had tasked him with retrieving it. Extremely reluctantly, ArcticCat explained his experience in full—-about the scorch marks and how he reacted to them. He explained why he thought the Heart of the Sea had caused him to interact with the scorch marks.

"And this is why I think there is some sort of similar item like the Heart of the Sea, something with a significant amount of power that would cause me to react with the scorch marks," ArcticCat said. "That is why I wanted to show Orion the marks—to find more clues, to see what or who has been doing this."

"How come no one has told us about this? Shouldn't the council have heard about this? I think something of this importance should not have been kept secret!" Fution spoke, harshly.

"More importantly, we need to find Orion as soon as possible. And now we know more exactly what this mysterious threat actually is!" PurpleTimeRift added.

Jojo nodded, "Though we council members do not appreciate being kept in the dark, I agree with PurpleTimeRift. We must deal with the threat at hand as soon as possible, starting with finding Orion. Starpig is leading a patrol that will head out tomorrow morning. I want you, Fution, to go with them."

"Can I go too?" ArcticCat asked.

"No, we need you here. We might need the Heart of the Sea in order to stop this threat," Jojo ordered.

"Well, Jojo, now that you are in charge of AquaCraft for the time being, I advise you to appoint other leaders. It would create better organization and there would be a chain of command in place," Fution advised.

"Good Idea. I will get on that." Jojo replied.

Chapter 13: The Trident of AquaCraft

Orion awoke in the rubble inside the respawn center. He looked around. It seemed as though the ceiling had collapsed on him. He couldn't remember anything, at least no recent events. *Where am I?* he thought. *How did I get here? What happened?* He slowly got up; he couldn't remember where he was or what had happened.

It was dark outside. *I need to find shelter*, he thought. *Wait, how do I know that?* He shook his head; he would worry about what had happened later. Right now, he wanted to find shelter and safety.

He left the respawn center and wandered a ways into the forest. Eventually he came to a small cave where he took shelter. He lit a torch and sat down. Slowly he checked through his inventory. The armor he had was damaged, and he didn't have many tools. He was also missing a sword. He was low on food, and he didn't know his way back to...to where? Orion couldn't remember where he had come from. He was too tired to think much more, so he lay down on the hard floor of the cave and fell asleep.

Morning came. The air was clear and crisp. Orion sat up slowly, stood up, and then walked outside. It was beautiful. There were pine trees on this side of the forest. He looked up. He saw the sky beyond the trees, which was dotted with clouds. Then something cold fell on him. Snow. It was snowing! Just lightly, but it made the world look amazing. Orion paused to enjoy the scenery. Then he walked northward, the opposite direction of the ruined respawn center, which was north of the city.

After half a day of traveling, Orion reached the end of the forest. The weather was starting to get colder. He hugged himself for warmth and moved on slowly. Eventually he came to a small village. This village seemed abandoned. *How weird!* Orion thought to himself. Then he thought he saw a light in one of the houses. Slowly and carefully, he approached the house; he opened the door slowly and went in. Just as he came inside, he was pushed against one of the walls. An iron sword was pointed at his head.

"Orion?" Said a voice. The sword was lowered abruptly.

"TheHappyBranch? What are you doing here?" Orion was very much surprised.

"I could ask you the same thing," said TheHappyBranch, sheathing her sword.

"It's good to see you!" Orion replied happily.

"Indeed! I didn't think I would find you here. I thought you would be in the city with all the other AquaCrafters. What are you doing here?" TheHappyBranch asked again.

"Well, I am not exactly sure. I can't seem to remember..." Orion's voice trailed off. Then he straightened up. "Of course! That is where I needed to go!" he exclaimed.

"How do you not know where the city is? We are in AquaCraft? You invited me to come to AquaCraft, you know, in your letter. Do you remember that?" TheHappyBranch asked curiously.

"That is a good question. All I know is I woke up under rubble in a ruined building. I left there quickly. I felt exhausted when I woke up, as if I had just been in a fight," Orion replied, still puzzled.

Orion and TheHappyBranch sat down on chairs inside the village house. It was a one-room house with just a chest in one corner and the door in another.

"Weird. It seems like you have had amnesia. But something serious must have caused that bad memory loss," TheHappyBranch pointed out, then went on to explain how and why she came to AquaCraft. "I came here to this village from northern Evenglade. I brought with me the map you sent. I decided to take a detour on the way to the city. You see, there is a story—more like a legend—that tells about a trident in the land of AquaCraft. According to the legend, the trident is in an underwater cave in an ice-spikes sea. I thought

I might find that in the northern areas of AquaCraft. I came east from Evenglade and then went north and eventually came here. Did you know AquaCraft is on the most eastern side of the known world? But I am getting side- tracked. The point is that this trident is said to hold incredible power, and we might be able to find it! I have been on that quest ever since I heard of the trident. I planned to come to the city after I had hopefully found the Trident."

"Wow! That sounds interesting! Hmmm. Do you suppose I could join you on your quest?" Orion looked at her hopefully.

"Sure! I wouldn't mind a bit of help!" TheHappyBranch replied. "We will set out tomorrow!"

The next day Orion and TheHappyBranch journeyed northwards. After a few hours they reached the sea. It was a semi-frozen sea with ice spikes sticking out from the water. There were icebergs dotted around as well. The two of them got in a boat and rowed through the sea, avoiding the ice and the spikes.

"According to the legend, the entrance to the ice temple where the trident is located should be pretty obvious. We should keep a lookout for any unusual icebergs," TheHappyBranch explained.

"Copy that," Orion replied.

The sky was overcast that day, the sea cold, and the ice even colder. Behind them in the distance was the land they had come from. Ahead and to the right and left of them was more ice, more water, more spikes, and more icebergs.

They had been traveling for about an hour when Orion pointed ahead and said, "Hey look over there! Is that it?"

In the direction where Orion was pointing was a massive iceberg. It wasn't like any other iceberg. This one wasn't just big; it also had ice spikes sticking out from it. And the obvious marker was the giant cave entrance at the front of it.

"That must be it!" TheHappyBranch exclaimed.

They rowed faster and arrived at the iceberg in record time. Cautiously they stepped onto the iceberg. TheHappyBranch pulled out and lit a torch. Orion drew an iron sword, which he had borrowed from TheHappyBranch. After walking through the ice cave for a while, they reached a chasm. The bottom of the chasm was too dark to see. A rickety old wooden bridge went from one side to the other.

"How stable do you reckon that bridge is?" Orion asked, testing the first step on the rickety rope bridge.

"Only one way to find out," TheHappyBranch said.

Orion started to say "I'm not sure you should do that..."

Too late. TheHappyBranch ran across the bridge without any sign of fear or nervousness. A few of the wooden steps broke under her weight, but she made it across, somehow. Orion stared across the bridge.

"Come on!" TheHappyBranch beckoned Orion to follow her.

Orion ran across the bridge, but the last step gave way, and just as he was about to fall, TheHappyBranch reached out and grabbed him. She pulled him up to safety.

"That is what I like to call a close call!" TheHappyBranch's eyes gleamed with amusement.

"All I can say is you may be fearless, but if you aren't careful, it might get the better of you someday!" Orion responded, shaking snow off himself.

TheHappyBranch's skin varied, depending on what season or environment she was in. Because they were in an icy location, she used a skin with blue eyes, white hair, and icy blue outfit. Every time Orion met her, she looked different. For example, in Evenglade, she used a more forest-like skin. It was one of the things that intrigued Orion about his friend.

Orion and TheHappyBranch continued on through the ice cave. The torch light glowed on the ice. They reached a bigger area; three passages went in different directions from there. Each passage had a symbol on the top of it. The left one had a symbol of parkour, which was a figure jumping from platform to platform. The middle had a symbol of a book. And the passage on the right had a symbol in an ancient language. Orion and TheHappyBranch examined the symbols.

"Well, I don't think we should go down the left one, I'm not that good at parkour. This middle one has a book. I wonder what that could mean. And this last one looks extremely familiar. I just can't recall where..." TheHappyBranch pondered on the choices.

Orion reached out and touched the symbol on the far right. Something about it reached out to him, as if calling him down that passage.

"So, what do you think? I want to go down the middle passage. Maybe the book involves knowledge, which is always helpful," TheHappyBranch said.

"I suggest we split up. I will go up this passage, and you can go down the one you want," Orion suggested.

"Are you sure that is a good idea, to split up?" THB (TheHappyBranch) questioned.

"Yeah, I think so. Just trust me about this," Orion said, looking at THB, then looking back at the passage that drew him so strongly.

"Oh OK, if you're sure," THB replied. Then she turned and walked toward the middle passage. Just before entering, she stopped and looked back. "Race you to the Trident!"

"You're on!" Orion exclaimed.

Orion ran down the right passage. Unknown to either of them, that specific symbol meant *To face thyself.* As Orion continued down the passage, each step felt as though something was calling out to him. He reached a large opening. It was lit up, a blue glow emanating from a center point. Around the large ice cave were spikes coming from the ground and coming from the ceiling. A small bridge-like ice walkway led up towards a podium. As Orion approached the podium, his heart began to pound. Upon the podium was a trident, THE Trident, the Trident of AquaCraft. Power and light were pulsating from it. It seemed like it was calling to him. In a trance-like state, Orion took one step, then another. With reverence he approached the Trident.

He reached out to grab it, but before he did, a voice spoke.

"So, you think that belongs to you, do you?" said the voice.

Orion turned around and saw himself.

"So, you think you deserve something so powerful, you think just because you were the first to arrive in AquaCraft it gives you some sort of right to take it? Or maybe you are just that legendary?" mocked the other Orion.

"I didn't...who are you?" Orion asked.

The other Orion looked surprised. "Don't you see? I'm you!"

"But that's not possible," Orion responded slowly.

"It's not? Why shouldn't it be possible? Didn't you read the symbol before coming down this passage?" The other Orion sounded so reasonable.

"I didn't understand it, I don't know the ancient language," Orion said.

"Yet if I'm you, then shouldn't you, er, be able to understand it?" The other Orion started to circle Orion.

Orion looked troubled then spoke. "What do you want?"

"Isn't it obvious? I want what you want! I want the Trident!" The other Orion hissed, hatred burning its gaze.

"Then why don't you take it?" Orion asked calmly.

"The Trident calls out to you, not me. I cannot wield a weapon of the water. I am your darkness, I am your fire. I cannot wield a weapon of that sort," said the other Orion. "I am destined to either destroy you or be destroyed by you."

"Why can't we just be friends? We don't have to kill one another. At least not without a respawn center," Orion offered.

"No, you do not understand. I am destined for either of those outcomes. There is no alternative. It's destiny!" the other Orion insisted.

"I don't believe there is such a thing as yes or no, black or white, good or evil," Orion argued, "It's not that simple."

The other Orion's gaze saddened for a second. "I wish that were true." Then his gaze hardened.

The other Orion leapt at Orion, his blue skin turning into orange and red, the red visor turning to blue. The other Orion drew a dark blade, a netherite sword.

Orion drew his iron sword and blocked the attack. The two battled, each striking and or blocking each other's attacks. But the netherite sword started to eat at the iron sword, the iron sword slowly breaking from the powerful netherite blade. Each Orion was skillful in combat, yet one Orion was a bit stronger. The Orion with the netherite sword knocked the iron sword out of Orion's hand, smashing it into pieces. The Orion that was winning showed no mercy; he slashed at Orion. Orion fell to the ground with a thump. Orion looked down at Orion.

"Please, you don't have to do this," said the Orion on the ground.

"But I do," the other Orion said.

Orion lifted the netherite sword for the finishing blow and started to bring it down. But Orion, who was lying on the ground, reached up and grabbed the Trident. As soon as he touched it, he was empowered by it. Orion moved with inhuman speed, and blocked the strike, the sword clashing at the Trident's end. Orion charged up the Trident, and shot a blast of water, sending the other Orion flying. Orion with the netherite sword landed on the ground winded. Orion with the Trident got up and walked over to the other Orion.

"Listen, I don't want to fight you, Orion," Orion said.

"My name is Nether Orion. I am your darkness, freed from inside you with the power of the Nether Star. I am your fate. I will be destroyed or will destroy you. Only one of us can live. We will meet again." Nether Orion spoke quietly, and then he vanished in a puff of smoke.

Greatly troubled, Orion left the cave with the legendary Trident in hand.

Outside the cave Orion met TheHappyBranch.

"You found it!" THB said, staring at the Trident with astonishment.

Orion stopped but didn't reply.

"You OK?" TheHappyBranch asked, "What happened there?"

Orion shook his head. "I'm fine. I just found the Trident on a podium and walked out. That's all. What did you find in your passage?"

THB wasn't satisfied, but not taking her eyes off the Trident, she told her tale, "I didn't find much, just an abandoned library. I did find some really old texts though! And even some enchantment books! I had to slay a few monsters, though."

"Ah. At least you got something," Orion replied.

Orion noticed an unusual text among the books THB was carrying.

"What's that?" Orion asked, pointing at the mysterious book.

"Oh this?" THB put a few books down and opened the mysterious orange book. "I'm not exactly sure. I found it behind some other books. The words are in an ancient language, and I can't decipher it yet. The only thing I could catch were the words command and block."

"Oh. Fascinating," Orion commented.

"Hey, could I, um, use the Trident? After all this was my quest..." THB asked, drawing his attention back to the Trident.

"Sure," Orion responded, handing THB the Trident, "Though I will want it back because I broke your sword."

"Oh? And how did you do that?" TheHappyBranch asked curiously, but her focus was on the Trident. She traced its surface carefully with her fingers, as if looking for something specific.

"Um, well, I must have accidently knocked against the ice, and it fell down a hole," Orion said.

"Oh sure." THB rolled her eyes. She handed back the Trident reluctantly.

They traveled until sunset before calling it a day. They set up camp on the edge of the forest, and they decided to try to find the city the next day. They talked about Evenglade and AquaCraft. Orion's amnesia seemed to have mostly disappeared, though he still couldn't recall what had happened at the respawn center or any other events on that day.

"I bought a whole family of cats," Orion told THB. "They now live in a treehouse in a more secluded part of the city. Away from all the excitement. You could buy some animals at Gestroyer's pet shop if you wanted to! Oh, and remind me to show you my sky base when we get there."

"Sounds fun. I may want a treehouse, too, sometime...or maybe a sky base," TheHappyBranch said. Then she yawned.

"Guess we should call it a day," Orion said tiredly.

"Goodnight," was THB's short response.

. . .

Starpig was at a gathering of his patrol of AquaCrafters, sitting around a fire.

"If we don't find Orion soon, we may have to return to the city," Fution said gravely.

"Yeah, I know. We will head north one more day, and if we don't find him, then we will turn back." Starpig replied.

The next morning, they headed out. They were about a day or two's journey from the ruined respawn center. Jojo had put PurpleTimeRift in charge of building a more secure respawn center. But until it was built, all the AquaCrafters would be unable to respawn. This is why Starpig and his patrol were so cautious, especially because of the strange events that had happened near there. They couldn't afford to take horses on the trip because there were not enough of them. The patrol was losing hope of finding Orion.

Starpig noticed that the oak forest had turned to pine. Why might Orion come in this direction? This was not the direction of the city. Then again, if what Jojo told him about ArcticCat's experience, then who knew what Orion was thinking, thought Starpig.

"OK, we will start heading west and circle back south," Starpig ordered.

"Wait! I found something!" shouted TactifulBelt.

Starpig ran over to where TactifulBelt was standing. TactifulBelt pointed at the footprints.

"Those are Orion's footprints!" Starpig announced.

Fution joined them and took a look.

"It seems as though Orion was dragging his feet, as if he were extremely tired. It seems that Orion was injured, close to exhaustion," Fution decided after studying the prints carefully.

"We must follow those footprints!" Starpig ordered.

The patrol followed the footprints to a cave. Then they moved farther into the forest.

"Where was Orion going? If we go much farther, this forest should end, unless it's endless," TactifulBelt said.

"Forests aren't endless," Starpig pointed out.

"All I meant is why would Orion go this far?" TactifulBelt asked.

Starpig answered, "That is a good question. Let's hope we find him so we can ask him."

Starpig's patrol continued onwards. Then they heard voices. They drew their weapons. Starpig signaled the patrol to spread out and surround the unknown voices. Starpig stalked forward, sword drawn. He came past a bush and stopped.

"Orion!" he exclaimed.

TheHappyBranch drew her sword.

Orion signaled for her to sheath her sword, "It's alright, it's the AquaCrafters!"

She hesitantly lowered her sword but did not sheath it. Starpig on the other hand did sheath his sword. The rest of the patrol emerged from the trees into the clearing.

"Orion, where have you been? What happened? Is it really you?" Starpig questioned.

"What do you mean? Of course, it's me! Can you not see that?" Orion was confused.

Starpig signaled for the patrol to lower their weapons. He looked at Orion levelly, then made a decision. "You must return to the city with us immediately. We've been under attack!"

Chapter 14: Herobrine?

Gestroyer was going about his daily business. Today he was checking on the animals in his pet shop. The dogs and cats were especially popular to adopt. Because his business was so successful, he was considering selling monsters as well. Mobs and monsters! That is what I can name my shop, thought Gestroyer. Then again, with all the chaos going on lately, it might make the perfect addition to add some excitement. If only he were in charge, then maybe order would actually be implemented and there wouldn't be deaths, destruction, and chaos, he thought. Lately, very strange things had been going on. Trees were missing their leaves, reports were coming in of glowing eyes hidden beyond the mist, and it almost seemed like...No way, it couldn't be, Gestroyer thought. That person wasn't real. All the strange things were just a coincidence. Besides, there were also buildings that were being pillaged and ransacked, and that kind of thing was done by ordinary people.

Just as Gestroyer was leaving his shop, someone walked in.

"Orion! You're here! Where have you been? We have been searching for you for days!" Gestroyer stared at Orion, hiding is surprise.

Orion looked around nervously. "We need to go somewhere private, away from everyone else. Do you have a room behind your shop? I have something important to discuss with you."

"Wait, you need to explain yourself! Where have you been?" Gestroyer said a bit angrily. "Is something wrong? You seem very upset."

"Come on, I will explain, but no one must see me here." Orion looked around one more time, then turned to Gestroyer, motioning for him to follow.

Gestroyer followed Orion reluctantly. He showed Orion the way to the room behind the shop, then locked the door, walked across the room and sat down in a chair. The room was a small room, mainly used as storage. But there was a wooden desk in one corner with two wooden chairs next to it. The room was dim, with only two lanterns lighting it up. Storage barrels and boxes were piled on the other side of the room. Something seemed strange about Orion, as if he wasn't himself Gestroyer thought, but he couldn't put his finger on what it was. Orion was tapping the table nervously. Finally, he spoke.

"Listen, Gestroyer, you can't tell anyone this yet; we can't trust anyone. There are forces that are working against us AquaCrafters. And unfortunately, the leader whom you trust is allying himself with the enemy," Orion began gravely.

"What do you mean?" Gestroyer focused his full attention on Orion, staring suspiciously. Something was off about Orion.

"The reason why I left..." Orion said, choosing his words carefully, "...is because they kept me from coming here. Even now, I may be in grave danger. Jojo, who is in charge of AquaCraft, is working with Herobrine. Jojo is the one who allows the attacks on the city to happen. He disarms all the defenses and lets Herobrine's forces invade and pillage the city."

"I knew it! I never liked Jojo, and him working with Herobrine? The trees without leaves, the weird sightings other AquaCrafters were talking about...I can't believe it! Herobrine, he's real! Herobrine is a legend!" Gestroyer responded, trying to process all this information.

Orion nodded. "Jojo is sneaky; he acts as if he is everyone's friend, but actually he has made a deal with Herobrine to enslave the server! He says he is doing the best he can to stop the attacks, but then why are they still happening?"

Gestroyer interrupted, very disturbed. "If Jojo is in control of the city and helping with the attacks, then what do you propose we do? How will we convince the people that Jojo is actually corrupt? The AquaCrafters support him..."

"That is why I came here. I need someone's help, someone who is on the inside, in the city. We must build something that will stop the attacks. I can deal with the people later. But first we must stop the attacks. It is almost impossible to enter the city without Herobrine and his forces or Jojo knowing that I am here. In fact, I almost got caught earlier! They are too powerful, but

I know a way to stop all this." Orion explained.

"What do you want me to do?" Gestroyer asked. He wanted to help, but at the same time he was catching a glimpse of an opportunity here.

"Well, first of all, I want you to join the ShadowCrafters; that is a group of Minecrafters who are trying to take over AquaCraft. Together we will form a new government, one that knows what it is doing. The ShadowCraft council might be willing to put you in charge of the AquaCraft City. If you prove yourself to them, maybe they will accept you," Orion suggested, as if reading Gestroyer's mind.

"Wow, um, I don't know what to say," Gestroyer was staring at Orion, his mind racing with the possibilities.

Orion said, "For now, do nothing. I will set up a way to contact you. I want you on standby until the time comes when we will stop Herobrine and overthrow Jojo. Are you in?"

And just like that, Gestroyer became part of something that he didn't know would have devastating consequences until it was too late.

Orion left Gestroyer's shop and walked through the shopping district cautiously, entering into a small, unlabeled building. He walked up to a contraption, a machine made with quartz, sea lanterns, and end rods. He flipped a lever and then waited, waiting for the hologram image to appear.

"It is done, my Master; the seeds have been planted. We may move along the plan to stage two. The AquaCrafters won't know what hit them," said the Orion that flared from an aqua blue to a fiery orange.

Many days passed. Jojo was sitting down at his desk in the police station. Starpig's patrol still hadn't returned. *If they hadn't already found Orion at this point, we may have to give up on him,* thought Jojo, leaning back, deeply in thought. *We don't have enough AquaCrafters to defend the city all the time. At least the attacks have stopped for now. But still, it seems like just the calm before the storm. Maybe soon we will find out who is behind all this. These are dark times indeed.*

The door to his office flew open, and Cicer walked in.

"Have you seen the invasion?" Cicer exclaimed.

Jojo sat up abruptly. "No, what's going on?"

"Come on, you really need to see this," Cicer replied emphatically, then walked out of the room.

Jojo followed, and they exited the police station into the daylight. Outside, he looked around, then gave a startled grunt of alarm. Hordes of monsters creeping up on them! The whole area around them was swarming with what seemed like endless numbers of monsters. He looked more closely and saw that monsters had started spawning in the shadows. Zombies limped towards them. Very alarmed now, Jojo drew his sword. Cicer pulled out his bow and shot an arrow, slaying a zombie.

"We need to find the others! We can't stay here!" Jojo shouted as he started to run.

They sprinted towards the mine cart station. Skeletons shot a storm of arrows in their direction. Jojo was hit in the side by one of the arrows. Cicer returned fire, striking down a few of the undead. They entered the station and locked the doors behind them, then leaped into the mine carts and were off.

"What was that!" Jojo turned around in his minecart to face Cicer, who was in the minecart behind him.

"I don't know! I told you something is happening!" Cicer replied.

Jojo said, "Well first things first. We definitely need to find the other AquaCrafters."

"You got hit out there; are you good?" Cicer asked.

"Yeah, I'll be alright," Jojo answered, turning back around to check on his wound.

"We should head to the armory; we could get equipped there," Cicer suggested.

"Good idea. Now that I think of it, we should also install an armory in the police station. If we start getting attacked there too, we need to be prepared." Jojo said.

They rode out of the tunnel onto a bridge. They looked left, in the direction where the main city was. Monsters had started spawning all over. On their right, more monsters. It was an apocalypse! It was as if it were nighttime out with all the monsters around. Something strange was going on.

"That's weird, monsters don't usually spawn on the surface, at least not in these numbers," Cicer pointed out.

"I have a feeling that this is more than just an invasion," Jojo stated.

They entered another tunnel. The ground underneath them flew by. Then the minecarts screeched to a stop, yet they still had a ways to go before the next station.

"Why did it stop?" Cicer exclaimed.

"I don't know, but we will have to walk the rest of the way," Jojo replied.

After 15 minutes or so, they exited the rail tracks tunnel. The armory was not far from here. They carefully sneaked through the city, trying not to draw any attention from any of the monsters. They entered the armory building, which was a stone structure near Orion's hotel. Jojo put on some armor, while Cicer grabbed a sword. Just then PurpleTimeRift ran through the door, closing it behind her.

She panted for breath, then spoke, "What in the world is going on? Why are there so many monsters around?"

"PurpleTimeRift! Glad you aren't dead! I mean not that you couldn't respawn, but lately I don't exactly trust respawning." Jojo exclaimed.

"I know, right! Just when I think the attacks have stopped, now this? Also, don't worry, the new respawn center is heavily guarded and hidden," PurpleTimeRift assured him, "So what's the plan?"

"Find the others and figure out what in the world is going on!" Jojo responded.

The three of them gathered their weapons and armor and walked out of the building fully equipped. Jojo blocked a shot from a skeleton. PurpleTimeRift quickly slew it. Cicer took out a few more monsters, making the path clear for them to run. And they ran, reaching the theater.

"Look over there!" Cicer pointed up towards the top of Orion's hotel.

On the highest floor, ArcticCat was being swarmed by phantoms. Phantoms were like flying stingrays, if stingrays were dark and spooky. They flew down on nights when people didn't sleep, swarming anyone who was in the open. Without hesitating Jojo and PurpleTimeRift, with Cicer close behind, ran to the rescue. They entered the hotel, and Jojo and PurpleTimeRift headed towards the elevator.

"Go! I will watch our backs!" Cicer shouted.

Jojo nodded. PurpleTimeRift reached the top floor first, shooting an offensive firework from her crossbow. It went off with a bang, killing a few phantoms and temporarily driving off the rest.

ArcticCat glanced over and gave a weak grin. "Thanks! I don't know how much longer I would have lasted!"

They looked around, watching the hordes of monsters that were attacking the defensive towers around the districts. Iron golems were being swarmed by the massive numbers of monsters. If any more monsters spawned, then the defenses would be overwhelmed.

Meanwhile Cicer was driving off a small group of zombies who were trying to get through the hotel entrance. A creeper exploded, destroying the front entrance of the hotel! The large hole left by the explosion made it easy for other monsters to push their way through. The other AquaCrafters soon joined Cicer in driving off the monsters. They built barriers, while shooting arrows and other projectiles at the monsters. Then the shadow started vanishing. As quickly as it came, the eclipse started to end. The monsters that still remained quickly began to burn up in the sunlight. (Monsters only spawned in darkness; normally, the sun kept them from existing.)

Jojo and the others walked slowly out of the hotel, through the hole the creeper had left.

"It's gone? What happened?" ArcticCat broke the silence.

The AquaCrafters just stared at each other.

"Is it over?" PurpleTimeRift asked, swinging around to look in all directions.

"I'm not sure." Cicer replied. He still had his sword in his hand.

Later that day The AquaCrafters gathered on the hill above the theater. Here they had built a council room for the council members to meet to discuss things. Today though, the AquaCrafters were using it as a meeting place for all AquaCrafters to gather.

"I believe everyone is here," Jojo said.

"Wait, where is Gestroyer?" ArcticCat asked.

"Yeah, where is he?" Cicer agreed.

Jojo looked around. "Does anyone know where he is?"

"No, I haven't seen him." PurpleTimeRift stated.

"Hey look, people are coming!" ArcticCat exclaimed.

Approaching from the northern mountains, a group of Minecrafters appeared. Cicer walked forward, ready to greet the newcomers. The group eventually came within a distance that one might clearly be able to see them.

"TactifulBelt! It's you!" Cicer exclaimed. "I'm so glad to see you!"

Behind TactifulBelt, Fution and many others approached.

"Did you find...Orion?" ArcticCat asked anxiously. No one answered.

The AquaCrafters gathered, greeting one another.

"Orion, where have you been!" someone asked. ArcticCat turned. Sure enough. Orion was there!

Questions upon questions poured out on all sides until Orion signaled for everyone to be quiet.

"I will answer all your questions soon, but we have all been on a long journey, and we need to rest." Orion smiled slightly. "First, though, I would like to introduce you all to my friend, TheHappyBranch."

Everyone greeted THB (TheHappyBranch), and then they turned to each other and got talking. ArcticCat sat with Orion while he ate.

"Well, we are all back together again!" ArcticCat said.

"Indeed. Do you want to or do you want me to..." Orion started.

"No go ahead, you can tell your story first," ArcticCat interrupted.

Across the room, Starpig and Jojo were at a table by themselves, chatting about current events.

"Well, maybe now that you all are back, maybe there will be some peace in the city for once." Jojo said.

"I hope so. But don't think that just because there are more of us here, that they won't try and attack again just because we might outnumber them..." Starpig said thoughtfully.

"True." Jojo stood and stretched. "Well, I'd better head out to my base. I need to gather more ores in the ravine. For armor," he said.

"Would you mind if I came too? I need some more resources as well," Starpig asked, always polite.

"Sure," Jojo responded.

And so, they headed out for Jojo's base. They took the mine cart track there. They arrived just as the sun had started going down. And this time, it was actually going down; it was not an eclipse. Jojo and Starpig entered the base, climbing down scaffolding into the ravine.

Jojo headed deeper down into the ravine, trying to find some iron ore or maybe some diamonds. He found a bunch of iron and began to gather it. This would help to make more armor to fight the threat, he thought.

A loud bang of thunder and a flash of lightning struck the base that was suspended above the ravine. Jojo turned around to look at a figure standing on the roof of his base. When the mist cleared, he saw the two bright white glowing eyes of a figure with a light blue shirt and dark blue pants. The figure was staring directly at Jojo. It was Herobrine. The name and the recognition pulsed through Jojo, sending a shiver throughout his body. Unbelievably, standing before him was the Herobrine. He blinked and looked again. Herobrine turned and stared at Starpig who was oblivious to what was going on. Jojo started to call out a warning, but he was too late. Herobrine leaped down and landed on the crevice where Starpig was. Starpig turned around, and Herobrine drew an enchanted dark sword out of his inventory. Herobrine pointed the sword at Starpig who had quickly drawn his own sword to defend himself. The dark nether sword pulsed, and fire shot out, striking Starpig, stunning him. Herobrine did not hesitate. He dashed in at lightning speed and stabbed Starpig right through the chest.

Jojo gasped, stunned. Herobrine collected Starpig's items, then turned to stare at Jojo. Then he just backed away and vanished into the shadows...

Chapter 15: Eclipse

Gestroyer was following Orion through a forest. Orion had said that he knew where Herobrine was and that Gestroyer might be able to help him stop Herobrine. He also promised Gestroyer a high position in the government if they succeeded. Now they talked as they wove their way through white birch trees and green pines.

"All Herobrine needs to do is to kill all the AquaCrafters at least once with the nether star's power. Once he has done that, he will have power over AquaCraft, for the nether star can then be used to turn all AquaCrafters to the nether side. We must stop that from happening," Orion said.

"How do you propose we do that?" Gestroyer asked, struggling to keep up with Orion's pace.

"I would like to introduce you to my friend. He can help us defeat Herobrine," Orion explained.

"Is this friend a DarkCrafter?" Gestroyer asked dubiously, pausing to catch his breath.

"He is the leader of the DarkCrafters," Orion answered confidently, looking back over his shoulder.

"And he is meeting with us? Wow!" Gestroyer exclaimed quietly, as if to himself. He began to think about what this might mean for him.

"Here is the place. Now be very respectful to him, for he is easily offended," Orion said.

"What is his name?" Gestroyer asked.

"Flamecat," Orion answered.

Orion and Gestroyer came into a clearing in the forest. Above them was the large cliff face of a hill. Next to the cliff face was a small wooden cabin. The floor of the cabin was supported by wooden plank pillars. Stairs led from the ground up to the cabin deck. The cabin was very plain—a very simple design. All the windows were dark, as if the light couldn't break through.

They entered through the cabin doors. Inside, a figure sat facing away from them. A fire burned in the fireplace at the end of the one-room cabin. The figure stood up and turned around. What Gestroyer saw surprised him. The figure looked as though lava were flowing through its armor.

"Master Flamecat, I bring you Gestroyer, the one I spoke of who might help us stop Herobrine," Orion said.

"Let us hope you are up to the task." Flamecat said, looking at Gestroyer.

"What do you want me to do?" Gestroyer asked, after some hesitation.

"There is a way to stop Herobrine, and we have the item strong enough to stop him, but without something to direct its power, the item is useless. We need you to build a giant statue of Herobrine. Above the statue, we will place the item. We cannot go too far into the city without Herobrine knowing or one of the AquaCrafters trying to stop us. That is why we need you to go and build this structure. Neth... I mean Orion will place the item at the top of the statue once it is built. Time is of the essence, so you must do this, and must not let anyone near the statue," Flamecat explained.

"Is, is that all?" Gestroyer asked. He seemed puzzled.

"One more thing; we cannot have you seen by the AquaCrafters," Orion started.

"Why not? If we are trying to stop Herobrine, shouldn't the AquaCrafters know?" Gestroyer interrupted.

"Don't interrupt. If the AquaCrafters knew, then so would Jojo, and he would stop us," Orion responded.

"Oh, OK." Gestroyer said.

"You must leave now," Flamecat said in a flat tone that allowed no argument.

Gestroyer left. He headed back to the city, leaving Orion and Flamecat in the cabin. He walked for some time. It was beginning to become evening when he realized he had reached Jojo's ravine base. Out of the corner of his eye he thought he saw movement. He looked around but didn't see anyone. He looked down the ravine. From where he was on the top of the hill, he saw the base. Down below it, two small figures stood in the ravine. The setting sun sent shadows down the ravine, the lighting making it hard to see. After some examination of the figures, he realized Starpig was the one higher up in the ravine, while it was Jojo at the bottom. Then he saw a third figure at the top of the ravine walk out of the bushes and climb onto the roof of Jojo's base. It was Herobrine! Gestroyer couldn't believe his eyes. Yet Herobrine wasn't as mysterious as Gestroyer remembered. He thought he would look more ominous. Then Herobrine summoned a lightning bolt, striking the roof. Gestroyer saw Jojo look up. Herobrine leapt down to where Starpig was mining. *Why doesn't Jojo do something*, thought Gestroyer. Herobrine killed Starpig with a flash. Of course! Jojo meant for this to happen, thought Gestroyer. Jojo must be luring AquaCrafters to their demise!

Gestroyer knew he had to do something. He needed to build the statue as soon as possible. He snuck down the hill and ran straight to the mine cart tracks. Jojo and Herobrine must be stopped!

Days passed. Gestroyer was feeling more secure. None of the AquaCrafters hadn't seen him since the incident at the ravine. Now that Orion was back, Jojo had stepped down to let him lead. Even though Starpig had respawned, the mood was still gloomy. Herobrine could strike at any moment, catching the AquaCrafters off guard. The AquaCraft Council Members had gathered to discuss what their next course of action would be.

"We must not let Herobrine find the new respawn center. Just imagine the damage that would be caused if he destroyed it," Fution said.

PurpleTimeRift piped in. "The real question is whether this Herobrine is the same Herobrine in the legends, or just a fake. Also, is this Herobrine the one who destroyed the first respawn center and killed Archan?"

"Indeed, but there doesn't seem a way to find that out unless we can somehow capture him." ArcticCat half smiled, "I doubt that will happen, especially if this is the real Herobrine!"

"Oh, come on! Surely, we aren't believing that this is the real Herobrine; that's just a myth!" Cicer said, rolling his eyes.

Jojo said, "I think we are forgetting something. What about Gestroyer? What happened to him?"

"These are all good points. It is unclear what we should do next, but before we do anything else, I would like to propose we have TheHappyBranch join the council," Orion said, "She comes from outside our group and may have a unique perspective on this crisis."

"Shouldn't we wait until we know more about her? I mean, we have only just met your friend," ArciticCat asked, ever the cautious one.

"No, I think in a time like this we need more than just the council to discuss things. At this time, I propose we have all the AquaCrafters gather and discuss these topics. During this crisis we will need all the help we can get," Cicer said.

"I agree. We should get all the AquaCrafters to help fight this threat. The only way we can defeat Herobrine is if we stand together, not apart," Jojo stated strongly.

To that the AquaCrafters were nodding their heads in agreement. And so the call was sent out, and not long after, all the AquaCrafters gathered in the council meeting room. It was packed, but everyone was cooperative, invested in protecting their realm. After the meeting, Orion began giving out orders.

"OK, I want THB, Starpig, and Cicer to leave on a patrol to find Gestroyer; we cannot be missing AquaCrafters, at least not while Herobrine is hunting us," Orion ordered.

"We will leave immediately," Starpig responded.

"Now PurpleTimeRift, please assign someone to guard the new respawn center, and make sure to assign shifts as well," Orion said. "Jojo, you are in charge of defense. You know your castle? I want you to extend the walls to protect the main areas of the city. We will place snow golems and iron golems on and near the walls to defend them."

The meeting broke up, and the AquaCrafters went off to their duties. TheHappyBranch, Starpig, and Cicer were off in the direction of Gestroyer's base, a good place to start searching. Arriving at Gestroyer's base by midday, the AquaCrafters split up. Gestroyer's castle was large, and he might be anywhere. Starpig looked up the giant stone wall stretching up at least 50 blocks. TheHappyBranch went up the left hill, and Cicer went up the right. Starpig could see the giant ender dragon head floating above Gestroyer's castle. It was still there from after the demise event. Starpig walked over to the tall doors at the base of the wall. He pulled on the door handle, and to his surprise, they were unlocked. Inside the walls, a large castle tower went up from the center of the base. Gestroyer's castle was built on a hill, so the walls were only on some parts of his base. THB would search the top, while Cicer would search in the giant dragon head structure. Starpig would check the tower. He looked left and right. On his left, he saw Gestroyer had built small village-like houses against the walls. On the right he saw that there were farms. *How medieval*, thought Starpig. Sneaking inside, he drew his sword to ward off any threat that might be waiting. He entered a dimly lit room, the only light coming from a few torches on the walls. Straight ahead he saw a staircase leading down, and to his right, a spiral staircase leading up. Just then Starpig heard footsteps coming from the staircase ahead of him. He ducked away into the small storage room to his left. He watched as Gestroyer emerged, carrying a stack of wool blocks. What would Gestroyer need wool blocks for? Starpig wondered. Starpig followed Gestroyer out of the tower. Gestroyer was heading out of his castle. Starpig pulled out a firework from his inventory and set it off.

Starpig then pointed his sword at Gestroyer and exclaimed, "Stop right there, Gestroyer!"

Gestroyer glanced back and then took off out of his base, going through the door in the wall. Starpig followed, running after him. TheHappyBranch and Cicer joined him outside the castle.

"We heard your signal, did you find him?" TheHappyBranch said, catching her breath.

"I did, but then he just took off! He ran in the direction of the mine cart station." Starpig replied.

"What has gotten into him?" Cicer asked.

"I don't know. Come on! We may be able to catch him on horseback." Starpig said.

The trio ran over to where they had left their horses underneath a tree. Starpig leapt onto his light brown horse, taking off. THB and Cicer weren't far behind him. Slowly but surely, they began to catch up with Gestroyer. Horseback riding was faster than running. Cicer pulled in front of the group.

"Come on Gestroyer, we just want to talk!" Cicer shouted.

Gestroyer, stopped, turned around, and shot an arrow from his crossbow, knocking Cicer off his horse. Then he entered the mine cart station and was gone.

"You take care of Cicer, I will stop Gestroyer!" TheHappyBranch exclaimed.

"Hey, wait," Starpig began, but she was already gone, "Oh, never mind."

TheHappyBranch got into a minecart, then pushed the button that powered the rails, sending the minecart off on its journey. Gestroyer had already had around a three-minute head start. THB would have to hurry if she wanted to catch him. Not long after, TheHappyBranch spotted Gestroyer in the distance on the track ahead of her.

"Can't this thing go any faster?" TheHappyBranch complained to herself.

TheHappyBranch followed Gestroyer through the shopping district, out of the city, and to a hill. On the hill rose a giant statue, created out of wool blocks. The feet were made out of black wool, the legs out of blue wool. The chest was made out of cyan colored wool. A statue of Herobrine! Except for the fact the white eyes were missing. Then she saw Gestroyer at the top of the statue, placing white wool blocks in, filling in the eyes. She looked even higher up to see the statue supporting a large grassy island with a house upon it. The statue had to be at least twice as tall as Gestroyer's castle. And that was saying something, thought THB.

Meanwhile, up top the giant statue in the house, Gestroyer met with an Orion who still gave him an uncomfortable, unfamiliar feeling.

"If you thought that first invasion was something, you haven't seen anything yet," this Orion said. He seemed to be boasting.

"I thought the invasions were bad things?" Gestroyer said, confused.

"Yeah, they are. But we need to do this in order to stop Herobrine. We must open the rift and force Herobrine back to where he has come," Orion explained.

"You mean the Nether," Gestroyer responded.

"Precisely," Orion said, "The Nether Star is the only thing strong enough to open the rift, the key to the nether. Last time we tried doing this, it didn't work because we didn't have the statue to direct its power."

"I see," Gestroyer said, "So what do you want me to do?"

"Well, once Herobrine arrives, you must direct the power of the Nether Star at him. That's why you built the house up here. To hide the Nether Star. You must not let any AquaCrafter stop us. They don't understand what is going on," Orion explained.

Orion placed the shulker box down on a pedestal in the house.

"Once I activate this, you will have to guard it. I have placed monsters to stop anyone from getting up this high. If someone attempts to climb up through the statue, the monsters should stop them. We can't let anyone interfere." Orion said.

"That seems...a bit harsh. Wouldn't it be easier just to warn the AquaCrafters?" Gestroyer wondered out loud.

"That um, well, the AquaCrafters wouldn't understand. Jojo has too much control over them," Orion stammered.

"I'm not sure about that," Gestroyer replied suspiciously.

"Don't be having doubts now! We must finish this now!" Orion exclaimed. "And don't forget, if we are successful, you will be rewarded."

Gestroyer left the house, surveying the landscape. Orion opened the shulker box, retrieving the Nether Star. He lifted it up, his form changing, becoming a fiery orange. Then his shape changed again, glowing white eyes replacing the visor. A blood red beam emitted from the Nether Star, like a beacon, flying upwards through the hole in the roof. A dark cloud formed, overcoming, overwhelming all the blue sky. Thunder and lightning sounded above him. The sun was totally eclipsed. The moon replaced the sun above, shining through the clouds. It was as if the sun had died, for it was eclipsed by the moon and the clouds. Monsters started spawning, zombies and skeletons rising from the ground. Spiders and creepers emerged from the forests.

TheHappyBranch had stopped at the foot of the statue. Now she watched as the eclipse spread over the whole world. She drew two swords, one in each hand. As the monsters approached her, she struck out at them, narrowly ducking underneath their outstretched arms. But the tide of monsters was endless, and she couldn't kill them fast enough. She brought her swords up, slaying two zombies at once. Then she backed away and settled into a fighting stance. She began to retreat towards the shopping district, eventually climbing onto a shop roof to get away from the torrents of monsters. She was growing tired now, not sure how much longer she could fight, and yet phantoms still flew down from the sky shrieking at her. Out of nowhere, an arrow flew over her head, singing as it flew, killing one of the phantoms coming down upon her. She turned around to see Cicer and Starpig bows drawn, shooting down monsters.

"Didn't think you would have all the fun for yourself, did you?" Starpig said, but he was breathing hard.

"Thanks. Where are all the monsters coming from? What happened to the sky?" TheHappyBranch asked, opening and shutting her hand to get rid of a cramp.

"I don't know. This has happened before, but not in these numbers. I think we should regroup with the others before we are overwhelmed," Cicer replied. He seemed his usual carefree self in spite of the stress.

"Good idea," THB answered, relieved.

They ran through the streets, fighting as they went. By the time they reached the council building, most of the AquaCrafter had already retreated inside the walls. Jojo had finished building a small stone wall around the most central part of the city. Orion, ArcticCat, and Jojo were gathered outside the council room when THB, Starpig, and Cicer reached them. TheHappyBranch gave a report of what she had seen, including the part where Gestroyer went up to the top of the statue.

"...and then the eclipse started!" TheHappyBranch reported.

"Well, I think we know where the origin of this threat is now," Orion pointed out. "Jojo, organize a patrol of AquaCrafters to attack this statue. Everyone else will stay here with Starpig. Starpig, we will send a messenger if we need back–up, but we need you to stay here for now to protect the main city area. There are too many monsters for a large group of AquaCrafters to reach the statue unnoticed."

Starpig nodded. "We will wait here until further notice."

Jojo had already gathered ArcticCat, PurpleTimeRift, and Cicer for the patrol.

"I will go with you," Orion said, bringing out the Trident. "We must stop this threat, and it's now or never!"

Orion and ArcticCat took the lead of the patrol. ArcticCat whispered to Orion, "Now might be a good time to use the Heart of the Sea. We need all the help we can get!"

"Then quickly now, retrieve it immediately. Whatever is causing the eclipse may only be destroyed by something the power of the Heart of the Sea has. We will try to destroy it on our own, but we may not succeed. I need you to get it quickly, because I don't know how long we will last out there on our own, especially if Herobrine is behind this." Orion replied.

ArcticCat ran off. Jojo walked up to Orion, and asked, "Where is he going?"

"To get something that may be able to stop this threat once and for all," Orion responded, then turned around. "AquaCrafters, I do not know if we will win this fight, nor do I know if we shall all survive it. All I want to say is that it is an honor to fight beside you." Orion lifted up the Trident, "For AquaCraft!"

"For AquaCraft!" The AquaCrafters responded.

The patrol neared the statue, walking cautiously. Jojo peered over the hill to look at the statue, examining the scene.

"There is a beam emitting from the house above the statue. I would say that is the source of the eclipse. I can't see any way up the statue though," Jojo reported.

"OK, in that case. Jojo and PurpleTimeRift, try to get a closer look at the way up the statue; Cicer and I will stay here and give you cover fire if you need it. I want to give ArcticCat as much time as we can," Orion ordered quietly.

PurpleTimeRift and Jojo approached the statue with caution. They left the shopping district, staying hidden underneath the trees in order to not be seen. It was dark, but not too dark to see. Not wanting to call attention to themselves, they did not light a torch. Swords drawn, they sneaked towards the statue.

"Here, this will allow us to get to the statue without being seen," PurpleTimeRift said, handing Jojo a potion of invisibility.

They both drank the potions, throwing the empty bottle on the ground. They took off their armor, for invisibility potion wouldn't make their armor invisible. They ran to the giant feet of the statue. Making their way around back, they found a door at the back of the feet, leading inside the statue. Their invisibility began to wear off at this point. Jojo entered the statue first, PurpleTimeRift watching their backs. They entered the weird structure, climbing up the ladders that led up into the legs of the statue. Just then, spiders leapt onto them from above. Jojo swiftly slew one spider. PurpleTimeRift, who was below Jojo, kicked a spider that was climbing up the ladder from below.

"Not a step farther!" shouted a voice from above.

"Gestroyer!" Jojo exclaimed in surprise.

Gestroyer glared down at Jojo, then stepped on Jojo's hand, forcing him to fall down to the bottom of the statue. He shot an arrow at PurpleTimeRift, who leapt off the ladder just in time, dodging the arrow. Gestroyer jumped down the leg, following them to the bottom. Jojo had his sword drawn, facing Gestroyer.

"You traitor!" Jojo exclaimed.

"Traitor? You're the one who is the traitor!" Gestroyer shouted, striking Jojo with his sword.

Jojo parried the attack. Their swords shone as they exchanged blows. Gestroyer landed one on Jojo's chestplate, which caused a loud clang. But Jojo answered with a blow just as mighty, landing it on Gestroyer's helmet. PurpleTimeRift shot a firework from her crossbow, sparks flying in all directions from the back of the firework. The firework reached its target and knocked Gestroyer against the wall.

"Surrender, Gestroyer." Jojo said, pointing his sword at Gestroyer who was lying against the wall, winded.

Gestroyer looked up, fear showing in his eyes, "Look out!"

Jojo turned around just in time to see a pair of glowing white eyes in the doorway. Herobrine was holding a sword of darkness. PurpleTimeRift, who was closest to him, turned her sword towards him to defend herself. Herobrine brought his sword upward, striking her iron sword, cutting right through it like it was nothing. Herobrine spun around and stabbed her right through the chest. She stared down at the sword protruding out of her chest, then looked up at him. He slowly pulled it out of her chest, before she crumpled to the ground.

Chapter 16: The Desert Temple

Orion and Cicer were watching Jojo and PurpleTimeRift sneak to the back of the statue beyond their sight.

"So, how long do you think ArcticCat will be gone?" Cicer asked. Things were pretty out of control as far as he was concerned.

"I'm not sure, but I am hoping he gets over here soon. If it comes down to fighting Herobrine, we will need what ArcticCat has," Orion replied.

ArcticCat had brought the Heart of the Sea closer to the city recently and had placed it somewhere that was easier to access. He had moved it after the incident at the ravine. Orion knew it had been moved, but he didn't know where.

Let's hope it is strong enough to defeat Herobrine with its power plus the power of the Trident, Orion thought. Maybe, just maybe, we can defeat him that way. He looked around and wondered how Jojo and PurpleTimeRift were doing in the statue. They still hadn't raised a signal that it was all clear or that they were in trouble.

"Something's wrong; surely they should have signaled by now," Cicer worried out loud.

"I bet they're doing fine," Orion said, but privately he shared Cicer's fears.

"I'm going to go take a look," Cicer said suddenly.

"Wait!" Orion exclaimed! But Cicer was already gone, making his way along the trees towards the statue.

"Oh, where is ArcticCat? He should be here by now!" Orion looked around, unsure about what to do.

Meanwhile, in the statue's leg, Jojo was staring in shock and disbelief.

"No! PurpleTimeRift!" he cried out. It had all happened in a flash, and there was nothing he could do. And now Herobrine had picked up all

PurpleTimeRift's items. He turned to stare at Jojo and Gestroyer, mocking them both with his look. Jojo's shock turned to fury. He was tired of all that had happened, and here, standing before him, was the culprit. The one who had caused all this destruction.

Jojo flung himself onto Herobrine, his diamond sword coming down with all his weight. Herobrine deflected the attack, and the two swords clashed. Jojo charged in with an onslaught of strokes, their two swords flying and sparking at contact. The two of them were battling at lightning speed. In their struggle, they had moved outside the statue and fought now on grass. Their swords clashed, and each of them was pushing with all his might, neither giving in. But then Herobrine lowered one of his arms, charged up a fireball from it and launched it at Jojo. The impact sent Jojo flying. He landed hard, his armor badly damaged. Herobrine walked up to him, preparing the finishing blow. But just as he was about to, an arrow flew out from among the trees. Herobrine turned swiftly and sliced the arrow in half. Then another arrow flew, and another. Herobrine deflected the arrows, walking backwards, and suddenly he disappeared into the darkness of the eclipse. Jojo looked over and saw Cicer with his bow drawn, pacing towards him.

"Are you alright?" Cicer asked.

Jojo groaned as Cicer pulled him up, "I will be in a minute," he managed to say. "Hey, where did Gestroyer run off to?"

"I don't know, but I think we have bigger things to worry about!" Cicer pointed up past the statue.

Herobrine was floating near the top of the statue, facing it. The dark clouds had parted now, revealing the true eclipse of the moon covering the sun. The day had turned into a dark night. In the distance, the shopping district could be seen. Behind them the river was flowing around the city. Thunder rumbled and lightning flashed high above them. Herobrine was now staring at the Nether Star at the top of the statue. Gestroyer was there, directing the energy beam that was emitting from the Nether Star to Herobrine. The red beam cut through the roof of the house, and when it came into position,

Herobrine shielded himself. It looked as if this was the end for Herobrine, but then Herobrine laughed. He opened his arms wide and began to absorb the energy, starting to glow with a bright white light. Then he raised his arms; dark red energy circled his arms, and then a dark red beam shot from them into the sky towards the moon. The moon began to glow darker. Yet it wasn't the moon, it was a portal—a portal to the nether. The portal circled like a hurricane, growing bigger by the second. Ghasts and blazes flew down from the portal, shooting fireballs down at the city. Magma cubes and zombie pigmen fell to the ground. Some died as they hit the ground. Others somehow survived. Herobrine stopped shooting out the beam, and flew at the house atop the statue, grabbing the Nether Star and breaking a hole in the other side of the house. He flew around and landed on the ground at the bottom of the statue, opposite the side where Jojo and Cicer were looking up in horror.

Jojo and Cicer ran around the statue to confront Herobrine. But they came late. A bright aqua beam hit Herobrine, knocking the Nether Star out of his hands. Orion leaped down from the small hill he was standing on, the Trident in his hands. ArcticCat ran up behind him.

"Get the Nether Star!" Orion yelled.

Jojo and Cicer both ran towards the Nether Star but were stopped by a horde of monsters. They charged through the monsters, slashing with their swords and killing multitudes of them. Yet the monsters were too many. They knocked Cicer down and forced Jojo back.

Meanwhile, Herobrine drew his dark nether sword. Orion ran to meet him, and their weapons clashed. Evenly matched they were; even their fighting styles were similar. Orion thrust the Trident forward, and Herobrine parried the strike. Then Orion brought the Trident up, striking Herobrine's arm and knocking him back.

Farther away, ArcticCat came on the scene, launched a water wave, using the power of the Heart of the Sea. The wave washed a bunch of monsters down the hill towards the river, knocking the monsters off Cicer and Jojo.

"Where did you get that thing?" Jojo exclaimed.

"You like it? It's the Heart of the Sea," ArcticCat replied happily.

Cicer was still looking at the Heart. "So that's what you went to get," he said.

Distracted by a group of zombie pigmen, ArcticCat pointed the Heart of the Sea towards them, and shot a jet of water. It impaled the pigmen. They collapsed onto the ground. ArcticCat smiled again.

"Come on you guys!" Jojo wasn't impressed. "We need to get that Nether Star!" he called out.

"You go, I will be right there," ArcticCat replied.

ArcticCat ran over to where Orion was in a fierce duel with Herobrine. Herobrine had knocked the Trident out of Orion's hand.

"Orion, here!" ArcticCat exclaimed, throwing the Heart of the Sea at Orion, who barely caught it.

Orion used the Heart of the Sea to grab the Trident with a water beam. Before he could react, Herobrine jumped up, bringing his dark sword down. The Trident and the Heart of the Sea fell out of Orion's grasp. Orion fell to the ground, barely conscious. Herobrine walked over and picked up the Heart of the Sea.

"I have been waiting a long time for this. With the power of the Heart of the Sea, I shall be able to kill you, permanently." Herobrine was speaking for the first time, his voice full of menace.

"Who...argh, who are you?" Orion mumbled.

"You know who I am," Herobrine replied.

Herobrine's figure then changed, his body melted away, revealing a dark red figure. Nether Orion.

"No one else can see me for who I truly am except you. Herobrine was the perfect cover. And now I shall fulfill my destiny!" Nether Orion exclaimed, raising his nether sword for the finishing blow.

The dark sword was empowered by the power of the Heart of the Sea, glowing with a bright blue shimmer.

"No!" ArcticCat exclaimed.

ArcticCat ran towards Orion, leaping over him, to be stabbed through the stomach by Herobrine's blade. ArcticCat collapsed on the ground, his body glowing with the energy from the blade. Orion reached to his side, and grabbed the Trident, swung it upwards, and struck Herobrine hard, causing him to step backwards. Orion leaped to his feet and shot a powerful jet beam of water at Herobrine, knocking Herobrine to the ground. Orion, who was now furious, grabbed the Heart of the Sea from the ground and merged it with the Trident. He walked over to Herobrine and swung the Trident down on him as he struggled to get up. The blow knocked him down again. Orion swung the Trident around, striking Herobrine again. Then he turned the trident around and got ready to deal the finishing blow. The Trident began to charge up with enormous energy.

"Do it. Kill me." Nether Orion said.

Orion hesitated, "No. Stop the eclipse which you have started. Close the portal!" Orion withdrew the Trident, motioning for Nether Orion to get up.

"What makes you think I would do that? Do you think I am unwilling to die?" Nether Orion said.

"Because I will not kill you. With the power of the Heart of the Sea and the Nether Star I will be able to imprison you permanently in a place where you will never ever harm AquaCraft again," Orion replied, "And tell me how to heal ArcticCat."

Nether Orion hesitated. "The, the only way to heal the damage that has been inflicted is to use the opposite power to balance out the energy. Otherwise, they will die, forever. In order to do this, I will need the Nether Star."

Orion walked over to where Jojo was standing.

"Hand Herobrine the Nether Star," Orion ordered.

"Have you lost your mind? Give Herobrine the..." Jojo started.

"Trust me." Orion looked steadily into Jojo's eyes. Then he turned to Herobrine and motioned him to take it.

Jojo hesitated, then he slowly and reluctantly handed Herobrine the Nether Star.

"Now, no funny business. If you try anything, I will be right here ready to strike," Orion said harshly.

They walked over to where ArcticCat was lying on the ground. Herobrine kneeled down and sent a small beam of energy from the Nether Star at ArcticCat. The nether energies combined with the energies from the Heart of the Sea. The energies evened out. ArcticCat opened his eyes, squinting.

"ArcticCat, are you alright?" Orion asked quietly.

"What, what happened." ArcticCat mumbled.

Orion didn't respond. Instead, he looked at Herobrine and said, "Now close the portal."

Herobrine didn't respond. Instead, he flew up and away with the power of the Nether Star.

"I told you this wasn't a good idea!" Jojo exclaimed.

"We'll talk about this later," Orion replied more harshly than he meant to.

With the power of the Heart of the Sea, Orion flew up, following Herobrine. Lifting up the Trident, Orion shot a jet beam of water at Herobrine. Herobrine dodged the attack by flying to the left. Orion shot more beams, just barely missing Herobrine. Herobrine stopped in midair, turning around and shooting fireballs at Orion, who deflected the blasts with his trident, swinging it around to disperse the flame. Then each of them charged up their own unique beams of energy and unleashed them upon each other. The beams collided, creating a large glowing ball of energy. The energy flew in all directions in a liquid-like motion. Nether Orion's disguise began to fade away because of the energy consumption. He was having to direct all the energy he had to the energy beam. Orion and Nether Orion were giving it their all. Neither one was backing down. Yet Orion's power was greater with the combined energies of the Heart of the Sea and the Trident. He began to be able to start moving the energy closer to Nether Orion. He pushed Nether Orion's beam backwards; slowly but steadily he began to destroy Nether Orion's beam. Nether Orion faltered in the air, losing control of his energy beam. Orion lunged farther forward with the Trident, drawing more energy into the beam. The beam glowed bright hot blue.

Suddenly, the Nether Star flew from Nether Orion, and he plunged down to the ground. Orion stopped the beam and flew down to catch Nether Orion. Shooting out a smaller, weaker beam, he created a water forcefield around Nether Orion. Detaching the Heart of the Sea from the Trident, he used it to send out a jet of water that caught the Nether Star and pulled it up to him. He caught the Nether Star, and attached both items to the Trident, creating the ultimate weapon. The Trident began to flash with the magnitude of its power. Still keeping Nether Orion in the forcefield, Orion shot a dark blue beam at the ginormous portal in the sky. The portal started shrinking, growing weaker, letting less monsters fly through. Eventually the portal vanished in a bright light. The dark clouds turned back to white, and the moon uncovered the sun, revealing a ray of sunlight, lighting up the whole area. Orion ended the beam. He flew with Nether Orion still trapped in the forcefield through the sky. Orion opened a small portal and flew through it. On the other side of the portal, he emerged in a desert biome, far away on the edge of the AquaCraft realm near the sea. Orion and Nether Orion flew to a temple, a deserted desert temple. Orion landed on the ground, dropping the forcefield around Nether Orion.

"You will come with me," Orion ordered.

Seeing no other choice, Nether Orion obeyed. They walked inside the dimly lit temple. They walked through the pyramid structure to its center. Light from the sun came down through a small hole at the top of the temple. Orion broke the clay block at the center of the temple. He jumped down into a new room. Nether Orion followed. They walked down a hallway. At the end of the hallway was a portal. A nether portal. Orion forced Nether Orion forward down the hallway.

"Walk through that portal," Orion said quietly.

Nether Orion slowly limped to the portal. Taking one glance back, he walked through the portal and disappeared. Orion exited the temple and sealed the entrance. Using all his power, he buried the temple in the desert sand. Looking back at his work, he was satisfied. He turned around and walked away. He built a sandstone arch, then created a portal by using the ultimate weapon. This portal would lead him back to the city. He hesitated a moment, then walked through the portal and emerged in a village. The village was an abandoned village, west of the city.

Orion sighed. It had been a long day. He walked slowly, heading home with the sun setting behind him. It was over, finally over.

I sure hope that is the last time we see Nether Orion, Orion thought. They had won, but why did he feel like they didn't win? His heart was heavy. Where would they go now? What was to happen now? After so much conflict, Orion didn't know what to do. Things had escalated so quickly. And what of the Heart of the Sea, the Nether Star, and the Trident? With the most powerful, ultimate weapon in his possession, he could create or destroy whatever he wanted. Where would the weapon be safe from the wrong hands? He needed to find a place that no AquaCrafter could find, he decided.

Chapter 17: The Aftermath

ArcticCat was sitting by the fireplace in the council chamber building when Orion returned. All the AquaCrafters had gathered in the small building to conduct an important gathering. PurpleTimeRift had respawned—thankfully the second respawn center hadn't been destroyed. Even though the main part of the fighting had been near the statue, the city had taken significant damage from the monsters, who at this point had now either been slain or had fled. Starpig was the city's hero. He had bravely defended it against the tides of monsters swarming through the huge portal, and when the tide turned, he had led a patrol out to destroy the remaining monsters. Many of the AquaCrafters had been injured, but luckily very few had had to respawn.

Orion walked over to the main table in the center of the room and sat down in one of the many seats.

"Orion. You're here," Starpig said, greeting him.

Jojo sat up. "Finally, we can start the meeting."

Orion nodded and looked around. After a moment he said, "I see you have gathered everyone here. Now I don't think there is a lot to discuss, so I will get right down to business. We need to start rebuilding. We need to start tomorrow."

"Actually, I think there is a lot to discuss. We have all been talking, and we need to make a decision about something," Fution interrupted.

"Oh?" Orion replied, surprised.

"To start out with, what do we do about Gestroyer?" Starpig asked.

"Oh, right. ArcticCat mentioned something about that," Orion said.

Gestroyer was sitting away from the rest of the group, against the far wall, deep in thought.

"Yes, well, Gestroyer here claims he has been following your orders to build the statue to stop Herobrine," Starpig explained.

"What?" Orion said, puzzled.

Gestroyer got up and walked forward to the table. He said, "Don't you remember? You took me to a small cabin in the woods. You wanted me to meet someone, what was his name? It went along the lines of Flame something."

"Orion, do you know anything about this? That statue was what was causing the eclipse, am I right? Or is my information incorrect?" TheHappyBranch looked at him quizzically.

Orion hesitated, "No, I don't remember any of this. Unless somehow it happened when I...Hey, ArcticCat, did I do anything when I was acting strange, you know at the old respawn center?"

"I'm not sure. I left as soon as...hmm, unless...," ArcticCat responded. "It's funny that you would bring that up, 'cause I don't know any other way for you to do this without your recollection."

"Gestroyer, please continue. What else happened?" Starpig looked thoughtful.

Gestroyer was looking confused. "Well, um, before the eclipse, Orion met with me and said that Herobrine was working with an AquaCrafter on the inside. He convinced me that I couldn't trust anyone because then Jojo would know."

Jojo stood up abruptly. "Wait, what's this? He told you what?" His voice growing angry.

"He said you were a traitor to AquaCraft and were working with Herobrine to destroy it," Gestroyer said.

Jojo was incredulous. "What sort of nonsense is this? Orion, explain yourself. Did you tell him this?"

"No, why would I do that?" Orion stammered. "I have no memory of that. Wait, when was this?"

Jojo began to grow more suspicious than angry. He sat back into his chair scowling, not knowing who to be angry at.

Gestroyer looked at Jojo, but he was speaking to Orion. "It happened during the first attacks on the city."

"Wait, but wasn't that when Orion was missing?" Jojo asked.

"That doesn't fit the timeline. We had almost found Orion in the far north with THB at that point. There is no way Orion could also have been in the city," Starpig reasoned.

"Unless he can teleport," Cicer said sarcastically.

Starpig looked at Cicer, annoyed. "Not helping."

Jojo was focused on Gestroyer. "What do you have to say about this?"

"I admit that doesn't make much sense. But I was sure that it was Orion. I was just trying to stop Herobrine!" Gestroyer responded.

A funny expression was beginning to take shape on Orion's face. But before ArcticCat could process what it meant, PurpleTimeRift spoke up.

She said, "Could it be that you were just confused about the date it occurred?"

"It's possible," Gestroyer replied.

"That still doesn't answer why whoever this Orion is was spreading lies," Jojo said.

"I suggest that we take a small break to let everyone contemplate these thoughts," Orion said, but what he really meant was that *he* needed some time to think.

"Agreed," ArcticCat said.

The meeting broke up. As everyone left the room, Orion pulled Gestroyer aside.

"Do you have a moment? Please come with me," Orion said politely, but he was holding Gestroyer by the arm.

"Sure," Gestroyer replied.

They walked down the small hallway out the door into the night air. Orion looked around to make sure no one else was there. The night was cool, stars could be seen in the sky above them. The moon shone but this time no monsters had spawned.

"Gestroyer, I have something important to ask you." Orion began.

"Sure, what is it?" Gestroyer said.

"What was this Orion like? Did he look exactly like me? Did he sound exactly like me? How did he act?" Orion questioned quietly.

"That's a weird thing to ask, but now that you mention it, he sounded a bit different than you. Not only that, but he seemed uncomfortable being in the shopping district," Gestroyer explained.

"Oh really? Well, how differently did he sound?" Orion asked.

"I'm not sure how to say this, but he sounded similar to you, but he had more of a rough-sounding voice," Gestroyer said.

"Hmm, did his visor sort of have a blue tint to it? Like behind the red visor?" Orion said.

"Exactly like that! Oh, and that person he had me meet, his name was Flamecat." Gestroyer added.

"Flamecat, Flamecat, where have I heard that name before?" Orion said to himself.

Orion looked back through his memories, trying to pinpoint where he had heard the name before. Suddenly his mind went back to the last time ArcticCat had gone with him to the old respawn center. He remembered a dark corridor, a dark flaming figure with lava flowing through its armor. Then the Nether Star, and a beam that went into his very self and had separated the good from the bad.

"Flamecat! Oh, this is not good," Orion said, something terrible beginning to dawn on him.

He turned away and walked back into the building. Gestroyer followed him, calling his name, but Orion didn't listen. He knew what had happened.

The AquaCrafters slowly gathered back into the council chambers. Orion was pacing the room, as he always did when deep in thought.

"Well?" Starpig said once everyone had gathered.

"Herobrine," Orion paused, "has the ability to disguise himself as other people. At least as far as I have learned. And his name isn't Herobrine. Herobrine isn't real, but this person used it as a disguise to scare us. Now I know you won't believe me, but this Herobrine is me. But not like–me, me, but also me."

"Orion, what are you saying? Are you saying you're Herobrine?" Fution asked.

"No, that isn't what I meant. This is a different Orion, one who wants to destroy me. One who wants to change AquaCraft into NetherCraft. This Orion is Nether Orion," Orion explained.

"So you're saying there is another Orion that has been trying to destroy us?" Jojo questioned.

"That is exactly what I am saying," Orion replied.

"And you expect us to believe this?" TactifulBelt spoke for the first time.

"I'm serious! There is a person, well I'm not even sure if I can call him a person, but there is a person who attacked me at the old ruins of the first respawn center. That person had the Nether Star, and he used it on me to create Nether Orion. I'm guessing he is the one who gave Nether Orion—Herobrine the Nether Star," Orion said.

"That sure would explain how two Orions are in different places," PurpleTimeRift pointed out.

"I'm not buying this! It's too strange for me," Jojo commented.

"Is this person a threat to AquaCraft? If they are allies with Herobrine, I mean Nether Orion, then are they still out there ready to attack?" Starpig asked.

ArcticCat got up. "I don't think so. At least not directly. None of us have seen this person. And does this person have a name?"

"Flamecat," Orion replied.

"That sounds like the opposite of ArcticCat," TheHappyBranch commented thoughtfully.

"Nah, that seems more coincidental than anything else," Starpig said.

"I think we are getting off topic. Is Flamecat a threat or not?" PurpleTimeRift asked.

"I don't know. But if he did this to me, then he will probably come back. I doubt he will just leave us alone," Orion said.

"Well, everyone can keep an eye out just to be safe," Cicer decided reasonably.

Everyone was silent, thinking this over. Then Jojo broke the silence.

"Well then, with that settled, I think we can finally move onto more important business." Jojo nodded to a few of the AquaCrafters. "Some of us AquaCrafters feel that Orion has too much power. He has possession of the Trident, the Heart of the Sea, and the Nether Star! Representing the majority's opinion, I am telling you, Orion, to hand over the items to be shared among the AquaCrafters."

Orion looked up, startled. "No way! We can't just let anyone use the items. You see what Herobrine, who is Nether Orion, did with them?" Orion pointed out.

"We will have management over them. Oh, and also, what did you do with Herobrine, who you say is Nether Orion?" Jojo asked.

"I, I imprisoned him in a desert temple. There is a map to it," Orion replied.

"With the Trident, the Heart of the Sea, and the Nether Star? What could we do if you decided we were threats and you started imprisoning us?" Jojo reasoned.

"I wouldn't..." Orion began.

Jojo interrupted. "Power corrupts; no one should be allowed to have all three powerful items."

"Jojo makes a good point, Orion. Nether Orion almost killed me with the Heart of the Sea, permanently!" ArcticCat agreed.

"As leader of the AquaCrafters, I can be trusted with all three items. Or, if necessary, I can place the items somewhere no one can access them," Orion said.

"I would be happy to help you with building or finding somewhere that no one can access the items," Starpig offered.

"Thank you; see, we can do it together," Orion suggested.

"Let's continue discussing this tomorrow. It is late, and I think we should all get our rest. It has been a long day." PurpleTimeRift stood up gracefully, yawning.

No one could argue that. So the meeting broke up, and the AquaCrafters left for their homes. ArcticCat left for his house in the forest. He had recently purchased a home from PurpleTimeRift, who had built a small cabin for him in the woods near her house. He hoped things would resolve quickly. There had been enough conflict lately. ArcticCat tried to shake off his thoughts while he walked, but they wouldn't shut down. There was Flamecat out there still, and what if Nether Orion broke out of the desert temple? ArcticCat sighed. Even if the AquaCrafters settled their differences, there were still other threats. ArcticCat opened the door to his cabin and walked inside. Maybe a good night's sleep would help.

Chapter 18: Memories Lost

Days had passed since the Eclipse. Almost a week. Orion knew that the Heart of the Sea and the Nether Star must be hidden away from everyone, away from all the AquaCrafters, in order to protect them from the temptation and the power. These things were too powerful; they could corrupt almost anyone. Because of this, he devised a plan with Starpig and PurpleTimeRift.

First, he contacted them and arranged a meeting at Starpig's base. There they would discuss the details of the plan. So, a couple of days later Orion and PurpleTimeRift arrived at Starpig's ground base; they came as quietly as they could. Starpig had built a base in the city. The base was made primarily of quartz, and was a magnificent site from both outside and in. Starpig used this base as a place to store all his resources. The building had a glass dome above the quartz supports. There was a walkway that ran from four sides of the circular structure. The walkway was above the main floor, and there were small staircases that led from the walkway down to each storage unit area.

Orion walked in and looked around. The base was more cluttered than when he had last seen it. There were more chests in the corners, and a mess of stuff was up against the wall behind him. Yet it still looked clean and futuristic. Starpig emerged from somewhere behind Orion and came up a quartz staircase to the walkway to meet him and PurpleTimeRift.

"Good, you're here! It's basically finished," Starpig greeted them.

"I can start feeling better, then," said PurpleTimeRift, tapping her hand on the hilt of her sword, then letting her arm fall loosely by her side. She turned to Orion. "Do you have the items?"

"Yes. Let's go before anyone misses us," Orion responded.

They made their way down the quartz stairs and came into a storage area. Starpig led them behind a couple of chests through a small gap between the chests and the wall. An unexpected onlooker would never notice them there. They moved into a passageway that led downwards to below his base, stepping carefully in the dim light. They rounded a corner and went down another flight of stairs into an even darker room where the quartz ended. In the dark room were a table and a few chairs. Other than that, the room was pretty much deserted. It had an entirely different feel from the modern aura of the earlier parts of the base. A few lanterns lit the room. Starpig went to one of the chairs and sat down. Orion and PurpleTimeRift sat down on the remaining chairs.

"So, you all know the basic idea of what we are about to do," began Orion. "Starpig, have you been able to complete your part?" Orion asked.

"Yes, the tunnel is complete," Starpig assured him.

"Good. Then we will be able to move on to the next phase of our plan. As you both know, we need to move the ultimate weapon to a place where no one will be able to find or get it. It is too powerful to keep with us. That is why I had you construct the secret base, PurpleTimeRift. From there we will transport the ultimate weapon to the ocean monument. Legend states that we will be able to travel there with the power of the Heart of the Sea. As you know, these temples—much like the desert temple I trapped Nether Orion in—are able to hold great power. They are one of the few types of building where we can place the ultimate weapon without worrying about someone finding or stealing it. These temples prevent the power from leaving the area and will keep intruders from taking it. The ocean monument is just one of these rare temples built by the ancients," Orion explained. He turned and looked at PurpleTimeRift." Is the portal setup?"

"Yes, I followed Fution's design precisely," she confirmed.

Starpig shifted in his seat. "Um, how confident are we that this will work?"

Orion sighed and shrugged. "We're not sure. But we don't really have any other options."

"Fine. Then let's get this over with quickly. I don't have a good feeling about it," Starpig said unhappily.

He got up and led them to the right, up to a quartz wall. He reached out his hand and pressed a button. To their surprise, the wall pulled apart out of their way into the walls on both sides of them. Hesitantly they walked through the opening. Starpig turned and flipped a lever, and the wall closed behind them, pistons sounding. Ahead of them was a minecart track. Many lanterns lit up the dirt tunnel. The tunnel was so long that you couldn't even see the end of it. Starpig motioned for Orion and PurpleTimeRift to get into two of the three minecarts on the track.

Once they were in, Starpig said, "Now, just press that button behind you, Orion."

Orion pressed the button. Click! And they were off. The powered rails jump-started the minecarts, and they began to gain momentum. Then they started gaining large amounts of speed until it seemed as if they were flying! The tunnel around them was a mere blur. Orion and PurpleTimeRift hung on grimly. They eventually rounded a corner, turning right. They flew past many stops and rode over large chasms; then they emerged into open air on the surface. They rode through a forest and then went into another tunnel. It was a long ride for a minecart track, but they wanted to be far away where no one might find them, and Starpig had really planned well for that. The end of the tunnel was up ahead, and the minecarts began slowing down.

"This is really impressive, Starpig!" Orion said in admiration. "Thanks for building it for us."

"Of course. I am loyal to you as our leader," Starpig answered soberly. "Maybe once we get rid of these items, the AquaCrafters might settle down."

Meanwhile, back in town it had been many days since that first meeting about the Ultimate Weapon. The AquaCrafters had been arguing about this issue hotly. This was why Orion had left before anyone could stop him. Now even ArcticCat, one of Orion's most loyal AquaCrafters, had agreed that maybe Orion was wrong this time. Jojo had been talking to the new Minecrafters that had recently joined AquaCraft. He had convinced them that he was right, and Orion was wrong, so at this point most of the AquaCrafters were loyal to Jojo's party. Their idea was to elect Jojo as the new leader of the AquaCrafters. He had led them well for a time, so why shouldn't he lead them again? And perhaps when Orion had been gone for such a long time, maybe his absence had left him unfamiliar with AquaCraft's needs. At least that is what many of the AquaCrafters were saying. A petition had been signed requesting that a vote be taken to elect a new leader, and so far, the majority of AquaCrafters were in favor of the change. If this petition was successful, then Orion would have 10 days to transition out before another leader took over. Jojo was of course the obvious choice for a new leader. If Orion refused, then he would have to be taken down forcefully.

Gestroyer was not one of the complainers. He had been forgiven for his deeds, but he was serving hours of community service. In spite of this judgment, Gestroyer had supported Orion's decision to get rid of the items of power instead of using them. Now Gestroyer continued to hold his ground, even though he was accused of treason by a few people. He was loyal to Orion, as he always had been, and he also figured that Orion would be the winner in the end, which would leave Gestroyer in a position where Orion owed him something. Orion, on the other hand, wasn't so sure he could win. He was still trying to get support to stop the petition, but he could see that he might be forced to step down, so he had decided to get rid of the items first while he still could.

The minecarts screeched to a stop, and Starpig, PurpleTimeRift, and Orion got out and entered a giant cave. In front of them was a stone archway, a stone bridge that led over a large chasm. Beyond the bridge was a frame of a portal. This portal frame was unlike anything Orion had ever seen before. It was made of prismarine, a special kind of ocean stone, the same stone that the ocean monument was made of.

Starpig explained, "Fution helped us with the design; he had a bit of the stuff, so I was able to construct a simple portal frame out of it. Now all we need is a power source to light the portal."

They walked over the bridge, and PurpleTimeRift examined the prismarine.

"It's real, alright. I don't know how Fution found this stuff, but it should be the right material for a portal to the ocean monument," PurpleTimeRift stated thoughtfully.

Orion pulled out the Heart of the Sea and the Trident. He attached the Heart to the tip of the Trident. PurpleTimeRift got out of the way, and Starpig made his way to a control panel for the redstone mechanism that helped guide the power of the Heart.

"I need to calibrate the machine really quickly. But when it is ready, Orion, you should shoot a small, focused beam at the center of the portal. Aim for the obsidian block behind the frame," Starpig explained.

"OK then." Orion nodded that he understood.

Starpig began to press a few buttons; then he flipped a lever and motioned for Orion to begin. Orion lifted his trident and pointed it at the portal frame. The Trident began to glow, and a bright blue beam shot from its tip, the beam hitting the obsidian block. Circles of energy began to emerge from the obsidian block. A faint sign of a portal began to show. The space within the frame began to shimmer like water. Slowly, water emitted from the portal and spiraled around until it took up the entire space within the frame.

"No, no, it's too unstable. We are losing the portal!" Starpig was panicking.

The portal glowed bright blue, and then an energy wave from the portal moved out like the ripples of water when disturbed. The whole cave vibrated. Orion was sent flying, Starpig fell to the ground, and PurpleTimeRift held on to the edge of the platform after she was sent flying as well. The portal shrank until it vanished in front of their eyes.

Orion slowly got up, "Argh, is everyone...is everyone alright?"

"No, the portal failed!" Starpig got up and began examining the control panel. "I don't understand what went wrong."

Orion walked over to where PurpleTimeRift was clinging to the edge and helped her back up onto the platform.

"I couldn't focus the energy while also trying to go through the portal. It just doesn't work. I would need someone else to go through the portal and take the items through," Orion reasoned.

"I'll do it," PurpleTimeRift said.

"But you would also need the Heart to keep the portal open. Once the Heart is not used to keep the portal open, the Trident can only keep the portal open for a moment." Starpig turned around from where he was fiddling with the redstone.

"I'll do it," PurpleTimeRift repeated.

"Are you sure? If the portal closes while you are on the other side, then there is no way back. It's too dangerous, something might go wrong." Orion replied.

"Listen, someone has to do it, and we don't have that much time. Let me do it; I can be fast. Just hand me the Nether Star and I will place it in the monument," PurpleTimeRift said.

"It might work, but I would have to calibrate the machine to make the portal inside the monument instead of at the monument," Starpig said.

"I don't like it. But I see no other choice. Will you need the Heart of the Sea to calibrate?" Orion asked.

"I don't think so, I just need to..." Starpig went back to the panel and began to adjust a few mechanisms.

Once it was calibrated, Orion, Starpig, and PurpleTimeRift got into position. Again, Orion shot a focused beam of energy, creating the portal once more.

PurpleTimeRift grabbed the Nether Star and ran towards the portal. She pulled out a clock from her inventory and leapt through the portal. If she was to do this, then she would need her timeclock to slow down time, just enough for her to place the items in and get out. Going through the portal was a sensation unlike any she had ever felt before. This wasn't like a nether portal or an ender portal, but something totally new. A bright light flashed, and she adjusted her eyes; there was the monument.

She was in an ocean, far away from the AquaCraft city. She turned around and saw the portal, just barely. She thought she could see the cave. But there was no time; she had to place the Nether Star in the monument before the portal closed. She swam with speed faster than normal. Her timeclock was working. She entered the deserted monument, holding her breath as she swam through to the vault room. She passed prismarine hallways and came to a square box in the middle of the monument. The vault. She went to place the Nether Star on the podium, only to realize that it had not gone through the portal! She swam back through the monument to the portal. She emerged out of the monument and swam up to the portal. She saw it, lying on the floor of the cave. She swam with all her might, but the timeclock fizzed out, and she slowed down, swimming at normal speed once again. This was not going to work! She swam frantically, trying to get back to the portal, but it began shrinking, growing smaller until no one could fit through it; it seemed as though it was getting farther away, more distant. She slowed her strokes. She couldn't hold her breath for much longer. Her lungs seemed to be bursting. Then her body gave way under the pressure of the ocean.

. . .

From Starpig's perspective, all he could see was a blue energy wall that was the portal. He heard Orion say something along the lines of, I can't hold it any longer. Starpig turned around to see Orion fall onto his knee, the Trident falling, and the portal dying. The portal began to grow unstable. Then there was a flash of blue light and then silence.

Orion groaned as he got up. "Starpig, are you there? Is PurpleTimeRift there?"

"Ugh, I don't know. PurpleTimeRift?" Starpig replied, then turned to face the portal. "PurpleTimeRift!"

Starpig ran to the portal, Orion not far behind. The portal frame was in ruins, the prismarine was cracked and the top of it had collapsed.

"We need to open the portal again," Orion murmured.

"It's no use. The frame is broken, and we don't have any more prismarine. Wherever PurpleTimeRift is, there is no way to get to her now," Starpig stated gravely. Then he pointed to the ground. "Look, the Nether Star didn't even make it through the portal."

"This...this has accomplished nothing." Orion got up from where he had fallen to the ground, his head lowered. He felt desperate, and he felt despondent. He looked up at Starpig. "Speak of this to nobody," he said slowly. "Close the tunnel and bury the entrance so no one can come here."

Starpig looked at him with gloom in his eyes. "I, I hope PurpleTimeRift is alright."

Orion shrugged and didn't say anything for a moment. Then he spoke slowly, as if talking to himself. "So do I. So do I. We can't say if she is dead or not. There may be hope. Maybe, just maybe we will see her again. The monument is in AquaCraft; we might find her again someday." He straightened up then. "Come on, let's go." But Orion suddenly felt hopeless, as if all the pressure around him was too much for him to carry...

• • •

There is one final thing to mention that will maybe be forgotten if it isn't said here. Unknown to the AquaCrafters then, that specific ocean monument was located at the center of the AquaCraft realm, and maybe someday it might become of some importance once more...

Part 3
Civil War

Chapter 19: AquaCraft HQ

Fution was at the construction site of the soon-to-be AquaCraft Headquarters. Despite the major disagreements going on, it was agreed that AquaCraft should have a headquarters where the council could conduct its meetings, a barracks, and a building for their every need. Starpig had been put in charge of its construction, with Fution and Cicer helping him. They were building it mainly of white concrete, and so far they had only built the foundations. Today Fution and Cicer would begin the full construction of the skyscraper. It would be by far the tallest, largest building in AquaCraft—a symbol of their accomplishments.

Unfortunately, the disagreements had only grown more intense. The AquaCrafters had split into two groups. Orion had a group who were staying loyal to him. The other group, Jojo's group, had the majority of AquaCrafters. Orion, Starpig, Fution, Cicer, Gestroyer, and a few others formed the TrustKeepers, which was the group that stayed loyal to the trust of Orion. Jojo, ArcticCat, TheHappyBranch, TactifulBelt, AngelOfDeath, and all the rest formed The Change, which was the group of AquaCrafters that felt there should be a change in how AquaCraft was run and who was in charge of it. The petition to make Jojo the leader of AquaCraft had received the majority of the votes, and Orion had been given 10 days to transition. By then, AquaCraft HQ should be finished—just in time for Jojo to take leadership.

It was a sunny day, and the sky was clear, making it the perfect environment to build. It wasn't hot either, for a gentle breeze was stirring. The foundation of AquaCraft HQ had been set in concrete, forming a 25 by 25 block platform. Cicer had begun to build a large archway that would be the entrance into the building. Starpig had just arrived to help Fution build up the walls. It would have to be at least 100 blocks tall. Each floor would be dedicated to a certain purpose, and at the very top would be a large meeting room for the council members.

It was tough work; scaffolding had to be set in place every 10 blocks up so that they could work on the walls. First Fution and Starpig started building up the back wall, which was around 25 blocks wide. They worked hard until sunset, and by then they had gotten the first wall up 70 blocks. Cicer had finished the archway on the opposite side from the first wall. He had done a masterful job. He had even begun to build the front wall around the arch. They had to build it at least five blocks deep in order to fortify it more. The build's walls had to be very thick so that nothing, but the strongest explosion could break through them. And it would certainly take a long time to mine through them. Unfortunately, getting the proper depth for the walls set them back a day. The next day, Fution and Starpig finished the back wall, and then went to help Cicer with the front wall. It took them several days to finish the outer walls, floor, and roof. Next, they had to light up the building on the inside because it was so dark that monsters might spawn. This took them another whole day. They used sea lanterns to light up the inside, and these created a very futuristic modern feel. Sea lanterns were aqua-rimmed blocks with moderate light that emitted from the center.

Fution was lying up against a wall eating his lunch when Orion came in through the archway. Starpig got up from his wall to greet Orion.

Orion looked around and then up. "Wow! You guys have been busy," he exclaimed. "The roof is like a mile away! How long did it take for you guys to build all this?"

"At least five days. And we still have to build each floor and the interior. We are behind schedule, and we may not be able to complete it before the transition of power takes place," Starpig explained.

"Well, you have done an amazing job so far! I am here now to help with the rest of it, so that should speed up the process a little bit," Orion replied. "Oh, and I really like the design you made on the front, on the outside."

Orion was referring to the amazing design on the front of AquaCraft HQ. Giant pillars came up from the ground all the way up to the top of the building. Between each pillar were sea lanterns that lit up the outside at night. On the side of the building was the huge sign that said HQ. On the other side, the right side from the front, was a gigantic arch that came down from almost the top of the building all the way to the ground. It was decorated with orange and blue concrete.

After lunch, the crew climbed up the scaffolding and began construction of the second floor. Then they moved on to the third floor, and the fourth, and the fifth. The ground floor was made to be a huge warehouse that would be used for storage and would be the entrance to the rest of the building. A bridge went from the entry arch to the water elevators and stairs at the end of the building. The floor dropped down on either side of the bridge into storage areas as well as an armory. It was still empty right now, but it would be filled up with stuff soon. The water bubble elevators at the end would take people to the very top floor, while the stairs led through each floor one by one. The second floor was smaller than the first and would be used as offices. There's not much else to say about the second floor except that it was one of the few floors with windows. The third floor was built as a vault area that could be used as storage for valuables or to hold large weapons, devices, contraptions, and in rare cases, to hold dangerous persons. The room was mostly empty except for the giant obsidian cube in the center of the tall floor. The next floor had not been given a purpose yet.

The top floor would be used as a meeting room for all the council members, with the leader of the AquaCrafters at the head of the giant table. The table took up most of the room, starting at one end of the room and going all the way to the large windows. Absolutely massive windows had been placed in the meeting room, and the light from these windows lit up the entire room. The windows provided a view of the whole valley below them, including the police station to the north and a small ravine near it. The top floor was one of the smallest floors, but it was still very grand, for the other floors had walls separating the rooms. This floor however was one gigantic room that had huge, vaulted ceilings with a sea lantern chandelier.

. . .

Too soon the day came when Orion was supposed to step down. Orion was in his sky base, thinking about recent events. He paced around on the glass floor. AquaCraft HQ had almost been completed. There were a few more finishing touches to make on the interior, but otherwise it was mostly finished, and they had made it an amazing structure. Orion thought about the building and then about the split that had happened. Orion had been surprised at first when ArcticCat sided with Jojo, but when he spoke with ArcticCat about it, he understood his point of view. ArcticCat knew firsthand how the power of the ultimate weapon could corrupt a person so much that it might take control of them. ArcticCat didn't think the weapon could be destroyed, so why not share it with a group of people so that the one who was using it would always be under a watchful eye. ArcticCat had convinced Orion to place the ultimate weapon in AquaCraft HQ's vault. That way Orion could be better trusted, and the weapon would be somewhere that was safe–at least temporarily. But Orion couldn't completely understand why TheHappyBranch had not sided with him. She just wasn't talking to him at all, for some reason. He sighed and shifted his weight on his chair and wished things could be different. But looking back, he didn't think he could have done any differently. He knew he would have to head over later in the day to meet the AquaCrafters at the bottom of AquaCraft HQ for the turnover of power ceremony. Orion wasn't sure exactly what he would do yet. He hadn't really spoken to anyone about it, but he guessed he was just expected to step down peacefully. He sighed again.

While Orion was thinking all this over, on the opposite side of the city, Jojo was also thinking over recent events. He was inside his ravine base, pacing around the room. The base was suspended above the ravine, and he had made it with stone pillars. The interior wasn't overly decorated, for Jojo wanted a functional base. Though he appreciated art and architecture, he needed something that could be resistant to attacks. He had had to fortify his base during the age of the eclipse and had never had the chance to add anything eye-pleasing. Now he was thinking hard. He hoped that Orion would step down peacefully. There had been so much conflict lately, and AquaCraft needed a time of peace. But Jojo understood that it would be tough for Orion to transition. They had known each other for a long time, and he didn't want this conflict to ruin their long friendship. Many years ago, Jojo had met Orion for the first time on a player versus player server. They had both ended up playing the same mini game, which happened to be a survival game, a game of last player standing wins. Jojo and Orion had met on the battlefield and decided to team up. They ended up winning the match, after which they became good friends. They had walked together exchanging stories about their battles and wins. They had shared many interests in the same kind of games. Eventually they had gone out to the realm of Evenglade, exploring its many forests, and Orion had introduced him to ArcticCat and Starpig.

Those were the good times, Jojo thought a bit sadly. He put aside his memories and focused on the task at hand. He needed to get ready for the ceremony of the opening of AquaCraft HQ and the transition of power.

He gathered his belongings and set out on horseback, riding to the new headquarters. He arrived to find Starpig, Fution, and Cicer already there. White tents had been set up for shade for the AquaCrafters to gather underneath when the ceremony occurred. Jojo got off his horse and handed the reins to a random AquaCrafter who politely nodded to Jojo and walked off to the horse pens. Not long after, TactifulBelt and ArcticCat also arrived. The ceremony would start in 30 minutes; meanwhile they were still waiting on Orion, AngelOfDeath, and a few others to show up.

It was the middle of the afternoon, but it wasn't hot. Dark clouds threatened to rain. Jojo walked over to speak with Fution, where he was standing by the entrance of the skyscraper.

"You said you would give me a tour sometime. Would you be willing to do that now?" Jojo asked.

"Uh, you don't want to go in there yet. Please wait until after the ceremony, and we will give you a proper tour," Fution replied.

"Well, then I order you to give me a tour," Jojo said more firmly.

Fution frowned and shook his head. "You're not in charge of AquaCraft yet."

Jojo gave up and walked away. He went back over to the platform and the tents that would hold the ceremony. He was afraid that Orion wouldn't show up, but then he saw him standing near ArcticCat underneath one of the tents. Jojo thought they were missing someone, but he couldn't put his finger on who it was. *Oh well, maybe it would come back to him.* Just then, it began to pour. *Great, the rain is just on time.* Jojo thought.

Then ArcticCat climbed up the steps of the temporary stage platform. He signaled for everyone's attention before he spoke.

"Attention everyone, attention. The ceremony is starting," ArcticCat began. "We have gathered here to celebrate the opening of the new AquaCraft headquarters! We want to thank the builders for their amazing work. They have done such a fantastic job!"

He paused for the applause. Then, making sure everyone was listening, he continued. "We also have gathered to hold the change of leadership, when our newly elected leader shall be put in charge of AquaCraft by the council's approval. And I shall be representing the council during this ceremony."

At this point there were at least 15-20 Minecrafters who had settled in AquaCraft. Only about seven or eight of them were council members. It was normal for a few Minecrafters to sometimes come and go. Now the city actually felt like a city instead of a small village, Jojo thought. And now he was going to lead them.

ArcticCat was still talking. "I would now like to ask Orion and Jojo to come up on the stage where we will first declare a new leader, then we shall open the new building."

Jojo and Orion made their way up the steps and sat down in chairs on either side of the podium where ArcticCat was speaking. Wait a minute, Jojo thought, where is THB? That's who we are missing!

"I would like to thank you all for coming, and now I am going to ask for your attention to Orion, who has prepared a small speech for this occasion," ArcticCat proclaimed.

Orion got up, and ArcticCat took a seat off the stage. Orion cleared his throat before he began. He fumbled with a sheet of paper that had been written out for him. He looked nervous, which was unlike Orion, for he was used to these kinds of events.

Orion looked around and then glanced back at his paper before finally beginning. "Today we have gathered to hold a changing of leadership. Um...I have been your leader for many months and I, I would like to thank the council's support during my time as a leader. As you know, I did not want to step down, but I respect the council's decision. We AquaCrafters have been through a lot together. From the first time we arrived here and conquered the great dragon to the tough times that Jojo led us through during the beginning of the eclipse."

Orion seemed to gain his footing again, but he didn't sound himself. The rain continued to soak the spectators below.

He continued, "Jojo has been elected to replace me as leader of the AquaCrafters. He has been chosen for his great leadership skills and his previous success earlier in this season. I hereby give my approval and surrender my title of leader and invite Jojo up to the podium."

Jojo then came up to the podium and gave his speech, stating how he would lead AquaCraft to the best of his abilities, and then he went on about how he would keep the promises he made, such as allowing anyone to access the ultimate weapon.

"But I feel like the word *weapon* is inaccurate in this case. I think it would be better called a creative tool that shall help all people—under the council's careful supervision, of course," Jojo spoke loudly and confidently, "As my first act as leader, I would like to officially declare the AquaCraft HQ as open to the public! There will be tours after this ceremony, in case you want to see it."

When Jojo finally ended his speech, the crowd clapped enthusiastically. Fution, Starpig, and Cicer then took many of the AquaCrafters on a tour. But as they went through each floor, Jojo noticed that it seemed like there were many things that he wasn't being shown. By this time, the rain had finally stopped. They ended the day at Orion's hotel, having a party to celebrate the occasion.

. . .

Starpig looked back in disgust on how the ceremony had gone. Orion had sounded terrible. He was pretty sure Orion had just read from a script that Jojo's election group had put together previously. Orion did not sound himself. He seemed uneasy, and he had sounded like a robot reading from the script. And then there was the way the crowd barely even clapped for Orion, but there was a standing ovation for Jojo becoming leader. Starpig moved restlessly around, feeling frustrated and angry. Fution certainly did not like how things had gone, either. He felt he could not just sit by while all this went down. He clenched his hand into a fist, then unclenched, then clenched again.

A few days after the ceremony, Starpig gathered with Fution, Cicer, and Gestroyer to discuss the matters at hand. They gathered in Starpig's dome base.

"This is outrageous! We can't just allow this to happen. Did you hear what Jojo planned to do with the ultimate weapon? He was going to just hand it out for anyone to use!" Starpig exclaimed.

Cicer nodded. "And after all that work we did in the HQ, we won't even be given access to our own building. I heard that Jojo planned to have a new election for council members! Everyone likes Jojo, so they are more likely to vote for ones that Jojo votes for!"

Gestroyer got up from where he was sitting. "I think we have no choice. We must act. Jojo can't just barge in and take over everything. Orion was the first leader, so why shouldn't he stay that way? I suggest we overthrow Jojo in his own headquarters."

"Hey, everyone, calm down. We should see what Orion thinks about this," Fution pointed out.

"Orion doesn't seem like he wants to be leader anymore. You saw him at the ceremony? I say we need a new leader," Gestroyer responded scornfully.

"I think we should at least talk to Orion before doing anything," Fution argued.

And so the meeting ended. Gestroyer was frustrated at the results. *He had hoped that they would actually do something. He walked away from Starpig's base thinking furiously. Fine! If no one else was going to do anything, then he would act.* He thought about it all afternoon, then made his decision. That night he went to the headquarters and snuck into the building through the back entrance. Security hadn't been implemented much yet because the building had just opened. He snuck up the stairs, making his way up to the vault floor.

He had never been on this floor before, but he was confident that he could find the ultimate weapon. He pried open an iron door and looked around. The room was dark; a great emptiness seemed to go on endlessly. Gestroyer could see security lasers that would detect an intruder who broke one of the red beams. In the center of the cube-shaped room was a podium that supported the Trident! He could see the Heart of the Sea and the Nether Star also on it. He placed a block down and used it to gain enough height to jump over the first laser. He landed with a soft thump. He used this tactic again and again to leap around the room, dodging the lasers and using blocks as parkour platforms until he was within reach of the ultimate weapon. He stretched out his arm and strained and strained to reach until he got hold of it. He took it out of its podium and leaped down to the floor below him. He used his previously placed blocks to get back to the entrance, but he slipped and fell down, breaking the beam of one of the lasers. A loud alarm went off, blaring a sound which echoed across the walls. Gestroyer ran out of the room as quickly as he could, hoping that no one was in the building. As suddenly as it came on, the alarm went off. He heard a voice call, "Up here!" So instead of going down the stairs, he went up. He came into the large council chamber room to find TheHappyBranch waiting for him.

"Do you have the Trident?" She asked.

"Yes," Gestroyer answered.

She led him to the water bubble elevator, and they went down the one that was labeled Down.

Once they reached the bottom floor, Gestroyer asked, "Did you switch off the alarm?"

"Yes," THB responded, not looking up from her work on one side of a wall.

"Will they be able to see what we did?" Gestroyer asked.

"No," She responded.

"Wait, what are you doing?" He asked.

"Will you stop asking questions and follow me?" THB said.

TheHappyBranch opened a panel and led Gestroyer through it. It was a small passageway that led outside of the building.

"Did you cover your tracks on the vault floor?" she asked.

"Yes, but how did you find this?" Gestroyer asked impatiently.

"If you stop asking me questions about my end of the deal, I will stop asking questions about your end of the deal," she said coldly.

They exited the building, and TheHappyBranch led him into the small row of trees nearby. She turned and faced him, lifting up her hands.

"What, what is it?" Gestroyer asked.

"The Trident. Give it to me." THB snapped.

Gestroyer handed the Trident to THB, and asked, "What are you going to do with that?"

"I need it to prove myself to my own people. This is the main reason why I came to AquaCraft in the first place. To find the Trident. That is why I went on the quest with Orion. But he took it for himself, and I wanted it back,"

TheHappyBranch explained. "What are you going to do with the Heart of the Sea and the Nether Star?"

"Nice doing business with you," Gestroyer replied, and walked away.

"Hey, come back! Aren't you going to tell me what you are going to do with the items?" THB yelled after him.

Gestroyer ignored her, climbed onto a horse he had stolen and rode off at a quick pace. Soon he arrived at a small wooden cabin in the woods. He climbed off his horse and went slowly into the cabin.

"Do you have something for me Gestroyer?" asked a voice.

"Yes, Master Flamecat. I return to you the Nether Star. But I would like to ask something," Gestroyer said quietly.

"What do you want?" the voice asked.

"I want to keep the Heart of the Sea," Gestroyer said.

The voice growled, "Fine." Then with more menace, "I will be calling on your service again, Gestroyer. Don't be too far away."

Gestroyer left the cabin and did not return...

Chapter 20: Tensions Tighten

Jojo had gathered the new AquaCraft council in the top floor of AquaCraft HQ for an important meeting. Jojo had previously held an election for new council members because he felt AquaCraft needed a new government. The new council was made up of Jojo, ArcticCat, TheHappyBranch, AngelOfDeath, TactifulBelt, Gestroyer, and Starpig. Jojo had appointed TheHappyBranch and ArcticCat as his seconds in command. Now, sitting at the head of the council table, he felt honored by all the support he had been given recently. He understood that AquaCraft needed a strong government, even if that meant more rules and laws would have to be implemented. This meeting would be discussing what some of these new laws might be. They would also be discussing any other important changes that needed to happen in the city.

Once everyone had taken a seat, Jojo stood up and spoke, "Welcome, everyone, to the New AquaCraft Government! We are entering a new age in AquaCraft—an age of peace, prosperity, and innovation! Before we begin this meeting, I would like to first thank the building team who constructed this headquarters for us all! They shall all be awarded 32 diamonds as a reward for their excellent and skillful work." Jojo looked over at Starpig and smiled. There was some applause from the other council members.

Starpig didn't say anything as he was not a talker, but he looked pleased about the reward.

Jojo went on. Having said that, now I would like each of you to come up with ideas that might help improve the order and safety of the city. Please write down your suggestions on a piece of paper, and the ideas that are most popular will be the ones that we will have to figure out a way to implement."

There was the sound of shuffling papers as people found paper and pens and wrote out their ideas. Once everyone had come up with them, Jojo collected them and read out the ones he thought would be the most useful.

"Here we have an idea. It suggests creating a new district for mini-games!" Jojo read out loud.

"That seems like a good idea. It would be fun to have some things to do with our friends. It would be a good change from all the violence we have had lately," ArcticCat commented.

Everyone seemed to agree with the mini-game idea. AngelOfDeath and TactifulBelt were put in charge of creating the district.

"OK. Next, we have an idea that suggests a number of things actually. Some laws about more restrictions on mining and where people can build. Yes, I agree that the main part of the city has become very crowded lately, so it might be a good idea to create some more restrictions on what people can do where," Jojo summarized.

Jojo ran down the list of ideas, and the ones that the council liked were put on a board near the table. Then Jojo assigned each member to different tasks. There was a lot of work still to be done. But with the new facilities, they were able to be much more efficient than they used to be.

"Now I think that covers everything. Thank you for gathering today, and you are all dismissed to your duties," Jojo finished.

And with that the meeting was finished, and the council members dispersed.

. . .

Two weeks after the council meeting, Starpig and Fution went to meet Orion.

"Did you hear about the new law? They are completely switching out the currency! Diamonds will be swapped out for emeralds as currency! It's outrageous! Some AquaCrafters already have thousands of emeralds thanks to villager trading! They claim that emeralds are more valuable than diamonds. But can emeralds make armor? No!" Starpig complained.

Orion blinked in surprise. "Wait, really? They are actually doing that?"

Fution and Starpig had gone to speak with Orion when they had heard about the new law that was to be implemented in a few days. They were gathered in Orion's new house. Orion had moved out of his old bases and found somewhere more secluded out in the taiga forests. He had bought a wooden tower from PurpleTimeRift a while back when she was still in AquaCraft. It wasn't far from ArcticCat's house. Nearby in the woods was a small stone memorial in PurpleTimeRift's memory, though it was unknown whether she had actually died. It seemed unlikely, however, that anyone could have survived what she had gone through. Before PurpleTimeRift vanished, she had run a housing company in the forest. Orion had bought the tower because he wanted somewhere out of the city where he could live. PurpleTimeRift had been a skilled builder. She created beautiful wooden houses and cabins, and Orion's tower was skillfully made. Presently, Fution and Starpig were gathered on the second floor of the tower in a small room. It was neatly decorated, but still simple.

"That's not the only things that they are planning on doing. There are a bunch of new regulations that they are creating. And many of them are bad," Fution added.

Orion responded carefully. "The new government needs to create a new order. There are bound to be new laws that they are creating to improve the city."

Starpig shook his head. "You don't understand how radical these laws are. And what about the ultimate weapon? Surely you can't just let them hand it out to just anyone?" Starpig was definitely concerned.

"I will see what I can do to convince the council that we shouldn't allow people to use the ultimate weapon," Orion stated calmly.

"Orion, listen! You are not even on the council anymore. Jojo recently held a new election for council members, and of course, the most popular candidates were elected. In fact, none of us are on the council anymore except for Starpig," Fution explained.

"Wait, I hadn't heard about this. Jojo did what?" Orion asked, his voice rising.

So now that they had Orion's attention, Fution and Starpig explained to him all the things that had occurred while he was away from the city. These ranged from the ultimate weapon to building constraints to new taxes to building the mini-game district. It also included a new system of rules that would insist that all citizens of the city must notify the government of what they were doing. Events would be mandatory, and all AquaCrafters would be rounded up to go to them. Much of the freedom that the AquaCrafters used to have seemed to be getting taken away with this new government.

"I, I didn't realize all that Jojo has been doing. This seems unlike him. But maybe after the events of the eclipse, Jojo might feel like he needs to control the realm more. We should head over to the AquaCraft headquarters immediately and find out what is going on," Orion suggested.

Relieved that they had finally got Orion's attention, the three of them left Orion's tower and rode off to the city. They rode through the forest swiftly. They eventually reached grassland near the police station, and they did not stop until they were actually at the police station. Once they arrived, Orion hopped off his horse and asked Fution to go find Cicer. Orion and Starpig would make their way to the railway that led from the police station to the headquarters.

It wasn't long before they reached the front entrance of the headquarters. They made their way inside, and Starpig led the way up the stairs. An AquaCrafter guarded the way up the second stairwell.

"It's OK, I'm a council member. I am allowed to pass," Starpig explained.

They brushed past the guard, who turned and yelled after them.

"Wait, I was given direct instructions not to..." The guard stammered.

Starpig and Orion ignored the guard and made their way up to the offices. They entered the next floor and looked around but couldn't find anyone. Each office was empty.

"Where is everyone?" Orion asked.

"I don't know; they just vanished," Starpig replied, puzzled. "Maybe they are in the council room."

They went up to the very top floor, but to their surprise, there was still no one there.

"I think we should ask that guard back there," Orion suggested.

They made their way down the building to find the guard panting up the stairs.

"You're not allowed up here..." The guard started.

Orion interrupted. "Where is everyone?"

"That's what I was trying to explain. Jojo gave me direct instructions not to let anyone up here. Jojo left a few hours ago with a whole patrol. There was a big commotion. It was as if they were chasing something," The guard explained.

"Hey, what's your name?" Orion asked.

"Talser, sir," The guard answered.

"OK Talser, please go downstairs and let us know when they return," Orion said kindly.

Reluctantly the guard obeyed and left Orion and Starpig in peace. The two of them took a seat in the council room.

"Strange, it's not like Jojo to just up and leave," Starpig commented.

"Agreed. And to only leave one guard behind," Orion said. "Say, these chairs are pretty comfortable." He stretched out his legs and leaned back. "You guys did really good work building this building."

Starpig leaned back too, then replied, "Thanks. Hey, you reminded me of something. Fution, Cicer, and I built in some special defenses in this building for practically any scenario. We were going to tell you, but didn't have a chance. Even Jojo doesn't know. Actually no one knows except for us TrustKeepers. We thought that if it ever came time that another invasion occurred or someone betrayed us, that we would have a place to go for safety. Like a safe house. I will have to show you all the functions."

"Oh really?" Orion sat up alertly and considered what Starpig had said. "That may prove very helpful," he decided.

Starpig elaborated on some of the defenses and showed Orion the secret control room for all of them. While they were still looking around, they heard a sound from a lower floor. Orion got up, uneasy. Then he sighed with relief.

"Ah, Fution, Cicer, it's you. Starpig was just telling me about the defensive mechanisms."

Fution replied, "Good, it's about time you knew."

"I don't know where Gestroyer is, but other than him, all of the TrustKeepers are here. We wanted to discuss with you what to do about the new government," Cicer said.

"Yeah. Well, after all that these guys have told me, I feel that AquaCraft has strayed away from where it was meant to be. I think that we need to have a big meeting and see if others feel the same way," Orion said.

Fution stood quietly and looked back in his mind. "I remember those first times when we first set foot on AquaCraft. Those were the good days, when times were simpler. Life was less crazy. We came here to create a realm where little government was needed, and people were free to do what they felt was needed. Now those times are gone."

"Maybe those times will come again," Cicer said hopefully.

"Let us hope so," Orion agreed.

Just then the guard came up the steps and announced that Jojo's patrol had returned. Quickly the TrustKeepers got up and Cicer rushed over to the opposite side of the room. Not long after, Jojo came in with ArcticCat, TheHappyBranch, and TactifulBelt behind him. Starpig noticed that Jojo had come in with his sword drawn and had not sheathed it.

Starpig cleared his throat. "I have brought all the TrustKeepers here, just as you ordered I should if such a time would occur."

"Good. Arrest them. Arrest them all. Orion and Fution you are coming with us. We already have Gestroyer," Jojo announced, "Good work,

Starpig. I know this is difficult for you."

The AquaCrafters surrounded Orion and Fution, who looked bewildered, and forced them down the stairs. Cicer had managed to slip away into another room.

"One of them is missing. Find him quickly," Jojo ordered.

ArcticCat and TactifulBelt moved to obey. They went around searching the large room. Jojo looked around and then vanished down the stairs. Starpig ran down to the water elevator and jumped down it. If the plan was going to work, he was going to have to be swift.

Hours earlier, Jojo had been sitting in the lounge room on the office floor of the AquaCraft headquarters. He was looking over some paperwork that showed the overview of the new laws that would soon be implemented. Just then the alarm went off, blaring loudly! Jojo ran over to the stairwell. ArcticCat met him on the stairs.

"What's going on?" Jojo yelled over the noise.

ArcticCat looked wide eyed and alarmed. "The ultimate weapon is gone! Someone stole it!"

"WHAT?" Jojo exclaimed, "Gather everyone in the barracks immediately."

Once everyone had gathered on the bottom floor, the alarm had been shut off. Jojo explained the situation to AquaCrafters who had gathered.

"Everyone get suited up," Jojo ordered. He spun around and said to a guard, "I want you to stay here and guard the HQ. Don't let anyone in under any circumstances. Understand? Good. Now everyone, let's go."

The whole patrol raced out of the HQ on horseback, riding quickly. Once everyone was outside, Jojo ordered each of his patrol members to different districts to interrogate any Minecrafter they came across to find out if they had seen anything. He ordered ArcticCat to stick with him. They were heading to the shopping district.

It did not take long for them to reach it. They began questioning every

AquaCrafter they came across, but to no avail, still nothing.

After half an hour, ArcticCat came to Jojo and said, "We have been looking at this all wrong. I just realized that there is no way for just any Minecrafter to get into the vault."

"Go on," Jojo encouraged.

"Well, now that I think about it, only a council member would have access to the vault. No one else would even be able to access that floor without a key," ArcticCat explained.

"You're right! That means we are looking for TheHappyBranch, TactifulBelt, AngelOfDeath, Gestroyer, or Starpig," Jojo reasoned.

"Yes. But you can eliminate TactifulBelt from the list, He rarely comes to the HQ except for meetings. And surely, we would have seen him if he were going to the vault floor," ArcticCat said.

"Hmm...I don't think it would be AngelOfDeath either, for he hardly knows about the ultimate weapon or its worth. He came to AquaCraft after the eclipse," Jojo added, "That means we must find Gestroyer, Starpig, and TheHappyBranch."

It took them another half an hour to gather back the patrol and journey to THB's base. Jojo sent part of the patrol to Gestroyer's base and Starpig's base.

TheHappyBranch came out of her base to meet them. She had built a skybase, so it took them a while before they could get her to come down. Finally, they saw THB coming down from her base using a waterfall to take her to the ground.

Once she reached them, she looked at the expressions on their faces, "What? Come on! You know I don't like elytra. It takes me time for me to get down from my sky base without it, but that's your problem. I am guessing this is about something urgent?"

"Yes, it is. Do you know anything about the stolen ultimate weapon?" Jojo asked bluntly.

"No...has something happened to it?" THB replied slowly.

"Well, it was stolen from the vault and only a council member could have taken it," ArcticCat explained.

"Now that you mention it, I thought I saw someone suspicious leave the headquarters earlier. I think they went in the direction of Gestroyer's base," THB said.

"And you didn't think to report it?" Jojo was incredulous.

"In fact, I think they were wearing business attire. They were dressed in a suit and tie," THB added.

"That sure sounds like Gestroyer," ArcticCat commented.

And with that, the three of them got on their horses and journeyed off in the direction of Gestroyer's and Starpig's bases. They met the patrol at Starpig's base and took them with them along the way to the Gestroyer's base. The patrol of six people entered into Gestroyer's castle. It didn't take them long to find Gestroyer though. He was just waiting for them, sitting on a rock in his gardens.

Jojo motioned for his patrol to surround Gestroyer. Once Jojo was convinced Gestroyer had no escape, he spoke.

"Hand over the ultimate weapon, Gestroyer," Jojo ordered coldly.

"And what makes you think I would do that?" Gestroyer smiled a sinister smile.

"So you don't deny it! You were the one who stole it!" ArcticCat exclaimed.

"Far be it from me to deny it. It is a feat that is almost impossible to accomplish. To get through one of the most complex security systems in the realm? Unfortunately, I cannot say that I did it alone though," Gestroyer smirked.

"What do you mean?" Jojo asked.

"Well, I couldn't get in there alone. At least I couldn't escape without help. That is where the ones that helped build it came into play," Gestroyer said, taking his time.

Jojo was beginning to get frustrated, "Just tell us what happened!"

"Alright, alright. I stole the ultimate weapon for Orion. The TrustKeepers wanted it back. They were plotting to overthrow you, so they needed the power in order to do so. They aren't strong enough to do it without the power," Gestroyer explained.

"Orion would never do that. I know him. This isn't him." ArcticCat looked at Jojo.

"Well, I guess you don't know your friend very well then. We have been meeting for ages, waiting for this moment to overthrow you, Jojo. And now that you are distracted, the HQ shall be theirs!" Gestroyer laughed.

"I have heard enough. Silence him and arrest him. We must return to the AquaCraft HQ immediately. It seems as if Orion has betrayed us..." Jojo spoke gravely.

As the patrol converged on Gestroyer, he brought out the Heart of the Sea, threatening to use it. But before he could, in a lightning-swift move, ArcticCat managed to snatch it out of his hands. ArcticCat turned and handed it over to Jojo.

As the patrol took Gestroyer into custody, Jojo turned away and said, "We're finished here."

Chapter 21: All-Out War

TheHappyBranch hadn't meant for things to turn out this way. All she wanted was the Trident. She hadn't meant to help frame Orion for something he hadn't done. It was Gestroyer. He was the problem. That evil genius! He had helped turn the AquaCrafters against themselves. He was the issue. He needed to be taken care of. But surely, she wouldn't be allowed to kill him. She would surely be seen, and even if she did kill him, he would just respawn. She would have to get rid of his spawn point. But that would only make matters worse. She couldn't destroy his spawn point without possibly destroying someone else's spawn point, too. Plus, she might get caught. Things were tense right now. She would have to find another way to take care of Gestroyer. Until then, she would have to help in whatever way she could.

TheHappyBranch was sitting by a tree, thinking about what to do. Suddenly she got up and walked over to her horse. At this point, few people used elytra anymore; the use of elytra was forbidden except for quests. She had never liked elytra anyway; it seemed unnatural.

She rode like the wind, traversing the terrain quickly to make up for the time she had wasted. It wasn't long before she came into view of the police station. The TrustKeepers had been imprisoned until a proper trial could be conducted. She stopped and got off her horse. She snuck over to one of the stone walls that surrounded the prison area of the police station. Taking out her pickaxe, she mined a small hole in the wall and climbed through. Careful not to be seen from the large watch tower in the center of the station, she pressed her body flat against the inside wall. Now she was in the small prison yard that was outside the cells. She made her way by each cell, peering into each window to see if someone was there. Finally, she found someone; it was Fution! She made her way around the yard until she came to the doorway that separated the interior of the police station from the yard. She pried open the door and went inside. Thanks to her elvish background, she was able to be more silent than any Minecrafter could be. The interior of the prison was very bland. There were rows of single person cells lined up on either side of the prison. On the far side she could see the offices near the front of the police station. There was a ladder in the center of the large room that led down to what probably was a basement.

Following the edge of the cells, she made her way past Fution's cell and found Orion in the next-door cell.

"THB? What are you doing here?" Orion whispered.

"Getting you out of here," She replied.

TheHappyBranch flipped the lever next to the cell door, and it opened. But she didn't stay to see her friends out. Carefully, she went over to the opposite row of cells. Looking around the identical stone cells, she finally found who she was looking for. She flipped another lever and dragged out Gestroyer, who was lying inside.

"You will follow me, and not a word, or I will cut you open and serve you to hoglin," She whispered fiercely into his ear.

Gestroyer got up in utter surprise. He said nothing, but his eyes were wide as THB moved him out of the prison the way she had come in. She had a mini-sword touching the small of his back, and she forced him forward, moving them both quietly but surely. Gestroyer, who was unarmed, followed THB's instructions very carefully. Eventually, they made their way to where THB had left her horse.

TheHappyBranch spoke harshly. "Now listen to me carefully. This is what you are going to do..."

Orion was extremely confused. Slowly he made his way out of his cell. He sneaked over to Fution's cell and opened it. Once out, Fution followed Orion out of the prison. They made their way to a chest which had a few tools and weapons that were used by the guards. Once armed, they walked over to the yard and made a run for it.

They didn't make it far when someone shouted, "The prisoners are escaping! Guards, stop them!"

Orion and Fution broke into a sprint, running over to the door on the far wall. Just then, an iron golem guard leapt down from the wall and stalked toward them.

"Quickly, break down that door! I will distract the golem," Fution exclaimed.

Orion ran to the door and started whacking it with an ax. Meanwhile, Fution leapt onto the golem swinging his sword in a downward motion. The golem was thrown off balance causing it to fall backwards but was unharmed. Fution jumped back out of the reach of the golems' huge arms. Orion had broken down the door at this point, and they exited the prison, running as fast as they could. An AquaCrafter shot arrows at them from their crossbow. Arrows rained down upon them, as they easily dodged the badly aimed shots. It wouldn't be long before the guards caught up with them. and Jojo would be alerted soon. They needed a quick escape, and fast.

Looking around, Orion noticed the small ravine next to them. He motioned for Fution to follow him, and they ran over to it. Thinking fast, Orion saw a small ledge not far down.

"If we jump, we might be able to make it to that ledge over there," Orion pointed to the other side of the ravine.

"Are you crazy? There's no way we'll make it there," Fution responded.

Orion looked behind him, seeing an AquaCrafter running towards them. He said, "I don't think we have a choice."

Orion hunched down and then flung himself over the edge; he tumbled through the air and landed hard on the granite below. Fution joined him not a moment too late.

"Argh, that hurt," Orion complained.

Fution just grunted, "We better get going."

They ran into the cave in front of them and followed it down into the earth. They passed many turn offs and took the path that led back up to the surface. They squinted as they emerged, their eyes adjusting to the light.

"Hi guys, glad you made it," said a voice from the surface.

"Who's there?" Orion asked.

Once Orion's eyes fully adjusted, he realized that the person standing in front of him was Cicer.

"Where did you come from? How did you find us?" Fution asked surprised.

Cicer helped them up, then said, "I came looking for you guys after I escaped from the HQ. I thought I heard that you guys were placed in the police station. But when I came near, all the guards had gone off to the small ravine. You're lucky that I just happened to know where those caves went."

Once they caught their breath, Fution asked, "Well, what now?"

"Now we must find the ultimate weapon. We must destroy it before anyone gets a hold of it. If Jojo decides to use it, he could defeat any of us. We wouldn't even be able to draw our sword before he disarmed us. We won't stand a chance unless we can remove it from the equation," Orion said.

"Surely Jojo wouldn't use the weapon on us? No one is supposed to take hold of it," Cicer commented.

"I wouldn't be so sure about that. He might think of it as an easy way to end the conflict," Fution said.

"Well, I know that the Heart of the Sea is at the AquaCraft HQ. Jojo had it with him when I snuck out of there," Cicer said.

"Then that's where we need to go. Before we do anything, we need to plan out what we are going to do," Orion said.

"OK, then you will thank me for bringing these from the armory before I left," Cicer said, pulling out two full sets of iron armor and weapons from his inventory.

The three of them walked over to a tree and pulled on the armor and suited up for a fight. Once they were ready, Fution explained the layout of the headquarters.

"We actually designed the HQ as an ultimate fortress. In case of an attack, we could retreat there and use it as a base. It is secretly equipped with TNT cannons, complex defensive mechanisms, and even a whole room of operations. We should contact Starpig and have him prep the base to use it against those inside," Fution explained.

"Wait, I thought Starpig betrayed us," Orion said, surprised.

"Oh, did we forget to tell you the plan? Gestroyer was supposed to inform you," Cicer said.

"No, I didn't know," Orion replied.

"Well, Starpig is our inside man. We were planning to overthrow Jojo's government by using the HQ against them. We may not have the numbers, but we have the equipment to outplay Jojo and retake the headquarters," Fution explained.

"Are you suggesting all-out war? We can't just take over the HQ and not expect conflict," Orion exclaimed.

Fution hesitated. "Orion, do you want to get the ultimate weapon back or not? It's in the vault where you left it. This is the only way."

Orion sighed, "If this is the only way. But no killing. And no sabotaging the respawn centers. I want to reduce the fighting as much as possible. But we must destroy the ultimate weapon. It is too powerful to be used."

Orion, Fusion, and Cicer neared the AquaCraft Headquarters. The plan was to meet up with Starpig and get to the control center. Once that was completed, they might be able to lock down the building, essentially trapping everyone inside on separate floors. Then it would be easy to get to the vault without any issue. Now it would be incredibly difficult to enter the building from the bottom because they would surely be spotted. Besides, the control center happened to be at the top of the building. So, they would have to climb to the very top of the skyscraper.

"OK, so you all know the plan. Get out your climbing gear and get over to the arc," Orion instructed quietly.

They ran over to the giant archway that came down from the top of the building. It would be easier to scale the building on something that wasn't completely vertical. So, the arch was the perfect choice. Fution and Cicer took out wooden ladders and bamboo scaffolding. They would use the equipment to climb up the side of the archway. Orion would keep watch, and make sure they weren't seen. Fution placed a ladder and climbed up it; he placed another piece of ladder and then another. Then he climbed onto the lowest ledge. He helped Cicer and Orion up. Cicer and Fution then began repeating the process. Five blocks in the air, then ten. They kept on climbing. It was exhausting work, especially with the sun boiling down on them. For some parts, the ladders wouldn't stay up without falling over, so Cicer took out some scaffolding and used it to climb the larger stretches. Unfortunately, that had limited scaffolding, so they had to be careful how much they used. It took them what seemed like an infinite amount of time to climb up the archway, but they finally made it. Placing the final ladder, they heaved themselves on the roof.

"Wow, don't look down!" Orion shuddered at the thought of falling down that far. The ground was at least eighty or ninety blocks below them.

They slowly dragged themselves over to a small trapdoor in the roof. Together, they opened the trapdoor and went down. They had entered a small dark room. Orion pushed a button, and a redstone lantern came on. They went through the wooden door in the wall. On the other side of the door was a decently sized room. The ceiling in this room wasn't very high, and there weren't any windows either. In the center of the room were a few control consoles with buttons and levers and redstone mechanisms. The room was smaller than any of the other floors in the HQ, and not very well lit.

"Welcome to the control room. Here you can control basically any of the functions of the entire headquarters. Fution helped a lot with most of the mechanisms," Cicer said.

"Interesting. It's kind of easy to access if someone attacks from the sky," Orion pointed out.

"Not many people have elytra anymore, remember? Only the Original AquaCrafters would have one," Fution replied.

"I see your point," Orion said.

Suddenly a section of the wall opened up, and Starpig came in.

"Guys, chill, it's just me. Like the piston door, Orion? One of your own designs actually," Starpig said.

"It's good to see you, Starpig," Orion replied.

"Oh, sorry about earlier. I had to play along; they needed to believe I was on their side. Otherwise, I would have been arrested like the rest of you," Starpig said.

"It's fine. What is the status down below? How many people are we dealing with? Do you know where the ultimate weapon is?" Orion asked.

"Well, we haven't much time. But here is the situation." Starpig was matter-of-fact. "Most of Jojo's governmental officials are here. At least all of his council. In fact, they were having a meeting right now, so I had to make an excuse to leave in order to get out of there. They have just learned about your escape, actually."

"OK, that means we must hurry. Fution, I want you to stay here in the control center, and when the signal goes off, I want you to lock down the building. Cicer and I will distract them and lead them onto one of the floors. While we do that, Starpig will go and get the ultimate weapon from the vault." Orion was laying out a plan.

"Um, yeah, I think I forgot to mention that the ultimate weapon isn't here anymore, but the Heart of the Sea is," Starpig said uncomfortably.

"Wait what? But that's the whole plan! To get the ultimate weapon!" Cicer exclaimed.

Orion thought fast, "OK, that complicates things. Then where is the Heart of the Sea? Is it accessible?"

"Kind of...Well, Jojo has it on him," Starpig explained.

"Oh, great. In that case I want you, Starpig and Cicer to distract everyone and trap them on a floor. Meanwhile, I will lead Jojo to the training floor. I don't think I can beat Jojo in combat, but I might if I have an advantage. Fution, I will need you to initiate certain battle scenarios so that I can get the Heart of the Sea from Jojo," Orion explained.

"I think I can do that. There are security cameras on each floor, so I will be able to see and hear you. Just tell me what you need once you have gotten him there," Fution said.

"Good. So in review, Cicer and Starpig will distract them, leading them into a trap here," Orion said, pointing to a place on the map on the table in the control room. "Meanwhile I will catch Jojo's attention and have him chase me to the training floor. Cicer will stay here and use the controls to lock down the building once we have everyone in the right place. Once everyone is trapped, take the hidden passageways back to here and we will figure it out from there. Does everyone understand?"

Everyone nodded. Fution ran over to the control panel and readied the systems. Orion took the piston door passageway to get down. Cicer and Starpig ran over to the secret vents that went into the meeting room. It didn't take long for Starpig and Cicer to make their way through the ventilation system to the floor below, which happened to be the meeting room. They could hear voices below them.

"We tracked them to a ravine, but they lost us in the tunnels," said a voice.

"Send a search party to check that area. We must find them at once!" said another voice.

Cicer whispered to Starpig, "Hey, that sounds like Jojo."

"You're right. OK, Cicer, here is what we are going to do. You're going to go down first and draw their attention. We must draw them away to a lower level so that they are out of Orion's way..." Starpig started.

Cicer interrupted. "Wait, how come I have to be the first one to go? Why shouldn't you go first?"

"Well, they wouldn't realize something is wrong when they first see me. Never mind, we are wasting time. Just go!" Starpig replied urgently.

Cicer crawled a bit forward through the dark vents.

"Seriously, I think you should go first…" Cicer began.

Suddenly the vent panel that Cicer was on flipped open, and Cicer fell down to the floor below. The council members all looked up as Cicer fell down, bringing the chandelier with him. TactifulBelt, and AngelOfDeath leaped out of the way, while Jojo shouted an exclamation of alarm. The chandelier hit the table with a crash, and Cicer hit the table with a loud thump. Everyone in the room just stood there in utter shock, frozen with disbelief, just staring at Cicer. Cicer took a moment to recuperate before looking around.

"Um, hi, everyone! Gotta go. Bye!" Cicer jumped to his feet on the broken table and ran as fast as he could down the stairs.

"Don't just stand there! After him!" Jojo exclaimed.

AquaCrafter guards ran down after Cicer, with TactifulBelt and ArcticCat not far behind. AngelOfDeath pulled out his sword and made his way down. Jojo slowly followed but stopped when he heard another thump behind him. He turned around just in time to see Starpig's sword coming down on him. Jojo just barely parried the attack and retreated down the stairs. Starpig quickly followed, meaning to help Cicer.

Meanwhile Cicer had made his way down to the office floors. He ran, jumping over desks and chairs, evading all the AquaCrafters who were after him. He dodged attacks from all directions, barely escaping each time. Then the AquaCrafters surrounded him, and he was forced closer to one corner of the room. He jumped off a desk and landed neatly on the ground. He turned around to find himself surrounded with swords pointed towards his chest.

"Surrender, Cicer," TactifulBelt ordered.

"Guys, we can talk about this," Cicer said desperately.

Then Starpig came out of nowhere with Jojo running after him. Starpig leaped on one of the AquaCrafters, knocking them out.

"Cicer, we need to get them to the bottom floor!" Starpig hissed in Cicer's ear.

Then Starpig went back into combat with another AquaCrafter. This gave Cicer the chance to escape. Running past the guards, he made it to the stairs to go to even lower floors. The majority of the AquaCrafters ran after him. Only Jojo and one other were left in front of Starpig. Starpig was soon overwhelmed by both of their attacks. He turned and ran off, with both of them on his trail.

Jojo was making his way down the stairs after Starpig when he heard his name being called.

"Jojo!" Orion exclaimed.

Jojo stopped and turned. "Orion. I see you finally decided to show up." He stood on the stairs looking at Orion doubtfully.

"It's just you and me now. Just like old times," Orion said, lifting up his sword as challenge.

"You know, I am better than you with a sword, right?" Jojo replied, drawing his sword.

"We'll see this time," Orion said.

Orion jumped down the flight of stairs, swinging a strike along the way, allowing him to get in and get out without risk. Jojo blocked the attack, and soon ran after Orion down the stairs. Orion saw the Heart of the Sea on Jojo's belt as he passed. He needed to get it. Orion ran over to the entrance to the training floor, which was a large cube space that was the size of a mini-stadium. Orion flung open the door and walked in.

"Fution, now! Lock down the building!" Orion exclaimed.

Jojo walked in just in time to hear a loud alarm go off, and the door behind him sealed shut just like all the entryways and exits of the building. Orion had a mini two-way communicator on his wrist that spoke up with Fution's voice.

"Orion, all the AquaCrafters are trapped in the armory except for you and Jojo. But AngelOfDeath escaped out of the building. What do you want me to do?" Fution said.

"Forgot about that right now. Activate training scenario parkour number 105," Orion ordered.

Blocks throughout the room began to lift out of the ground and come out of the walls, creating an obstacle course all the way to a platform at the top. Orion jumped onto the blocks and leaped upwards with Jojo close behind.

"I don't know what you are trying to do, Orion, but it won't work," Jojo exclaimed.

Orion paid no attention to him. Instead, he said, "Fution give me kit number seven."

A chest appeared on the platform above Orion. He leaped up and hauled himself onto it. He opened the chest and pulled out a fishing rod. He turned around and flung the line at Jojo and it caught hold of the Heart of the Sea. He reeled it in and grabbed the Heart of the Sea out of the air and put it on his own belt.

"No!" Jojo shouted.

Jojo pulled out a bow and shot three shots at Orion. Two of which missed, the last one hit Orion, knocking him off the platform. He fell the long way onto the ground and collapsed on the floor. Jojo parkoured down and landed heavily a few blocks from Orion. He walked over to Orion slowly, dragging his sword behind him making a sharp noise of iron hitting iron. Orion pulled himself up, groaning from the effort. He drew his sword and the two Original AquaCrafters launched themselves into combat. Their swords clashed, causing sparks to fly every which way. Jojo brought out a shield and blocked a heavy blow from Orion. He stabbed his sword forward barely nicking Orion, but Orion swung his sword around to stop the attack from penetrating any deeper.

"Fution, switch training scenario to fort variation two," Orion said.

The terrain in the room changed, and all the parkour blocks went back into the walls and floor, and grass emerged below them. A small wooden fort was constructed out of the ground behind Orion. Orion ran over to the fort and closed the door behind him. Jojo banged against the door, trying to burst it open. Orion ran up to the top of the fort. He leaped over the edge, landing on the soft ground carefully. Jojo had just broken down the door in time to see Orion leap off. He retraced his steps and sprinted over to Orion. He jumped up and swung his sword mightily. Orion parried the attack, but not without consequence. He staggered backwards and lifted his head in time to block another strike. Jojo unleashed a furious onslaught of attacks. Each strike was harder to parry than that last. Then Jojo twisted his sword at a weird angle, flinging Orion's sword out of his hands and onto the dry grass.

Orion backed into a wall, looking around desperately for an escape. But Jojo's sword was already pointed at his head.

"Forgive me, Jojo," Orion said.

He pulled up the Heart of the Sea and shot a small beam of energy that sent Jojo flying across the room. Jojo flew through the air and collapsed hard on the ground.

"Fution, flush him out," Orion ordered, breathing heavily.

The block beneath Jojo collapsed into the ground and Jojo fell into a tunnel tube that ran all the way to the bottom floor, which was the armory. Orion dragged himself out of the training room, and slowly went down the stairs. He came down into the armory to find Starpig and Cicer standing over the rest of the AquaCrafters. Iron golems had surrounded the rest of the AquaCrafters, who had all dropped their weapons and surrendered. Jojo was limping towards them. Thanks to the advanced security system which included the iron golems, the TrustKeepers were able to retake the headquarters.

"So, what now? We have trapped all the council members, and they have surrendered. But the rest of the AquaCrafters are still out there," Starpig explained.

"I'm not sure. We never planned this far," Orion said hesitantly.

"Well, we can't just leave them here," Cicer pointed out.

Suddenly the main door exploded, and AngelOfDeath leading a patrol of AquaCrafters walked in. They shot arrows at the golems and gave the new council members a chance to run.

"Stop them!" Starpig ordered the golems.

The golems started approaching the patrol.

"Quickly Jojo, ArcticCat, this way. TactifulBelt, help the others!" AngelOfDeath exclaimed.

The group ran out of the headquarters, but Jojo glanced back for one moment.

"You don't know what you have started, Orion! You will regret this. This is all-out war!" Jojo shouted, before vanishing out of sight.

"Should we go after them?" Cicer asked.

"There's no point. We wouldn't be able to stop them if we tried. Jojo is right. This is war at this point. He will not stop until he gets the Heart of the Sea back. Fortify the headquarters immediately. We must prepare for battle. This isn't over," Orion said gravely.

Chapter 22: Recuperation

Jojo and his allies had retreated to the city. Now that the TrustKeepers had taken over AquaCraft HQ, the AquaCraft government would need a new place to use as a command center. Though the AquaCrafters vastly outnumbered the TrustKeepers, the TrustKeepers did have a few advantages. First, they had the HQ, which gave them an almost impenetrable fortress. Also, they had a full barracks with tons of resources. In fact, the AquaCraft government had few resources remaining. They had moved almost all their resources to the HQ, and now the TrustKeepers had them all. They would have to regroup and gather more resources if they wanted to survive. Because of all these things, it was a suicide to try and reclaim the headquarters at this point. So, they would set up camp and evaluate the situation. Luckily, the TrustKeepers had their own problems. Because there were so few of them, they couldn't launch any attacks or control large areas of land. The TrustKeepers were mainly keeping to themselves in the area around the HQ.

Jojo's government decided to regroup at the old barracks and gather the remaining supplies to that place. They decided to set up a camp outside the city, so it would be easier to watch the headquarters. The headquarters was south of the city, so they set up camp south of the city as well. Separating the headquarters and the city was a small ridge, the police station, and a large field. They set up camp near the ridge not far from the police station. From there, they could see the headquarters in the distance.

"We have control over the entire city and the land up to the police station. The TrustKeepers wouldn't dare attack us with so few numbers," TactifulBelt reported.

Jojo leaned back in his seat and looked around the room. TactifulBelt, ArcticCat, AngelOfDeath, and an AquaCrafter called SwankPrism had gathered to discuss the situation. They had gathered at the camp in the leader's tent.

"Then why don't we attack right away?" AngelOfDeath asked.

"Do you know how hard it would be to invade the HQ? It's a fortress. There is no way we can go up to the headquarters and expect to just walk right in," Jojo explained.

"Then how did Orion and the TrustKeepers infiltrate the HQ and kick us out?" AngelOfDeath protested.

ArcticCat's expression was dark. "Because they were the ones who built it. They know its layout like the back of their hand. I wouldn't be surprised if there are secret passageways and mechanisms we don't know about."

"Then we will have to find those secrets if we want to attack. For now, though, we must recuperate. Even if we could somehow get inside the HQ, we would still be completely outplayed by their superior tools and weapons," Jojo added.

"Agreed. I suggest that we set up defenses on the field that separates us from them. We should also keep people on watch in case they decide to attack. That might give us enough time to gather the might to bring the fight to them," TactifulBelt suggested.

"Good. Then I will leave you, TactifulBelt, in charge of the defenses. Meanwhile, I want a patrol to go around the city and see if we can find any more supplies. Also, I want a few spies to go investigate the HQ and see what we can find out. I think we have a few potions of invisibility and swiftness left," Jojo ordered.

He motioned for them to leave, sending them off to their duties. As they were walking out, Jojo stopped ArcticCat.

He said, "ArcticCat, one moment if you can."

"Yes, what is it?" ArcticCat asked quietly, turning around.

Jojo sighed and stared directly at ArcticCat. "Listen, I know this is tough. For both of us. It's hard to think of Orion and the others as enemies, but they made their choice. They betrayed the government. Nothing we can say can change that fact. But I need to know if I can rely on you."

"We both believe that the Heart of the Sea, the Nether Star, and the Trident must not be held by any one group or people. And we can't destroy them in case more evil threats return. It is too bad if Orion has forgotten that. I would have made sure that it wouldn't land in the wrong hands," ArcticCat replied heavily.

"We both would. Maybe Orion can still be reasoned with. But unless he hands over the Heart of the Sea and the Nether Star, I'm afraid we might have to use force. I would let him keep the Trident though," Jojo said.

"I understand," ArcticCat said.

"Good. Now I won't keep you any longer," Jojo finished.

It didn't take long for TactifulBelt to organize and build the defenses. Unfortunately, due to lack of necessary resources, they were unable to cover the entire field. They were able to place in many rows of lava, trenches, and spikes. If those didn't stop the TrustKeepers, they would certainly delay them or force them to go the long way around.

Many Minecrafters had left AquaCraft due to the conflict and the present situation. Those who stayed were committed to the cause. They would reclaim the headquarters and retake the Heart of the Sea and the Nether Star.

The camp had also progressed significantly from when it first started. It now had an obsidian wall surrounding it, with a lava moat that was sure to stop many intruders. They had also built watch towers on the edge of the field behind the defenses where they could be alerted if an attack was imminent. It would be difficult now for any attack to take place.

The next morning, the AquaCrafter called Nulfan walked out onto the stretch of land between the lava moats. He was supposed to keep watch around the area, in case the TrustKeepers decided to attack. The crisp morning air was refreshing after an uncomfortable night. The living quarters were adequate, but only barely. Since the government was so low on resources, their meals were bland and tasteless. In fact, most of their materials were run down by this point. He finished his inspections in the area and headed back towards the camp. On his way there, he ran into the AquaCrafter SwankPrism.

"SwankPrism, what are you doing here?" Nulfan asked curiously.

"Hi Nulfan. I'm supposed to take your shift to keep watch. They want you back at camp," SwankPrism explained.

"Why? I haven't been out here for very long," Nulfan asked, surprised.

SwankPrism shrugged, "I don't know. It doesn't seem like our leaders know what they are doing. Hmph, I don't even know why we are even fighting each other anyway. If the TrustKeepers would just hand over the Ultimate Weapon, then we wouldn't have any problems."

"Yeah, you're right about that one; well, I'd better be going," Nulfan replied.

Nulfan left SwankPrism and headed back to camp. *What could be so important to bring me back to camp already?* Nulfan wondered. He would soon find out.

Back at camp, Jojo had gathered AngelOfDeath, Nulfan, and one other AquaCrafter.

"I have a mission for all of you. AngelOfDeath, you will lead this mission. Your goal is to infiltrate the AquaCraft HQ and report back on its defenses and weaknesses. Nulfan, who is one of our defense builders, is here to brief you on the best path through our traps. Once you make your way past the defenses, you will continue to the HQ," Jojo explained thoroughly. "Good luck."

As the three exited, Nulfan muttered under his breath, "As if luck will help us complete the mission."

They slowly made their way out of the camp. Once they reached the edge of the defenses, Nulfan pointed out their way with careful instructions., Then he started to walk away.

"You're not coming?" AngelOfDeath asked.

"This is your mission, not mine. Good luck," Nulfan said gruffly, without turning around or slowing his pace back to camp.

AngelOfDeath looked around helplessly, before giving up and

continued down the path Nulfan pointed out.

And so it was two lone figures who rode out past the towers and defenses. AngelOfDeath and Galen—one of the new AquaCrafters—had volunteered for the daring adventure, and now they journeyed stealthily across the land. As they drew near the giant skyscraper, AngelOfDeath motioned for them to stop.

"We leave the horses here. From now on, we will use our invisibility and swiftness potions. They should last around five to eight minutes, so we have to be quick. Our goal is to find any weaknesses in the building where we can attack when the time is right. But you have to be swift, because I can't help you if you get caught," AngelOfDeath instructed. "Do you understand?"

Galen nodded. AngelOfDeath and Galen then drank their potions, grimacing from its taste. Then their bodies shivered in the air and vanished all together. They ran as fast as any horse thanks to the swiftness in the draught, and they approached the HQ.

Once they got there, AngelOfDeath flattened himself against the wall. Even though no one could see him, particles could still be seen in the air around him. The two of them had to inspect the entire outside area of the building in a very short time. Walking around the first wall, the one in front, he came to the second wall. He brought out a pickaxe and hacked at different sections of it. The more he dug, the more he realized how thick the wall was. It would be extremely difficult to get in that way. Giving up on penetrating the wall, he sneaked over to the giant archway that came down from the top of the building. Coming around its side, he noticed the arch wasn't that steep. A person might be able to climb up it with the right equipment. Next AngelOfDeath walked over to the front doorway. He would have to wait until someone opened the door, or else it would look like a ghost opened the door. He waited for a while, examining every inch of the space. Then he saw Cicer walking by towards the door. Cicer pressed the buttons on the control panel, imputing the correct code. Pistons sounded, and the giant door collapsed into the floor. AngelOfDeath took the opportunity to sneak in after Cicer. They emerged into the barracks. Maybe AngelOfDeath would be able to steal some equipment on the way out. But he focused on the main objective and kept an eye out for any secrets. He hopped off the bridge that went over the lower parts of the floor and looked around. On one wall was a rack of weapons. Next to it were armor stands with shiny new armor all hung up on them. Ignoring these, AngelOfDeath walked around to the other wall, feeling around it to see if he could find any variations. Then he came across an air vent near the floor. Or what seemed like an air vent. He pulled on the vent. It came out. Leaning down, he stared into it. It was a passageway! Looking behind him to make sure no one had noticed him, he crawled in and found himself in a whole secret passageway system. There were even signs labeling where each passageway went.

After exploring for some time, he noticed his invisibility was wearing off. He would have to stay hidden if he wanted to escape. He had no clue what floor he was on. He must have taken a wrong turn. He looked around, then pushed on a vent panel. It fell to the floor. Greatly relieved, he crawled out and stretched, happy to find himself in an open room. The room was dark and lifeless. There were control panels and mechanisms all over. Confused, he wandered around the strange space. He came to a ladder and climbed up it. When he opened the trapdoor above him, he realized he was on the roof of the HQ! If they were somehow able to climb up to the top of the building, they would be able to sneak into the HQ without being seen. This must have been how Orion and the others snuck into the building. He climbed back down and checked out each of the redstone mechanisms. One panel, he realized, was a row of security cameras. This must be the security room or something like that! Looking closer at the blurry image on the panel, he realized that it was Galen! And Fution and Starpig were escorting him down the hall. He must have been caught. AngelOfDeath knew he had to escape immediately.

He went back to the ladder that led to the roof. He scrambled up as quickly and quietly as he could. Once on the roof, he walked over to the edge.

This had better work! He had borrowed Jojo's elytra for the mission in case he needed a quick escape. If necessary, he would be able to fly away and get back to the camp quickly.

Taking a deep breath, he stepped onto the ledge, and jumped off. Activating the wings, he felt the air pressure build up around him. He flew downwards, gaining speed before steadying out. He landed on the ground near the horses. He quickly unequipped the elytra and got on his horse and rode off. He rode swiftly, hoping to make up for lost time. Jojo needed to hear of this at once. Though Galen had been captured, they had been given a chance to reclaim the headquarters. It was time to formulate strategies for battle and prepare for war. If they wished to survive, they would have to end the war quickly.

On the completely opposite side of AquaCraft, TheHappyBranch and Gestroyer were walking through the woods.

"You had better be right about this," THB growled.

"It's not much farther. Just keep going that way." Gestroyer pointed down the path deeper into the woods.

"Why did you stop? You are going with me!" TheHappyBranch said.

"I don't think that is a good idea," Gestroyer began.

TheHappyBranch wasn't having any of it. "And let you run off? I don't think so."

"Why do you want to see him, anyway?" Gestroyer asked.

"Let's just say that we have met before, and I would like to settle a few scores," she said.

TheHappyBranch drew the Trident and made sure Gestroyer walked in front of her. The trees here were pines, but they all looked dead. It wasn't long before they came to a cabin near a rock wall. They stopped.

"Go on and open the door," THB ordered.

Gestroyer gulped and hesitantly approached the door. He opened it slowly, the door creaking as he did so. He went inside with THB on the porch behind him.

"Hello? Are you there?" Gestroyer called out softly.

TheHappyBranch followed Gestroyer into the dark cabin. It was silent. The fireplace was unlit, and the chair was empty. Looking around, THB noticed there was hardly anything in the cabin. Then, a loud creaky sound came from behind them. The door creaked open. Red eyes, and a dark figure stood at the doorway.

"It seems as if someone has ventured too far into the woods..." said a mysterious low voice.

"Who goes there? Show yourself!" THB exclaimed

Instead of responding, a blood red beam shot out, knocking THB back against the wood, splintering it. THB struggled to her feet as the figure stepped into view. It was a knight, with lava flowing through its armor. TheHappyBranch lifted up the Trident and shot out a jet of water. The figure blocked the attack with its arm, breaking the beam of water, sending it flying all over the place. The beam broke when THB's concentration broke. The figure then created a ball of dark red energy and flung it out, causing the entire cabin to explode. Blocks went flying. THB landed on the ground heavily. Gestroyer vanished. Squinting, she saw the figure leap up into the air and spread its arms, revealing the Nether Star in its chest. Energy charged up, and the figure got ready to deal the finishing blow.

"I shall destroy you beyond the point from where you can respawn," the knight stated ominously.

Refusing to give up, THB charged up all her remaining energy, and lifted the Trident, shooting out a beam of water more powerful than she had thought possible. There was a deafening sound when the beams collided. The energy knocked back both of the users. A mere mortal would have been knocked out, but TheHappyBranch was not a mere mortal. She staggered to her feet. Using inhuman strength, she launched the Trident like a javelin, sending it at the knight as he rose from the rubble. As it struck the knight, lightning came down from the sky, knocking the knight to the ground.

TheHappyBranch took a deep breath and straightened up. She limped over to the knight and lifted the Trident off of his body. Turning around, she saw Gestroyer looking at her warily. He backed up and ran into the forest, disappearing from view.

Gestroyer would be back. She knew that. But she would be ready when he did. She walked back to the trail, but just as she thought she had won, the knight rose to his feet. She turned to face him again. He looked at her with one eye flickering. The lava flowing out of him looked as if it had almost completely drained his body. His power had been weakened.

"This is not over, TheHappyBranch. This is not the last you have seen of me. I shall return stronger than ever. Until we meet again," Flamecat growled with hate.

He backed away, using what power he had left to create a Nether Portal. A purple mist rose around him, and then he vanished back to his own world.

With that, THB walked away back to the city with the Trident. She knew that that wasn't the last time she would meet Flamecat, but it would certainly be a while before he dared to torment AquaCraft again. She really disliked the nether and hoped to never have to visit that wretched place.

Chapter 23: Battle Plans

Back at AquaCraft HQ, the TrustKeepers had gathered in the council room. Orion stood up as Starpig and Fution dragged in an AquaCrafter. It was Galen. They threw him to the ground.

"Orion, look who we found snooping around," Starpig announced.

"Let him get up. Well? What do you have to say for yourself?" Orion exclaimed.

Galen got up and shook the dust off of him. Then he looked up and dipped his head as a sign of respect.

"Sir, I was sent on a mission to spy on the HQ," Galen said politely.

"Go on," Orion replied.

"Well, Sir, AngelOfDeath was tasked with finding any weaknesses in the headquarters for the time that we might attack the TrustKeepers. I volunteered to join him on the mission," Galen explained. "You haven't caught him yet, have you?"

Orion felt a jolt of anxiety but didn't show it. He signaled to Cicer, who immediately ran out of the room. Then Orion spoke.

He said, "That is not of your concern yet. We need to know if we can trust what you say."

"Please, sir, you can trust me. The real reason why I volunteered in the first place was so I could have an excuse to join the TrustKeepers," Galen explained earnestly.

Orion hid his surprise. This was interesting. But all he said was, "Then please tell us all you know."

"Well, after the TrustKeepers took over the HQ, the AquaCraft government retreated to the city. Once we gathered enough resources, we set up camp on the far side of this plain," Galen explained, pointing out the window at the far side of the plain. "After that, Jojo and his advisers started planning how to reclaim the HQ. He sent AngelOfDeath and me here to find how to invade when the time came. AngelOfDeath and I were equipped with invisibility and swiftness potions. I wasn't invited to their meetings, but what I understand is that they want to reclaim the Heart of the Sea, the Nether Star, and the Trident."

Orion thought about that for a minute. Then he asked, "How are their defenses?"

"They set up lava moats and other ground defenses all across the plain. There is no way you can get past them without getting spotted."

Orion then turned to Starpig and Fution. "It seems like they are farther along than expected. Prepare the tunnel. We must stop them before they get here."

Starpig and Fution rushed off down the stairs. Orion motioned for Galen to follow him. Orion jumped down the bubble elevator with Galen was close behind. They emerged out of the elevator into the armory at the bottom of the building.

"What's your name?" Orion asked.

"Galen, Sir," Galen replied.

"Well, Galen, if you would really like to help the TrustKeepers, then I need you to follow me. We are more desperate than you would think. We need all the help we can get. Get suited up and come quickly," Orion ordered.

Galen did not hesitate. He grabbed the armor off the armor stand and pulled it on. Then he grabbed an iron sword off the wall and sheathed it. Orion also suited up, but with diamond gear. Then Orion led Galen to the far side of the armory. They went off the walkway down a flight of stairs. Starpig was waiting for them at the bottom. It was the entrance of a tunnel that led below the building. They walked down into it and followed it around a few turns until it straightened out into a long passageway.

"This tunnel leads almost all the way to the city. We have been working on it for weeks now. I need you to take me to where many of the AquaCrafters are. I want to speak with them and see if I can convince any of them to join our cause," Orion explained.

"Oh? There are a few AquaCrafters I know that, like me, don't support the use of the ultimate weapon," Galen replied.

Orion nodded to that, then said to Starpig, "I need you to hold the fort while I am gone. Don't let anyone in or out until we get back. Activate full security except for the tunnel. Hopefully we will have a few more helping hands when this is all said and done."

"Good. I will make sure nothing bad happens here until you get back," Starpig responded with absolute confidence. He moved away from the tunnel. Orion looked after him for a moment, feeling warmed by Starpig's unconditional loyalty. Starpig could be counted on. Then Orion turned back to Galen.

Orion and Galen ran through the tunnel, passing by dirt walls and dimly lit lanterns. They ran for what seemed like ages, though one wouldn't know how much time they spent traveling through the tunnel. When they eventually reached the end, they were exhausted and out of breath. They stood there breathing hard for a few minutes. Then Orion showed Galen the way to exit. The tunnel became narrower as it came closer to the surface. At what seemed a dead end, Orion pulled out a shovel and started digging out the dirt above them. Once a space big enough to fit through was cleared, they climbed out. The bright light from the day blinded them. A few moments later when his vision cleared, Galen realized where they were. They had come out at the small ridge on the side of the camp which was closest to the city.

"Now, can you take me to the AquaCrafters which you spoke of?" Orion asked.

"I don't know exactly where they are, but I know where we might find them," Galen replied.

Galen led the way into the south side of the city. You see, the city was north of the police station, Jojo's camp, and the HQ. It wasn't long before Orion saw his hotel come into view. They passed by it, heading deeper into the city. Galen was leading them the long way around the city in order not to be seen. Orion noticed that the city was more developed then when he had last seen it. There were more shops in the shopping district, more governmental buildings in the central district, and more houses and bases throughout the outskirts of the city. Galen led the way to the train station at the center of the city.

To the north of the city were small mountain ranges that ran from west to east. A river flowed from the far east all the way to the police station, past the ridge into the southern areas of the city and out into the plains and wetlands that lay west of the city. To the east, large ravines carved through the landscape, and forests existed beyond them.

Galen was taking them to the higher area in the northwest where many AquaCrafters had decided to settle in the low mountains. The railway system connected the northern, western, and eastern areas to the city. It was one of the main ways AquaCrafters got around. In order not to get caught, Galen and Orion took off their armor and disguised themselves in leather armor to make them look like poor Minecrafters.

It did not take them long to arrive in the northwestern region. They got off the railway and began to walk over to the bases of Fulkin and Erune.

"As you might already know," explained Galen, "we are new to AquaCraft. Most of us do not support any powerful items. That was kind of the reason we came to AquaCraft. We heard about the new realm and wanted to go somewhere that gave us more freedom, somewhere without strict government oversight and threats of violence, AquaCraft has become known as the free realm. And we don't want that to change." Galen kept talking as they walked over to the bases.

The bases mirrored each other, lying side by side. They both had cube-shaped architecture with a sleek and modern design. Each cube base had its own color pallet. Fulkin's was orange and blue while Erune's was green and yellow. The door to the green and yellow base opened, and Erune walked out. He was older than most of Orion's friends and looked calm by nature. Now he was curious.

"Galen! What are you doing here? I thought you were helping with the war effort?" Erune asked, staring at Orion and raising his eyebrows.

"Erune!" Galen acknowledged him. "This is Orion, the founder of AquaCraft."

Orion laughed. "Is that what people are calling me now?"

Galen nodded and looked back at Erune. "Where is Fulkin?"

"He should be here soon. Interesting! The founder of AquaCraft. Everyone has heard about you." Erune frowned then. "And also, about the so-called war between you and Jojo. Can I help you?"

Fulkin emerged from his base and said grumpily, "Who is disturbing our peace and quiet?"

Erune said to Orion, "Don't mind him. He just dislikes it when people disturb him."

"Well, you can help. But I don't want to force you to fight if you don't want to," Orion replied.

"We may not fight, but is there anything else we can do for you?" Erune asked kindly.

"Actually, there is something you could do. Could you go around the city and see if you can promote anti-war? The TrustKeepers want this war to end, just like everyone else. Jojo has made it almost impossible to negotiate. If we could convince him to open up diplomatic relations, then maybe we could settle this pointless conflict. Also, see if anyone else would support the TrustKeepers if we retook power," Orion suggested.

"Yeah, we could do that!" Erune responded nodding thoughtfully.

"Thank you. I really appreciate that," Orion said, slightly bowing toward Erune with careful courtesy.

On the way back, Galen told Orion a bit more about Erune, Fulkin, and some of the other new AquaCrafters. Fulkin and Erune had come from a faraway land that had been occupied by a cruel and oppressive government. They came to AquaCraft to be free from it. Other Minecrafters had come to AquaCraft for similar reasons, whether for the freedom that AquaCraft stood for, or for the vast new land that brought adventurers from all over. The stories

Galen told touched Orion to the core, and he resolved to try his best to bring an age of peace and prosperity to AquaCraft.

Orion and Galen returned the way they had come through the tunnel. By the time they returned, the sun had set and the darkness of the night lay over all the land. Starpig, Fution, and Cicer were waiting for them in the council chambers.

As Orion entered, he said, "I trust that everything went well while we were gone?"

"Yes. So far, we have gone without incident," Starpig reported.

"Good. Now we must discuss plans," Orion said quickly.

The TrustKeepers were spread out around the room. Orion motioned for everyone to sit down. Orion took a seat at the head of the table, while everyone else sat down on either side of him. Only when everyone had sat down did Orion begin speaking.

"Our trip was a success. It seems like we still have AquaCrafters who support us. Though we may be few in number, we are still strong. Now I do not want to prolong this war, so I would like to open up negotiations soon with the AquaCraft government. Hopefully we will be able to reach a suitable agreement."

Fusion interrupted. "I am not sure that they would be willing to open up peaceful negotiations. Things have escalated quickly, and I'm afraid that they think of us as a threat."

"I understand your concern, but if we do not settle this peacefully, then however this war ends, it will end in disaster. I have learned from my previous mistakes. I will not let power corrupt me, and I have realized we need to listen more carefully. We have always been governed by the people. The whole point of AquaCraft was that we are all equals. But that has not become the case now." Orion paused to take a deep breath. "The TrustKeepers were formed to make sure that ultimate weapons would be destroyed. But this war is no longer just about that. It is a pointless war. Neither of us are our enemies. Speaking of the ultimate weapon, we will never use it again. Even if we could destroy it, we can't anymore. The Trident and the Nether Star are out of our control. Whoever has them wields great power and must be stopped. That is why I believe that we need to get the help of the AquaCraft government, and maybe we could agree at least on this point—that we need to find the rest of the ultimate weapon."

The TrustKeepers were silent after Orion spoke. Each of them was thinking deeply about the situation. Patiently waiting, Orion looked outside and admired the scenery. It was too bad that things had gotten to the point where they couldn't even share the beautiful land without arguing every second.

Galen shifted in his chair and then spoke. "I agree with what you say Orion. This war was a mistake. But what do we do now?"

"Right now, not much. Jojo has made no move against us yet. Tomorrow we shall reach out to them to see if we can open up negotiations. But there is one thing that we need to do. We must get the Heart of the Sea to a more secure location. I want to send it to our friends Erune and Fulkin. They are peacekeepers and wouldn't use it. Cicer, I want you to take the Heart of the Sea through the tunnels to them. The sooner we move it the better," Orion explained.

"But wouldn't I be more use where the action is?" Cicer asked, unwilling to miss anything.

"Galen and I are exhausted from our trip all the way there and back. Besides, you know the tunnels well and can sneak through the city without being spotted. If you leave now, then you can get there by dawn," Orion pointed out.

"OK," Cicer replied, getting up reluctantly from the room and walking down the stairs.

Meanwhile, at camp, Jojo was preparing the invasion. AngelOfDeath's news about the capture of Galen had disturbed him. If they didn't attack now, then they might not have another chance to retake the HQ.

Luckily, AngelOfDeath had brought back news about weaknesses in their defenses. Jojo, AngelOfDeath, ArcticCat, TactifulBelt, TheHappyBranch, and other AquaCrafters that had joined the war effort gathered around in a large tent.

"As you can see on the map, we have a lot of distance to cover to get from here to the headquarters. It is farther away than the city because of its design. AngelOfDeath, please hand me the blueprints," Jojo began.

AngelOfDeath handed over the blueprints he had stolen.

Jojo continued, "It was designed as a fortress. A place where AquaCrafters could retreat to in case of another world-wide threat. That makes it almost impenetrable. Notice that I said almost. As AngelOfDeath found out, you can climb up the decorative arch to get in through the roof. You can also enter in through secret emergency exits that are located at the base of the building. Remember to take a look at the blueprints before you are sent out."

"Question!" said a voice.

"Yes?" Jojo replied.

An AquaCrafter stood up. "Won't they notice us if we walk up to one of the entrances or exits?"

"I was just getting to that," Jojo said, then asked, "What was your name again?"

"Nulfan, Sir," said the AquaCrafter.

"Well, Nulfan, we will split up into different groups," Jojo began, then faced the entire group before continuing. "I will lead a small patrol of AquaCrafters that will sneak in through the top of the building. We will sneak into the vault and try to retake the Heart of the Sea, the Nether Star, and the Trident. Meanwhile, AngelOfDeath will lead a larger patrol that will be used as a distraction. I want TheHappyBranch and TactifulBelt to join me. Everyone else will be with AngelOfDeath. We leave at dawn."

Jojo then sent everyone off to get prepared for the invasion. TactifulBelt and Borin walked over to the training area of camp.

"Wanna spar?" asked Borin. He was a large, but somewhat slow new AquaCrafter.

"Sure," TactifulBelt replied.

Once they had pulled on armor, they walked over to the empty space in the training area and drew swords. For sparring they used stone swords because they needed to save the stronger ones for actual battle.

For a moment, neither one of them moved. Then Borin pushed forward to attack TactifulBelt. TactifulBelt easily sidestepped and counterattacked. Borin faltered and stepped back, back as the blow struck his armor. TactifulBelt struck again, then stepped back to get out of the way of Borin's sword.

"You need to be quicker on your feet, or one of the TrustKeepers will just run past your defense," TactifulBelt suggested.

Borin huffed, then rushed in, and their swords met. They danced back and forth, the movements becoming fluid. Then they disengaged, each of them breathing hard.

"Not bad. That was a good match," TactifulBelt commented.

After the match, they decided to polish their armor and sharpen their battle swords. While they did so, they discussed the upcoming battle and its implications.

"I wonder what Jojo will do once we recapture the HQ. Like how will he punish the so-called TrustKeepers for what they did? Not only have they betrayed AquaCraft, but they also insist on keeping power. Why not just surrender?" Borin pondered out loud.

"I don't know. They certainly have a lot to answer for. But don't underestimate them. If they decide to use the ultimate weapon, then you'd better run because there is no way we can defeat them then. That is why surprise is key to our victory," TactifulBelt replied thoughtfully.

"I hadn't thought about that. I guess all we can do is hope that that doesn't happen," Borin said, his voice lowering. He scratched his head absent-mindedly and rested his heavy hands on his legs.

Borin looked up as SwankPrism approached.

"That was a nice match there. We should spar sometime," SwankPrism challenged, looking from Borin to TactifulBelt.

"It will have to wait until after the big invasion. We'd better get some rest before dawn," TactifulBelt suggested.

And with that they went their separate ways to each of their tents, and the stars shone down on them watchfully.

• • •

The next day, Gestroyer was walking through the mountain region. He had heard rumors about peace negotiations and could not let that happen. That sense-forsaken THB had ruined his plans. He needed to get back into the power struggle so that he could claim his rightful place as leader of AquaCraft. He was in a tricky spot because since he was considered a TrustKeeper, he couldn't walk freely in the city. But in the mountain region, the AquaCrafters were more favored by TrustKeepers.

It wasn't long before he made his way to Erune and Fulkin's base. He despised pacifists. They were weak and couldn't stand up for what they believed in. But he would keep this to himself for now.

Fulkin looked up from his farm. It lay next to his base, and he was weeding a crop of vegetables.

"Gestroyer! What are you doing here? I didn't expect a TrustKeeper to be on this side of the realm!" Fulkin exclaimed.

"Oh well, you know, we TrustKeepers need to help out our fellow AquaCrafters once in a while," Gestroyer said, smiling.

Fulkin motioned for Gestroyer to follow him.

"It isn't safe to be seen with a TrustKeeper. Please come inside," Fulkin explained.

Once inside, they sat down at a table and Fulkin served Gestroyer a few pieces of bread and some stew. While they ate, they discussed the war.

"So, I heard that the AquaCraft government has launched a full-on invasion of headquarters and the TrustKeepers," Fulkin was saying.

"Oh really?" Gestroyer said.

"Yeah, they are trying to get the ultimate weapon back, but of course they won't succeed," Fulkin added.

"What do you mean?" Gestroyer asked curiously.

"Well, as you know, being a TrustKeeper, that the Nether Star and the Trident were stolen, and the Heart of the Sea has been moved here," Fulkin went on.

"What's this?" Gestroyer cried excitedly.

"I'm surprised you haven't heard?" Fulkin asked, starting to become suspicious.

Gestroyer realized his mistake and stammered, "Well, I was, um, sent on a secret mission. Yeah, a secret mission, but you aren't allowed to know. I wasn't there when this happened."

"Hm. Well, anyway, the AquaCraft government will be confused when they realize that the TrustKeepers don't have the ultimate weapon. In fact, they might even call off the entire invasion once they realize the TrustKeepers aren't a threat," Fulkin explained.

"Really..." Gestroyer said trying to hide his alarm, "Um, I'm not sure that it's going to happen that way."

"Why do you say that?" Fulkin asked, surprised.

"Peace isn't that simple to come by, and I'm afraid they might try and come after the Heart of the Sea. I may have to take it before they capture the HQ," Gestroyer explained.

Fulkin frowned. "Do you really think that is necessary? The Heart of the Sea is in Erune's base. He can show you where it is. But surely it is safer there," Fulkin said, starting to sound worried.

"Well, I think it can wait a bit longer, but I should head out soon with the Heart of the Sea," Gestroyer said. He stood up and thanked Fulkin for the meal. Then he left, trying to hide his excitement.

A few minutes later Gestroyer exited Erune's base with the Heart of the Sea. With this new power finally in his hands, he would be able to shape AquaCraft the way he wanted. Now he could finally get rid of THB and all the others who bothered him. But before he could do anything else, he needed to stop the war from ending. If the AquaCrafters settled things peacefully, then he would lose all his chance at taking AquaCraft...

Chapter 24: Invasion

Jojo's patrol had reached the HQ without any trouble. In a few moments AngelOfDeath's patrol would attack straight on to draw out the TrustKeepers from their fortress. That would give Jojo's patrol just enough time to get to the vault and get out without being noticed. Jojo was slowly climbing up the side of the building with TheHappyBranch and TactifulBelt behind him. They were about halfway up the decorative arch that came from the top of the building to the very bottom.

Jojo stopped and turned his head, "Signal AngelOfDeath,"

"Is it time?" TheHappyBranch asked.

"It's time," Jojo said quietly.

TheHappyBranch set off a firework that flew into the air and exploded in blue and green colors. Even if the TrustKeepers saw the firework, they would still have to deal with the full force of AngelOfDeath's patrol. As soon as the firework went off, Jojo returned to climbing up the arch. Not long after, the group reached the top of the building and prepared to break inside. The rooftop was flat, with a few TNT cannons facing in the direction of their camp.

"Disable the cannons. We don't want them to explode in our faces, and we can't allow the TrustKeepers to use them against us. I will go find a way in," Jojo ordered quickly.

He turned around and walked away past the cannons. Meanwhile, TheHappyBranch ran over to one of the cannons and examined the redstone circuitry. TactifulBelt went to the other cannon and did the same. First, they removed the TNT carefully so it wouldn't come in contact with the trigger mechanism. Then they broke the switch or the redstone repeaters, which made the cannon unable to fire again. Because they were short on time, they weren't able to thoroughly destroy the cannons. During this time, Jojo had found the trapdoor. THB and TactifulBelt soon joined Jojo at the trapdoor. Jojo opened it and went down first. TactifulBelt stayed behind to keep watch.

They were expecting to enter the control room, which was what the blueprints had shown, but instead they came into a brightly lit room. The fiery light blinded Jojo and THB for a second before their eyes adjusted. When he could see clearly, Jojo realized they had entered a room full of lava! Jojo clung onto the ladder, careful not to fall into the lava just below him.

Jojo growled, leaping up to avoid the splatters of lava flying up from the floor. "You don't happen to have a water bucket or anything?"

"No...But I do have a fire resistance potion," THB replied, handing over a bottle.

They gulped down the potions and tossed the empty bottles into the lava. Then taking a deep breath, Jojo jumped down into the lava with THB close behind. They landed in the lava unharmed; the potion ensured that. But that didn't prevent them from feeling the immense heat that emanated from the room. It was hard to tell how large the room was because even the walls were covered in lava. It was crazy that the building didn't catch on fire, or the floor melt up. The only probable explanation was the room was made out of obsidian, which would be bad news for Jojo's patrol because it would take a while to mine through it. Wading through the lava brought weird sensations throughout their bodies. On one hand, Jojo knew that the lava wouldn't burn him, but on the other hand, it was too easy to imagine that it would happen at any moment.

"How long do these potions last?" Jojo asked.

"About eight minutes or so," THB replied.

"Then we had better hurry," Jojo said, hiding his worry.

They came around a corner and entered a similar room. But strange yellow heads floated up from the lava with golden rods floating around them.

"Blazes!" THB exclaimed, alarmed.

A storm of fireballs flew at them, hitting them before they could react. Jojo brought out a shield, attempting to stop the barrage of fire that was flung at them. THB rushed behind Jojo, drawing out her bow and started picking off each of the blazes one by one.

Once all were slain, THB asked, "How in the world did the TrustKeepers capture blazes and place them up here?"

"I don't know. But we have underestimated them. I was wondering why we hadn't been attacked yet. Let's hope AngelOfDeath is doing better than we are," Jojo responded, breathing hard.

In fact, AngelOfDeath's patrol was not faring any better than Jojo. They had entered the headquarters without trouble. They came into the armory and found it empty—empty of all life, as if life had just vanished from existence. The entire patrol went up an elevator that bounced them up to the second floor. At least they thought it was the second floor until they realized they had been elevated all the way up to the training floor. The TrustKeepers had trapped them the same way Orion had trapped Jojo in there before. They now had to deal with a bunch of different training scenarios involving monsters attacking them or the room shifting all over the place. Hordes of monsters began to attack them, pouring into the room from all directions. The patrol could have easily defeated a single horde of monsters, but the room kept shifting, making it difficult to navigate though. Eventually they became tired of the endless barrage of monsters and were able to break through a small section of the wall that led onto the stairway. As soon as they had escaped, though, they found the TrustKeepers surrounding them on all sides.

"Surrender!" Orion exclaimed, pointing a sword up at them.

AngelOfDeath looked around, trying to find a place to escape. He noticed that the numbers were about even, and they might be able to beat the TrustKeepers or at least keep them busy.

AngelOfDeath swung around and whispered to Borin and SwankPrism, "Watch our backs." Then he exclaimed, "Charge!"

AngelOfDeath flung himself down upon Cicer, their swords' collision forcing Cicer back. The room erupted into chaos, fierce shouts and exclamations echoing around the stairwell. Behind AngelOfDeath, Borin was fighting as hard as he could to stop Orion and Starpig from overwhelming them. On the other end of the room, Cicer and Fution were being pushed back down the stairs. A figure leaped from higher up on the stairs and landed on the AquaCrafter Nulfan, knocking him out.

"Galen, you traitor! How could you?" Borin said furiously between lunges and sword strokes.

"I'm sorry, but you're on the wrong side of this war," Galen responded, moving down quickly.

"Less talking, more fighting," Starpig ordered, twisting Borin's sword out of his hand.

AngelOfDeath had disarmed Cicer who had retreated and gained enough time to switch to a bow. Fution was struggling to slow down the patrol that was forcing them down the stairs. Moments later they ended up on an office floor with half of them disarmed and the other half guarding the disarmed half. Starpig was guarding Borin, who had surrendered his arms. On the other side, Cicer and Fution were trapped by three of AngelOfDeath's patrolmen. Only Orion, Galen, and AngelOfDeath himself remained free.

"Galen, listen, we'll take him together," Orion said, pacing forward.

AngelOfDeath glanced from one to the other, not saying a word. Then he threw something up into the air and a bottle shattered on the ground. Red particles appeared around his armor. He rushed forward, careless about his own well-being and brought his sword down with all his might. Galen brought his sword up just in time to block the attack. But his iron sword shattered from AngelOfDeath's strike.

"What the..." Orion said, staring in surprise.

Galen fell to the ground and Orion brought himself back to his senses before AngelOfDeath could take the opportunity to get a similar blow on him. He dodged a few strikes and retaliated with a well-sequenced attack. What bothered Orion was that AngelOfDeath also had an iron sword. Galen's sword was newly forged and shouldn't have broken like that. But then he saw what he thought was a splash potion fly into the air. It must have been a strength potion or something Orion concluded.

Orion and AngelOfDeath exchanged fierce blows, fighting until both of them were breathing heavily from the exercise. Nearby, SwankPrism leaped onto Galen, pinning him to the ground, preventing Galen from running to Orion's aid. Orion knew he had to end the fight quickly if he expected to win. AngelOfDeath was better at combat than he had expected. They jumped into battle again. Their swords clashed, sending a shuddering sensation through Orion's body. They both backed away and collapsed on the floor. Orion used his diamond sword to support him, beginning to feel faint from exhaustion. AngelOfDeath wasn't doing much better but tried to hide it.

Meanwhile, Jojo, and THB had finally escaped the lava-filled rooms. By this point, TactifulBelt had joined them somehow. They had difficulty navigating through the HQ. It seemed like the TrustKeepers had added floors, converting the headquarters into a fortress. The top few floors were completely devoted to defenses, as if they knew that someone might enter from the top. Thanks to THB though, they were able to disable or avoid traps and monsters that were set up to prevent someone from getting to the lower floors.

They jumped down and found themselves in the council meeting room. They ran through the room to the stairs and made their way down the floors one by one. They ran past countless hallways and climbed down dozens of flights of stairs until they finally reached the floor that they were looking for. The vault. They stopped in front of the door of the vault and Jojo reached out his hand to open the door.

"I guess it's too much to ask for it to be unlocked," Jojo said.

To his surprise, the door flung open and they were able to walk right in. As they came into the large rectangular room, they looked around. It was empty. Absolutely nothing was there. They looked around in case there were any secret compartments where the Heart of the Sea, the Nether Star, or the Trident could be hidden. After a few minutes, they gave up and left the room.

"If it's not here, then where?" TactifulBelt asked, looking at Jojo.

"I don't know. But unless the ultimate weapon is with Orion himself, I doubt it's here," Jojo responded.

"We should get back to the others in case they need our help," TheHappyBranch suggested, as if reluctant to stay where they were.

"You're right. Let's go," Jojo replied.

It didn't take them long to make their way down the next few floors. They came down one more flight of stairs and emerged on the office floor. Jojo paused and surveyed the scene. Orion and AngelOfDeath were locked in fierce combat, but within seconds, both of them staggered to the ground exhausted. All the other AquaCrafters in the room were standing next to each other with one of them holding a sword on the other, or else they were knocked out on the floor.

AngelOfDeath was just about to lift his sword for another strike when Jojo exclaimed, "Stop!"

Everyone in the room turned to face Jojo, TheHappyBranch, and TactifulBelt.

"Lay down your weapons and stop this madness!" Jojo ordered loudly.

Reluctantly, AngelOfDeath and those with him put their weapons on the ground. The TrustKeepers however did not. Jojo took a step forward then another down the stairs and into the room.

"Please, Orion, can we talk?" Jojo said, sheathing his sword.

"I don't know Jojo, can we? You have made no move on peace negotiations and have just attacked us in our own base?" Orion said, exasperated.

"I made a mistake, and for that I am sorry. This war has been pointless. Let's talk and see if we can come to some sort of an agreement?" Jojo apologized.

When Orion didn't move. Jojo said, "At least hear me out, will you?"

Orion sheathed his sword and gestured to the TrustKeepers to do the same. Orion slowly walked over to a table that had been knocked over during the fight and put it back up. Then he grabbed a chair and pulled it up. Jojo did the same. For a while they were silent, staring at each other. They were both exhausted and sore. The AquaCrafters around them slowly split into two groups. The TrustKeepers went to one side of the room while the other AquaCrafters went to the other.

Jojo sighed, then broke the silence by saying, "You don't have the Heart of the Sea, do you?"

"No. And we haven't ever had the Nether Star or the Trident either," Orion replied. He looked steadily at Jojo. "We weren't planning on using the items as weapons, anyway. To tell you the truth, we were actually planning to reach out today to open up discussions for a peace treaty. But then you attacked."

"I see," Jojo said. Then he asked, "So what now?"

"Now," Orion paused to take a breath, "Now we should try to repair and mend the tension between us. Maybe now we can actually discuss peace."

"Orion, I am tired. And I don't think I am the only one. Let's dismiss the AquaCrafters and gather the original council members to discuss peace," Jojo suggested.

"Sounds good to me. Meet me in the council chambers in an hour to conduct the meeting. That should give enough time for all the council members to gather and the AquaCrafters to leave," Orion responded tiredly. He shrugged his shoulders, got up from the table, and walked away.

Chapter 25: Negotiations

It took a while for all the AquaCrafters to leave. It was the middle of the afternoon by this point. The TrustKeepers and the rest of the AquaCrafters kept glancing suspiciously at each other. Council members Orion, Jojo, ArcticCat, Starpig, TheHappyBranch, AngelOfDeath, and Cicer gathered in the meeting room at the top of AquaCraft headquarters. The other council members couldn't make it for various reasons. Some were too injured from the battle or were too busy managing the AquaCrafters so that the fighting wouldn't start again.

The council members sat down at the table, but none sat at its head, for all were equal as far as they were concerned.

ArcticCat stood up, cleared his throat, then spoke in a low, level voice. "Welcome, everyone. I'm not exactly sure where to begin, but...first I would like to say that we have been through a lot together. From when we first arrived in AquaCraft, to the dark ages during the eclipse, to now in our civil war. But in order to survive, we must move on. We must put behind us these conflicts and attempt to mend the broken pieces. We have made many mistakes, and now that we are at our very lowest, we must rise together or not at all. And today, we must work together and try to make peace with one another."

The council members clapped, and ArcticCat sat down, his face quiet, calm. The council took turns bringing up various topics of importance. These ranged from governmental issues to a proposal of a new peace treaty. In order to prevent further conflicts, many changes would have to be implemented.

"I believe that the first topic that we need to discuss is the peace treaty. We need to make sure conflicts do not arise again," Orion said, looking down at a note.

"Yes, but how do we do that?" Cicer asked.

Fution looked thoughtful, and Starpig noticed, so he said, "Fution, there seems to be something on your mind. Would you like to share?"

"Yes, I have thought about this for a while. We need a more organized way of leadership. We do need people in charge, yes, but not just one. We need multiple people in charge of different areas," Fution explained.

"Like someone in charge of building!" Cicer commented.

"Yes, that could work. We could have people in charge of building, defense, entertainment," Orion stopped, still figuring it out in his mind.

"Military too," Starpig added.

"Exactly. But we would also need someone for the AquaCrafters to speak to for their needs," Fution continued.

The bright, quartz room grew quiet. The council members were focused, thinking through the topic.

ArcticCat broke the silence, "We need a government. A government that is run by the people, and not the other way around."

"But wouldn't that make AquaCraft just like all the other realms?" THB pointed out.

"Not if we learn from the mistakes we made these last few months," ArcticCat countered.

"ArcticCat is right. This could be the solution to our problem. Of course, we would have to figure out all the specifics, but this could be the peace treaty that will hold us together. If we officially agree to a specific kind of government and make a physical document that we all must comply with," Orion agreed.

"You're suggesting the peace treaty be a guide for our government?" Fution asked.

"That's exactly what I am suggesting," Orion responded.

Jojo, who had stayed silent the entire time, began to grow impatient. He finally caught the attention of the council.

Leaning forward in his seat, he said, "I think there is a more important matter of business that needs to be attended to."

"Oh? And what might that be?" ArcticCat asked curiously.

Jojo replied instantly. "What of the ultimate weapon? It would be best to get this issue over with right away."

Orion nodded, "Agreed. The TrustKeepers have had possession of the Heart of the Sea, but no longer. The original reason why the TrustKeepers were formed was to make sure that the ultimate weapon would be destroyed. It's too powerful to just leave out in the open."

"At this point, I tend to agree with you Orion. The ultimate weapon was stolen right before the TrustKeepers captured the headquarters. We thought you were the ones who stole it," Jojo explained.

Orion looked surprised, then asked, "What makes you think that? Does anyone even know where the Nether Star or the Trident are?"

As he looked around, he noticed TheHappyBranch nervously shifting in her seat. He was about to say something when Cicer spoke up.

"I think we should send out search patrols. Or maybe ask around; one of the AquaCrafters might know something," He suggested.

"But what good would that do? It's been too long since the ultimate weapon was stolen. Whoever stole it, it is probably long gone by now," Starpig argued.

"Do you have a better idea?" Cicer asked.

"No..." Starpig began but was interrupted by a loud sound from the door.

The door to the council room flew open, crashing against the wall. In walked Gestroyer. He had a sword on his belt. He was fully equipped with armor as well, unlike the council members in the room. He stood in front of them all, seeming different from the Gestroyer they thought they knew. Now he seemed bigger, menacing, somewhat evil.

AngelOfDeath exclaimed, "This is a private meeting!"

"In case some of you have forgotten, I was a council member," Gestroyer snapped back. He walked over to the table and sat down at its head. He looked confidently, almost contemptuously at all of them.

"Hey you can't just..." ArcticCat started.

Gestroyer ignored him. Instead, he addressed the group. "You may be wondering where the ultimate weapon went. The fact is, I know who stole it and why."

The AquaCrafters were silent. Gestroyer slammed the table with his fist.

"The person who stole it is here among us now. She has betrayed us all. To the enemy himself!" Gestroyer exclaimed, pointing at TheHappyBranch. "You gave the ultimate weapon to Flamecat himself!"

The AquaCrafters stared at each other, shocked. Then TheHappyBranch rose from her seat furiously.

"How dare you? What right do you have to barge in here and make accusations such as these?" THB demanded.

Gestroyer also stood up and drew his sword smoothly. "I will take care of this traitor myself," he announced calmly.

He drew out the Heart of the Sea and attached it to his sword. Stepping to the side of the table, he raised his sword and swung it to one side, sending a blue shock wave of energy that knocked THB back. She flew through the air, crashing through the window, shattering the glass as she fell out of the building. The glass fell to the ground and broke into even smaller pieces. Everyone at the table froze in place. As she fell through the air, THB brought out the Trident and thrust it into the building. Starpig, who was closest to the window, rushed over to it. He saw her clutching the Trident. She was elevated almost 100 blocks in the air from the ground, holding on to the Trident for dear life, because respawning was unbearingly painful. Starpig moved frantically, searching for something to lower to help THB back up. The rest of the AquaCrafters were looking around still stunned, not knowing what to do. Some of them rose from their seats and moved to the window to stare.

Then Gestroyer made his next move. He jumped onto the table and ran over to the window. To the amazement of the AquaCrafters, he launched himself out into space. As he fell, he flung his sword out of his hand. It spun around in the air and struck the Trident, which was impaled in the building.

The instant it was hit, the Trident broke free from the building, and THB, the Trident, and Gestroyer all were in free-fall.

The ground below them got closer and closer as each second passed. In a few seconds they would impact the ground like squashed bugs. Those seconds passed as if they were minutes, which felt like hours. The world seemed to slow down. THB felt her life flash before her eyes. The ground was 50 blocks below them. Then 40 blocks below them. Then 30, 20, 15, 10, five, four... TheHappyBranch closed her eyes and prepared to welcome the darkness of death.

Just at that moment, Gestroyer brought out the Heart of the Sea, and clasping both hands on it, he formed a sphere of water around him much like a bubble. He landed first. The water that was being held in place suddenly was released, and it splashed across the floor. The bubble broke his fall, leaving him unharmed. He lifted his arm and shot a jet of water-energy from the Heart of the Sea, which formed a small pool of water that caught THB as she collapsed on the ground.

Gestroyer rushed forward and picked up the Trident from where it had hit the ground, cracking the dirt. He twirled it around and attached the Heart of the Sea to the Trident. This created an ultimate aqua weapon. He shot a beam of energy toward TheHappyBranch; it caught her with its grip. Then Gestroyer spun the Trident around and launched off the ground. With the power of the Aqua Weapon, Gestroyer flew through the sky with THB trailing behind. They flew all the way to the war camp on the other side of the large field.

Gestroyer landed on the coarse dirt with thump. He turned then and cut off the flow of energy from the Aqua Weapon. TheHappyBranch fell out of the sky where the energy had been holding her a few blocks up in the air. She landed badly. Picking herself up painfully, she looked around. Gestroyer had taken them to the camp on the far side of the field from AquaCraft Headquarters. He had made sure to surround them with lava moats on either side. Looking back, she saw Gestroyer facing her with the Aqua Weapon in his grasp.

"Why have you taken me here, Gestroyer?!" TheHappyBranch demanded. She managed to invest anger into her voice.

"So that I might get revenge on you, the one who ruined my plans. I also need to get rid the one who could tell the true side of my intentions," Gestroyer responded bitterly. He motioned at the Trident. "As you know, with the power of the Aqua Weapon, I will be able to slay anyone I wish without too much resistance from them. Not only that, but only a weapon like this is able to kill one permanently. And that is exactly what I intend to do."

THB stiffened. "Surely, we can negotiate this! You aren't as barbaric as to deny some sort of deal?"

"What could you offer?" Gestroyer asked.

"Well, what do you want?" TheHappyBranch asked back.

Gestroyer paused, then said, "You will not speak of any my activities. And you will not betray who I truly am to the rest of the AquaCrafters. Instead, you will serve me and help me take over AquaCraft."

TheHappyBranch stared at him, eyes widening. She spoke in a low, threatening tone of voice. "Never!"

"Then you will die," Gestroyer exclaimed, emphasizing each syllable deliberately.

He turned the Trident toward her and let out a dozen short energy bursts from its tip. Thanks to her elven agility and speed, THB dodged each blast as it flew by her. Falling into a kneeling position, she took out her bow and shot two arrows with one shot. Gestroyer spun the Trident around and sliced each arrow in half in a smooth fluid motion. Then he detached the Heart of the Sea from the Trident and launched it like a javelin. Multiple lightning strikes came down from the dark clouds above them, splitting the ground. THB flung herself to the side, barely avoiding the lightning as it struck the ground next to her. Gestroyer rushed forward, picking up the Trident from where it had stuck in the ground. He lifted it up above his head then brought it down in a deadly blow. TheHappyBranch brought up her bow to block the attack. The Trident came down, snapping the bow in half. Frustrated, Gestroyer swung it around, and the base of the trident wacked THB on the head. She fell to the ground with such force that she was knocked unconscious.

Meanwhile, back at the HQ, Jojo was discussing the situation with Orion and ArcticCat.

"Listen, if we go in bringing a whole army, Gestroyer will surely notice. Trust me, let me go alone to fight him. That way no one else has to get hurt, and he won't notice me until it's too late," Jojo argued.

"But if you go alone, there is no way you can beat him. He has the Heart of the Sea!" ArcticCat reasoned.

"One AquaCrafter or ten won't make a difference. Someone has to get in close and take him out. There is no other way," Jojo replied.

"Go then. We have spent too much time speaking among ourselves. Take two of your fiercest warriors and return with the Heart of the Sea. If you don't return in an hour, we will send a patrol to help," Orion agreed reluctantly.

Jojo ran off, leaving Orion and ArcticCat alone.

Orion smiled wryly. "Well, the negotiations were short."

Chapter 26: The Final Battle

Jojo, TactifulBelt, and AngelOfDeath set out, riding on horseback. They rode swiftly, and none of them said a word. It was as if they knew they were riding to their deaths. A grim silence set in. Normally they would be able to respawn, but from past experience with the Heart of the Sea or the Trident, they knew they couldn't survive a hit from one of those immense power generators. Research had been conducted after The Eclipse to better understand why you couldn't respawn. It involved researching past deaths and deaths by the ultimate weapons, and then comparing them. It turned out that these ultimate powers disrupted the connections between the parts of the body. In order to respawn, or at least respawn correctly, one needed all of their body to be connected. Without being connected, only part of one's body would respawn or none of the body at all.

Jojo and his team rode hard, forcing the horses to their limits. They followed the direction in which they saw Gestroyer go. Jojo didn't know what Gestroyer was going to do with THB, or why he was doing what he was doing. He just hoped to resolve the conflict quickly and reclaim the Heart of the Sea and the Trident. Eventually Jojo's group of elite fighters reached the lava moats. There were at least a dozen moats scattered across the landscape, destroying the beauty of the field. In the distance, Jojo thought he could see two figures, with one leaning over the other. Jojo signaled to his group to get off their horses. They would have to approach on foot from now on. They were equipped with the best armor AquaCraft had to offer at the time, which was diamond armor. Jojo drew his enchanted diamond sword, and each member of his group did the same. Once they had crossed over a few moats, they could clearly see the figures before them.

"Gestroyer! THB!" Jojo exclaimed, not knowing what else to say.

The sun was setting, and it cast long shadows upon the AquaCrafters. Gestroyer rose to his full stature. He had the Trident in one hand, and the

Heart of the Sea in the other.

"We come in peace! Please hand over the Heart of the Sea and the Trident!" Jojo ordered firmly.

"Then why are you so heavily armed? It seems to me that you are wearing the strongest armor we have. And you have your swords drawn. How is that peace?" Gestroyer retorted.

"It's just a precaution," Jojo tried to explain.

"The Ultimate Weapon doesn't belong to any AquaCrafter. It belongs to AquaCraft. You shouldn't be using it for your own gain!" TactifulBelt exclaimed.

"Oh? And why not? Do I not deserve to wield such a power?" Gestroyer said.

AngelOfDeath whispered to Jojo, "Careful..."

"Gestroyer, please, this is your last warning. If you do not hand over the Heart of the Sea and the Trident, then you will be considered a traitor to AquaCraft," Jojo said, trying to put a hint of threat in his voice.

"How dare you!" Gestroyer growled.

TactifulBelt and AngelOfDeath brought out their shields and stepped into fighting stances. Jojo, however, did not.

Gestroyer leapt into the air, up and over Jojo. He swung around and attempted to strike Jojo with a backwards motion while still facing TactifulBelt and AngelOfDeath. Jojo barely blocked the strike, which unsettled him. At the same moment, Gestroyer simultaneously attacked both TactifulBelt and AngelOfDeath, the aqua weapon giving him increased speed and strength. The two of them crouched behind their shields, trying to avoid getting absolutely destroyed by the flurry of attacks. When they could, they tried to get a strike in whenever Gestroyer was distracted by the other person. Only a few times did they succeed. Then Jojo rejoined the fight, launching himself upon Gestroyer. As soon as he attacked, TactifulBelt and AngelOfDeath launched themselves in a full-out attack on Gestroyer. Gestroyer couldn't block all the attacks at the same time. He dropped the

Trident and put both his hands on the Heart of the Sea. Gestroyer sort of curled into a ball and then brought back his shoulders; a blinding bright blue energy field exploded from him. The energy knocked all three of them back. Jojo and TactifulBelt landed on the grass safely, but AngelOfDeath almost fell into one of the lava-filled moats.

Breathing hard, Gestroyer picked up the Trident and looked around. He said. "Surrender now, and I might think about sparing your lives."

"Never," TactifulBelt growled, picking himself up quickly, for he was the one who had landed the softest.

"Are you sure? Think of how much I can offer you with this power at my fingertips." Gestroyer stood proud and sure.

"You're mad!" TactifulBelt responded.

"You are making a grave mistake," Gestroyer threatened.

TactifulBelt ran over to AngelOfDeath and helped him up before he could fall into the lava.

"Thanks," AngelOfDeath said, breathing heavily.

Then they looked over at Gestroyer, who let out a fierce cry. He jumped into the night sky. Then, lifting the Trident with one arm, he summoned lightning from the sky. It struck the tip of the Trident. Gestroyer laughed, then threw the Trident, and streaks of lightning came down wherever the Trident touched, burning the ground below. TactifulBelt jumped to one side and AngelOfDeath to the other. Gestroyer landed on the ground with a soft thump. He lifted the Heart of the Sea, and the Trident, which was stuck into the ground, now flew through the air toward the Heart's energy beam. He grabbed the Trident with his free hand, and started walking forward, using the Trident like a staff. Jojo had gotten up at this point.

"Oh, why can't you just die!" Gestroyer exclaimed, summoning more lightning.

He brought the lightning down on Jojo, who collapsed on the ground. Then he continued forward to confront AngelOfDeath and TactifulBelt. Just as they were getting up again, Gestroyer charged up the

Trident with power from the Heart of the Sea. He threw the Trident with all his might, and it struck TactifulBelt right in the middle of his chest.

TactifulBelt made a choking sound, and AngelOfDeath gasped. TactifulBelt looked down at the Trident which was wedged inside his chest. Gestroyer sent out a energy beam at AngelOfDeath which sent him flying across a lava moat and onto more burnt grass. Then he summoned the Trident with another beam from the Heart of the Sea. As the Trident left TactifulBelt's body, he fell backwards and landed in the lava. His body sizzled and began to smoke. Then the lava ate him up. He was completely submerged, and quickly disappeared from sight.

Jojo, who until now had managed to stay alive, picked himself up, silently watching what had just happened. He was appalled by what had happened to TactifulBelt. Gestroyer's power seemed unstoppable, and it was unbelievable that anyone could wield such power.

"I am definitely beginning to agree with Orion; the ultimate weapon is way too overpowered," Jojo murmured to himself, shaking himself off and trying to focus on what he had to do.

Once he got up, he summoned his courage and spoke.

"Gestroyer! It will take more than a little lightning to kill me!" Jojo raised his arms in challenge.

Gestroyer swung around from where he was on the bridge between the lava moats.

"I don't need to fight you. You're not even worth fighting. I have a different purpose for you," he said, capturing Jojo with the Heart of the Sea's energy. "As one of AquaCraft's greatest fighters, you will serve me. This is a little something I learned from Flamecat himself."

Jojo looked on in horror as Gestroyer sent energy through him, and everything went dark.

. . .

It had been hours since Jojo, AngelOfDeath, and TactifulBelt had set out from the AquaCraft Headquarters. There was still no sign of them. At this point, Orion knew he had to do something. So, he sent Starpig and Cicer out to gather the AquaCrafters and assemble an army. But that would take time, and time they did not have. Not only that, but what use would an army be against the power of the ultimate weapon or even part of the ultimate weapon. He would just be endangering more innocent lives. But what other choice did he have? If he did nothing, then Jojo, AngelOfDeath, and TactifulBelt would surely die, if they had not already. They should have contacted him by now, Orion was thinking worriedly as he looked out the window of the council room at the dark landscape. None of the AquaCrafters would even be awake right now. Or at least very few.

Orion turned around as ArcticCat came into the room. He was the only one other than Orion who was still at the HQ.

"Orion," ArcticCat greeted him.

"I'm glad you're here," sighed Orion. "I don't know what to do. Even if we gather enough AquaCrafters, what use would that be if we encounter the ultimate weapon? Something must have gone wrong if Jojo and his fighters aren't back yet. They should have taken the Heart of the Sea and The Trident peacefully," Orion said, his mind spiraling out of control.

"Orion, calm yourself. It won't help to worry about these things. We must prepare ourselves for battle in case Jojo, AngelOfDeath, or TactifulBelt has to retreat here," ArcticCat said.

"You're right. Of course, you're right," Orion replied.

They walked down the stairs of the HQ to the armory. They equipped themselves with the best armor they could find. They equipped themselves more heavily than they normally would in order to be prepared in case they had to face the might and power of the aqua weapon. Once they were fully clad in their new shining armor, they went to the roof of the headquarters. They had also enabled a full security system except for the entrance of the roof.

"You know, it would be nice if we had a device that allowed us to see farther," Orion commented.

"If only. Like maybe if we could magnify our vision," ArcticCat agreed.

They were looking out from the roof, with the TNT cannons armed and ready. A TNT cannon didn't look like a normal cannon. It involved a water stream and TNT placed on each side. Redstone connected the TNT dispensers and could be activated with a button or a lever.

It was difficult to see in the dark; luckily (or unluckily) the sun was rising over the horizon. Just then, a figure appeared in the far distance. It was too far to see who it was.

"If that's Gestroyer, then we should launch the TNT soon, or we might not get another chance," ArcticCat suggested.

"Not only that, but I doubt Jojo would return alone. I am willing to take the chance; launch the TNT!" Orion ordered.

He and ArcticCat lined up against one of the two TNT cannons and prepared to fire.

"Fire a warning shot!" Orion exclaimed.

ArcticCat pressed the button on his cannon, and TNT came out of the dispenser closer to the rear of the cannon. The TNT was lit, and it floated down the stream of water towards the front of the cannon. Then TNT came out of the dispenser device at the front of the cannon and that TNT also was lit. The TNT in the water exploded and launched the other TNT forward without damaging the rest of the machine. The reason it didn't damage the blocks next to it was thanks to the water stream. The TNT that had yet to explode flew through the air and traveled the long distance between them and the mysterious figure. It exploded in the air before it landed; it was a warning shot after all. Orion and ArcticCat watched on to see the reaction of the figure. The figure seemed unworried and unchanged from the warning shot. It kept on moving closer to the headquarters.

"It's a good thing we upgraded these things so that they would automatically reload. Because we may need to fire again soon if he does not slow down," Orion commented.

ArcticCat nodded his head in agreement. Then they looked back at the figure who had not slowed their pace towards the headquarters. As the figure ominously got closer and closer, Orion and ArcticCat realized they would not be able to fire TNT for much longer before the figure would be too close to shoot.

Orion sighed, "Well, this is it. Fire and do not stop until I say so."

Orion pressed the button of his contraption, and ArcticCat did the same a few seconds later. TNT began to rain down from the HQ, and large craters appeared on each side of the figure. When Orion realized the figure was not slowing his approach, he reluctantly fired at the figure directly, adjusting the redstone machine slightly to fire in the right place. Only then did the figure react, by jumping or leaping to the side. But still he continued on.

Orion noticed the figure's bashed up diamond armor and exclaimed, "Hold your fire!"

He looked closer, recognizing the gait. It was Jojo! He was alive! Orion looked at ArcticCat, and ArcticCat looked at him.

"Quickly now, take the water bubble elevator down and meet him. I will keep an eye out for a little longer to make sure he wasn't followed!" Orion ordered swiftly.

ArcticCat ran to the control room. There was now a safe passage between the dangerous top floors and the control room. Once there, he flipped the lever which opened the front door of the headquarters. Then he ran down to the council chamber room and jumped into the bubble elevator. He was sent whooshing down through the water, the bubbles allowing him to breath. It only took him a matter of seconds to travel from the chamber room to the armory. This was a secret elevator that only council members used in case of emergency.

Back on the roof, Orion waited another minute to make sure no one was following. Once he was satisfied that it was unlikely that anyone was following Jojo, he went down to the control room after ArcticCat. He stopped by the security cameras though, because something caught his eye. From the view of the front door, he saw that Jojo looked different. At least there was something off with his persona. Puzzled, Orion stayed fixed on the screen. He saw ArcticCat come into view on a different camera. ArcticCat was entering the armory. He watched as ArcticCat climbed up the steps from the lower area in the armory to the bridge. He watched him go over to greet Jojo. But even as he watched, he saw Jojo draw his sword. He watched in utter horror as Jojo attacked ArcticCat. Jojo's face was blank, as if he had no remorse for what he was doing. ArcticCat drew his sword to defend himself, but he was unprepared, and Jojo dismantled his defenses. ArcticCat's sword flew from his hand, and Jojo bluntly attacked ArcticCat's armor, which was denting from each blow.

Orion shook himself, as if to free himself from trance. He had to do something! He went over to a control panel that controlled the armory's defenses. He pressed a few buttons and flipped a switch and looked back at the security cameras as iron golems were activated and started moving out towards Jojo. Jojo looked up from his attacks and prepared to attack the iron golems.

Orion knew that this Jojo could take care of the iron golems quickly. So he had to move fast. He went over to another control panel and activated another few defenses that were on standby. Then he ran down to the council room and jumped into action. As he jumped down the bubble elevator, he drew his sword. He exited the bubble elevator a few seconds later and looked around.

Jojo had somehow killed one of the golems and was backing away from the second. Orion just needed to slow Jojo down long enough for Starpig, Cicer, and the rest of the AquaCrafters to arrive.

Orion exclaimed, "Hey Jojo! Over here!"

Orion watched as Jojo shifted his attention to Orion. Jojo narrowed his eyes and ran forward, ignoring the golem. Orion jumped off the bridge and ran to the bubble elevator that led upwards. Jojo swiftly followed. If Orion was any slower, Jojo would catch up to him. Orion looked down and saw Jojo enter the bottom of the tube. He exited the water elevator in a few seconds. Orion was in a tiny room full of buttons. Buttons covered all the walls. He had diverted the bubble elevator to a different location. This was one of the HQ's many defenses. Orion and Starpig were the only ones who knew the right button to press. He did so quickly. A gap in the floor opened up and Orion jumped down. Seconds later the gap vanished when a block covered it up, hiding the entrance. Orion was now in the vast secret passageways in the HQ. He climbed through quickly. Once Jojo arrived in the room, he would have no choice but to press each of the buttons. All the buttons that weren't the correct one would cause a dispenser to dispense negative potion effects. The walls were too thick for Jojo to break out quickly. This would at least keep Jojo busy for a while.

Orion climbed through the vents until he reached the council chamber. He realized then that a lot of passageways led to the council chamber. You could get almost anywhere from there. Once he was out of the vents, Orion took a moment to stretch. Getting out of the cramped space felt good.

Jojo had reached the buttons room and pressed a few to see what would happen. Once he realized what they did, he didn't dare press anymore. Jojo's armor was badly damaged so he couldn't take any risks. Instead, he started mining through the floor. He came across the secret vents pretty quickly. Unlike the walls, the floor happened not to be very thick.

The first warning Orion had was the sound of Jojo's armor clanking. He caught his breath, utterly surprised. He had thought he had more time. Looking around the council chambers, he couldn't see any escape he could get to in time. So instead, he ran over to the window and broke another hole in the glass with his pickaxe, careful not to get any glass shards on him. He walked out onto the small ledge the glass was on. He gulped as he looked down. He carefully placed a block against the wall and wedged it between the giant concrete pillars. Gingerly, he climbed onto it and hoped Jojo wouldn't notice the broken glass. He continued this technique to descend a few more blocks. Then he heard Jojo come into the council chambers. He held his breath, hoping Jojo wouldn't notice him. He carefully used his pickaxe to break the previous blocks above him.

Jojo was busy looking for Orion everywhere inside the room. He even climbed up into the control room. Still puzzled, he looked at the security cameras. Then he saw him. Orion was there, climbing in through a hole in the wall where it was weakest and climbing onto the grand staircase.

Orion ran down the stairs as quickly as he could and eventually found himself in the armory again. He waited a little while so that Jojo could catch up to him. He wanted Jojo to follow him. He waited until he saw Jojo enter the armory on the far side of the room. Then he turned and ran into the tunnels that led from the HQ to the close side of the city. Jojo saw him go and barreled after Orion through the dark and dirty tunnel. Orion rounded a corner and broke part of the wall of the tunnel, replacing the dirt behind him. He hated how much dirt surrounded him, but it was necessary in order to stay hidden. He heard Jojo run past him. He took a deep breath and made the big decision. He broke the dirt in front of him and walked back into the tunnel, his armor now filthy from the loose dirt in the tunnel. He turned and called after Jojo.

"Jojo. It's just you and me now," he said as calmly as he could.

Jojo turned around and stared at Orion like a wild animal. For a second, he hesitated, then he stepped forward.

"Prepare to die!" Jojo said coldly.

Orion drew his sword and prepared to do it again. Would he ever get a break from fighting Jojo? He quickly switched to his bow and shot a few arrows before Jojo got too close for him to use his bow comfortably. He parried a blow to his shoulder and retaliated with a series of strikes designed to disarm Jojo. But Jojo was too used to Orion's fighting style. He quickly disengaged and then re-engaged, striking from all sides. Orion struggled to block all the blows. So instead, he trapped Jojo's sword against the dirt wall and kicked him in the chest which sent him flying. But Jojo was not foolish enough to drop the sword. He quickly recovered and prepared to fight again. But he wasn't quick enough. Orion brought out an ax and chopped wooden supports that held the dirt up. He jumped back and a huge amount of dirt fell in, blocking the tunnel. Now he wouldn't have to fight Jojo; he had trapped him instead. By the time Jojo got free, Orion would at least have some help.

Back at the AquaCraft Headquarters, Orion ran to ArcticCat and helped him to his feet.

"Easy, easy. Don't want to rush things. We have a bit of time before Jojo gets back. Let's go out to the field and wait for the AquaCrafters there," Orion suggested gently.

"Good idea," ArcticCat groaned as he got up.

ArcticCat was obviously in no shape to fight. Slowly they made their way to the field, and ArcticCat sat down on a fallen log. Orion stayed standing. All the excitement of the day was keeping him energized. He stood there looking out at the broken landscape. Craters dotted the land around the HQ. Lava moats simmered at the farthest point he could see on the field. And he knew that the AquaCraft city had fallen into ruin during the traumatic times of the Eclipse and the Civil War. All that remained of their vision and effort were the AquaCrafters themselves. That was all. He sighed. It was a devastating sight, and for a moment everything felt hopeless. But AquaCraft was a vast land; maybe we could find another place... Orion shrugged his shoulders and shook himself. Maybe things would get better after all. Or maybe not. Orion turned around and saw the very filthy diamond armor of a certain Jojo who wanted vengeance, Orion thought.

"Jojo, come on. This has to end at some point," Orion said, exasperated and profoundly tired.

"Oh, it will. It ends now, for you and for your AquaCraft," Jojo replied.

Jojo was walking towards them from the entrance of the headquarters. He was limping, but still he carried on.

Orion drew his sword, hopefully for the last time. He stepped into his fighting stance, and Jojo stepped into his fighting stance. Then they circled each other. ArcticCat watched from afar, helpless to do anything. Jojo initiated the fight by going straight for a stab at Orion's chest. Orion parried the attack with some effort. This time, Orion waited for the next attack to come in. He was too tired to waste his energy on attacking. He needed to wait until he saw a weakness in Jojo's defenses. Orion and Jojo were already accomplished fighters, but Jojo's combat skills far exceeded Orion's. The only reason why Orion was even alive today was thanks to that accursed ultimate weapon.

Jojo tried to strike again, but this time he feinted to the side before going in for Orion's head. Orion barely had time to block the blow before Jojo struck again and again. But Orion refused to give up. Jojo had beaten him too many times already. He would not allow him to do it again, especially since this Jojo couldn't be the real Jojo. Then Orion made up his mind. Forgetting all regard for his own safety, he launched a furious number of strikes. Thanks to luck, or some other force, Orion was able to hold his own against Jojo. They fought for what seemed like hours. They fought until they were both heaving from the effort, unable to attack with well-designed blows. Instead, they attacked each other with crude, weak strikes that each could have easily taken advantage of if they were at their full strength.

Orion fought hard, but then Jojo managed a well-timed strike, which left a giant dent in Orion's armor. Their swords clashed, but this time Jojo stepped to the side and allowed Orion to fall forward. He took this opportunity to get an upward strike that sent Orion to the ground. Orion's sword clattered to the ground.

"Hey, Jojo, what in the world are you doing?" Starpig emerged from the trees near them, and his patrol surrounded Orion and Jojo.

Jojo looked around from AquaCrafter to AquaCrafter. There were too many to fight. Five, no ten, no twenty or more AquaCrafters gathered around, surrounding Jojo. Before he could react, Cicer came up behind him and wacked him on the head with a stick. An exhausted Jojo fell to the ground, knocked unconscious.

Starpig walked over to Orion, and held out a hand, which Orion gratefully grabbed and pulled himself up.

"I thought you could use some help. Though I must say, it was enjoyable to watch you beat Jojo for a while," Starpig said with a grin.

Orion replied, "Thanks. Though I could have used your help much sooner. I do not know what is going on with Gestroyer nor why Jojo attacked us."

Starpig looked troubled but didn't say a word. He ordered a few of the AquaCrafters to start circling the area in case anyone else showed up.

Jojo began to stir. Orion stood near him, and a few of the AquaCrafters kept their hands close to their weapons.

"Jojo, is it you?" Orion asked quietly.

"Who else would it be?" Jojo replied, groaning, "Ugh what happened? Everything hurts."

"You tell us. Do you not remember anything?" Orion asked.

Jojo sat up; he blinked, once, then twice, "The last thing I remember is riding out with TactifulBelt and AngelOfDeath. Then I woke up here."

Orion motioned for the other AquaCrafters not to draw their weapons.

"It's like there is a fuzzy spot in my memory. Wait, has TactifulBelt or AngelOfDeath returned yet?" Jojo asked, worry creeping into his voice.

"No, not yet." Orion replied.

Orion stared out into the horizon and wondered what could have happened during the time between when Jojo left and now.

. . .

AngelOfDeath woke with a start. He looked around and remembered where he was. Gestroyer was waiting by the lava moats. Gestroyer had combined the Heart of the Sea and the Trident, creating the Aqua Weapon again, which he was holding like a staff. He was staring into the Heart of the Sea as if he were watching something.

"No! How could you fail! Wait why isn't this thing working anymore?" Gestroyer raged as he watched the image of Jojo vanish from the Heart of the Sea.

AngelOfDeath was careful not to move, in case Gestroyer realized he was alive. Then AngelOfDeath heard another voice.

"Ah, so your enchantment of Jojo didn't work. You really aren't as good as Flamecat then," TheHappyBranch said from somewhere AngelOfDeath couldn't see.

Gestroyer started, then turned around to see THB on the hill above them.

"Have you been there the entire time?" Gestroyer exclaimed in shock.

"It takes a lot more than the Heart of the Sea and a fancy stick to kill me. I've seen all of it—from the killing TactifulBelt and AngelOfDeath to Jojo. Guess there are ways to get rid of the evil version of someone without having to have an entire eclipse," TheHappyBranch said.

"If you were standing there the entire time, then why wouldn't you try and stop me?" Gestroyer asked in confusion.

"Wow, you really don't know me, do you? I am not who you think I am. Now hand over that Aqua Weapon," THB said quietly, but it was a command.

"Excuse me?" Gestroyer said.

"You heard me." THB held out her hand.

"You would have to force me," Gestroyer replied.

"Fine, have it your way," THB said.

She jumped into the air and launched two arrows with one pull of the bow. Gestroyer quickly deflected them. As she landed, she rolled. Then she turned around and attacked Gestroyer with two swords. She was too close for Gestroyer to use the Trident very well, and too quick for him to get many hits in. Eventually she managed to dislodge the Heart of the Sea from the Trident. She dropped one of her swords and picked it up, while blocking a blow from the Trident with her remaining sword. She then leaped back out of Gestroyer's reach.

She dropped her other sword, too, in order to fully use the Heart of the Sea. Using the orb, she shot a powerful beam of energy at Gestroyer, which he blocked by spinning the Trident in a circle. Now it was a battle of wills. With unlimited power at their fingertips, it was who could be most creative with their power. She ended the beam and allowed him to counterattack. He shot a jet beam of water at her from the tip of the Trident, which she just redirected with the Heart of the Sea back at him. The force knocked him back. TheHappyBranch seemed to know that the Trident was merely a director of the power, and the Heart of the Sea was the one with the real power. With this knowledge, she could defeat Gestroyer. It came in handy to study ancient texts about these powers.

She walked over to Gestroyer and summoned another beam of energy and launched it at Gestroyer. He blocked the attack with the Trident, straining with the effort. Energy forces flew past him on either side of the Trident.

"Surrender, you can't win!" TheHappyBranch exclaimed.

"Never!" Gestroyer replied, groaning inwardly.

"If you hand over the Trident to me right now, I will not tell the others of your treachery," THB promised.

"And why would I believe you? You're an AquaCrafter, through and through," Gestroyer said.

"I am loyal to no one except myself. I help others when I can and take revenge on those who wrong me. And I will not break this promise as long as you stop attacking people," TheHappyBranch spoke strongly.

Gestroyer persisted for a moment more, then said, "Fine. I give in this time."

THB ended the beam and grabbed the Trident from an exhausted Gestroyer.

"You made the right decision," she said.

AngelOfDeath watched as she turned around.

"It seems like we are not alone. AngelOfDeath, I am glad to know that you aren't dead," THB said.

AngelOfDeath began to get up; he had to get out of here if she decided he was a threat. No one was able to defeat the one wielding the ultimate weapon.

She turned back to Gestroyer. "As I promised, no one will know of your treachery from me. I am giving you a second chance. Do you understand? Do with it as you wish but I will not be giving any more. Therefore, I will have to clear the memory of AngelOfDeath of these moments."

AngelOfDeath stared at her in confusion, horror, and a look no better described as *who is she*?

TheHappyBranch then went to AngelOfDeath and using the energy from the Heart of the Sea, cleared his memory of the battle. It was an elven technique she knew from her past. Then she walked with him to the rest of the AquaCrafters, leaving Gestroyer alone with nothing but his own defeat.

When they came in sight of the AquaCrafters, some of them ran up to TheHappyBranch and AngelOfDeath, and started asking dozens of questions. TheHappyBranch waited until Orion, Jojo, and Starpig arrived.

"THB, you're back," Orion nodded acknowledgment to her. "Where is Gestroyer? What happened?"

TheHappyBranch spoke evenly, choosing her words carefully. "Gestroyer and I settled our differences. And we learned it's a bad idea if we keep the Heart of the Sea and the Trident together. That's what caused Jojo to go berserk."

"So, you know about that," Orion commented.

"Yes," THB replied, "Here, this belongs to the AquaCrafters."

She handed the Heart of the Sea to Orion. But when she didn't hand over the Trident, Orion gave her a questioning look.

She looked back at him without smiling. "Again, it's a bad idea for these to be even a thousand blocks close together. Someone could cause too much damage. I will keep the Trident safe. Also, I found AngelOfDeath," she explained.

"Did you find TactifulBelt?" Jojo asked.

She shook her head.

There was silence among the AquaCrafters. Jojo's face showed a certain heaviness. He was the one that had led TactifulBelt to his doom.

"Well then. We have some things that need sorting out," Starpig commented, trying to change the mood. But the AquaCrafters were still silent and downcast.

Chapter 27: The Peace Treaty

All the AquaCraft Council members as well as most of the other AquaCrafters gathered in the AquaCraft HQ. The meeting was very disorganized. AquaCrafters were crammed into the council chambers or in the floors below. After so many weeks of conflict, it was difficult to find an agreement on what to do next. Every single AquaCrafter was somewhere in or around the headquarters. It was rare for so many people to be in one place. Especially in AquaCraft.

Inside the council chambers, voices erupted into chaos...

"Who is in charge now?" someone asked.

"The city has fallen into ruin; we can't live here anymore!" someone else complained.

"What are we going to do next?" another person asked.

The torrent of questions, complaints, and statements overwhelmed Orion. It seemed like an impossible task; how would they move on from this? How could they prevent another conflict, whether that involved the ultimate weapons or not? Orion couldn't seem to find the place to start.

At last, ArcticCat stood up. He was a lean, somber figure, and he commanded respect. "Everyone, everyone, please settle down. We won't solve anything if we are all shouting at each other. We should have learned that by now!" He stood there silently watching until everyone had quieted down. Then he looked at Jojo.

Jojo stood up from where he was seated at the council table. The rest of the AquaCrafters that weren't council members were gathered around the table or throughout the room.

Jojo said, "ArcticCat is right. We shouldn't be fighting among ourselves."

"Indeed," Orion agreed, relieved that things were finally calming down. "I think that first we should list the issues we are facing. There is the matter of the ultimate weapon, we have the city in ruins, what else..."

"Also, who will lead us now?" ArcticCat suggested.

"Thank you, ArcticCat. Who will lead us now? These are only a few of the issues we are all facing," Orion continued, "Now let's all start brainstorming ideas for solutions to each of these issues."

"Don't forget, how are we going to prevent conflicts like this in the future?" Fution added thoughtfully.

Jojo looked over at Orion across the table. They were old friends and old enemies. For a moment the tension between them wavered, then died down. "What would you think of a peace treaty?" Jojo offered. "We were going to make one anyway. There could be terms to the treaty that everyone has to agree upon."

Orion started nodding. "Yeah, that could work. But what would the terms be?"

"No more war among ourselves?" Cicer suggested.

"Yeah, but how could we enforce that?" ArcticCat asked.

The room went silent for a moment. Then Orion spoke up.

"The council members were discussing an idea earlier; we need a way to settle our disagreements without them resulting in war. Maybe the solution involves a diplomatic democracy, just like what we were in the process of discussing before we were interrupted," he suggested.

"But I thought the whole point of AquaCraft was that it wouldn't have a government in the same way other realms do. Otherwise, we wouldn't be any different than the other realms," someone shouted from beyond the council table.

"Yeah, AquaCraft is supposed to give freedom to its members," someone else added.

Orion looked thoughtful. "Well, what if we make it so all of the AquaCrafters have some say in the government? We might have to have some rules or regulations that prevent all-out war, but neither do we want an oppressive government."

"So then, we need to have a small government, but limit the government's power. It could work as long as there aren't too many AquaCrafters. It would get more difficult if there were too many of us," Cicer responded.

"But it would work for now. We can always figure that out down the road if we get bigger. But we need a solution for now. What does everyone think about that?" Orion asked.

Jojo replied, "Possibly. But we would still need a leader to organize things, only they can't have too much power."

"We could have a mayor! Just in charge of the main city? We could hold elections every month and rotate the person who is the mayor that way," Orion exclaimed excitedly.

Everyone thought about the concept.

"That might work!" ArcticCat replied. There were others around the room starting to nod.

"Then, if everyone agrees, we should sign a treaty to declare the new system," Orion said, preparing to tally votes.

Fution still looked troubled. "What about the city, though? It's fallen into ruin; it would take ages to rebuild it. And we certainly don't have the supplies here."

"We can rebuild! If we work together, it won't take long," Cicer insisted.

TheHappyBranch, who had stayed silent for a while, spoke up for the first time. "I think we are forgetting something. What about the ultimate weapon? As I have said before, it would be bad if the Heart of Sea and the Trident stayed too close. Not only because they would be tempting to use, but also because the power can corrupt."

"TheHappyBranch is right," AngelOfDeath said. "And what happened to the Nether Star?"

"The Nether Star! How could we forget!" Orion exclaimed.

"Does anyone even know where that is?" Jojo asked.

Orion looked around the room, just as everyone else also did so. No one moved or made a sound.

"It doesn't seem like anyone knows where it is. I don't think we can do much about it except hope that it is lost where no one can find it," ArcticCat said helplessly.

Orion said, "I hate being so helpless about this, but I tend to agree with ArcticCat. We need to focus on what we do know. How can we keep the weapons apart from each other and also keep them safe? We can't be in two places at once."

The room was again silent.

"Unless we can," THB said quietly.

Orion stared at her. "What do you mean?"

"I mean, what if I stayed here in the city. It's obviously in no shape to be used as a home for all these people. The AquaCrafters need to move on. I could hide and guard the Trident pretty well in the ruins of the city. The AquaCrafters obviously need a new home; you could take the Heart of the Sea with the AquaCrafters wherever you go and use it in case there is another attack on AquaCraft..." TheHappyBranch explained.

"But what about you? That would mean leaving you behind while the rest of the AquaCrafters continue without you," Orion began.

Jojo interrupted. His expression was serious. "But it would work. It seems like the most suitable solution."

"Yeah," Starpig agreed, "It would solve all our problems. We could start anew, find a new better place to live, leave all this behind, and set up a new government system."

Orion didn't say anything. He was looking at THB with a question in his eyes. She looked back at him steadily, as though trying to reassure him. Finally, he turned to the rest of the room and reluctantly nodded. The tenseness in the room slowly relaxed. Now they could focus on the treaty, what it would entail, how to say it in writing, how to make everyone understand it. Then everyone would have to sign on.

"ArcticCat," said Orion finally, "could you write up the treaty for us?"

Everyone turned to look at ArcticCat. "It would be an honor," he said simply.

After the meeting finally dispersed, Orion left to find THB. He found her sitting alone underneath one of the trees near the HQ. As he drew closer, she stood up.

"Orion," She greeted him.

"THB, why are you staying behind? Surely someone else would be willing to do so. We could at least leave someone else behind with you." Orion questioned, confused.

"Orion, you know that wouldn't work. I always work alone. Well, almost always. It's who I am. And I am more separate from the rest of the AquaCrafters, not so much one of them. Her tone was pretty matter of fact. Then she smiled at Orion slightly. "You could visit me?" Her voice lifted.

Orion thought about this for a bit, but he knew she was right. "OK, if you insist on this," Orion finally said grudgingly.

"Thank you for understanding," THB said.

Orion held up a hand. "One more thing. At the beginning of the meeting, you explained to the AquaCrafters what transpired with you and Gestroyer, but I am not buying it. There is something you are hiding from me," Orion added.

Orion thought he saw something change on her face, but he might have imagined it.

"Well," she began, "it wasn't completely peaceful. We fought for a while, but I beat him. Then I let him go, and just like I told the others, he did leave AquaCraft after that. I even went back to make sure he wasn't lurking, but sure enough, he was gone."

Orion wasn't sure he had heard the entire truth, but he trusted THB and didn't push her.

"Thanks, THB," Orion said.

"Of course," TheHappyBranch replied, then walked away.

Epilogue

The decision to leave was unanimous in the end. It would be a huge enterprise, but the AquaCrafters had been conducting their preparations for a few days already. It was difficult to leave. Each day when they were about to leave, there was something else that needed to be done. Everyone had to make sure they had everything they wanted to take with them. Not only that, but many of the AquaCrafters had decided not to come. This only delayed things even more. Some of them didn't want to leave because of how attached they were to what they had built or didn't want to journey even deeper into AquaCraft.

After the treaty had been signed, the council members gathered (except for THB) to discuss in which direction they should journey. To the west was the edge of AquaCraft. To the north was a frozen tundra. So no for both of those. To the south was one of the only deserts in AquaCraft. There were only wastelands and sand in that direction. That left the east. Of all the places in AquaCraft, the east had been the least explored. No one had wanted to journey too far into AquaCraft yet. Neither did anyone know what existed in that direction. They only knew that the AquaCraft river that ran from the edge of AquaCraft in the west came from somewhere in the east. And water didn't come from nowhere. They had decided to follow the river upstream to the east.

Besides, Orion, ArcticCat, Jojo, Starpig, and a few others wanted to see what was at the center of AquaCraft. They had only settled on the very edge of the realm. They had yet to explore the majority of it. But then again, they didn't want to travel too far from the original city. If they did so, they would leave society behind and be in the wilderness without being able to get supplies from the other realms. Therefore, they would travel only far enough to separate the Heart of the Sea from the Trident and settle on a new piece of land.

Now that all the plans had been made, and the preparations and packing were almost complete, Orion and the AquaCrafters took the first step. They had set camp on the farthest east side of the city against the river. TheHappyBranch and a few of the AquaCrafters that were staying behind came to say their farewells.

Orion exited his tent and walked over to where a small group had gathered. THB, ArcticCat, Jojo, Starpig, Cicer, and Fution were standing upon the grass talking in bright voices. As Orion neared, he heard what they were saying.

"We have been through a lot together. And I'm glad that I have been able to be a part of all these adventures," ArcticCat said gratefully.

"Yeah, and now we are moving on to a new chapter in AquaCraft history! Soon we will be going on a lot of more adventures!" Cicer exclaimed happily.

AngelOfDeath was standing a little apart and had been unusually quiet. Now he spoke up. "There's one who will not be with us," he said sadly. "TactifulBelt. He fought bravely for us, but now he is gone."

Everyone sobered, and there was a quiet spell.

Then Jojo looked from AngelOfDeath to Orion. "Ah Orion, glad that you could join us!"

As Orion walked into the circle of friends, he said, "Well, the preparations are basically complete. We can leave whenever people are ready."

TheHappyBranch looked straight at Orion as she spoke. "It's too bad you couldn't stay longer, but I know you have to get going soon or you might never leave!"

ArcticCat laughed. "You're right about that one. We need to get going soon if we want to travel while the sun is still shining."

"Agreed. We want to make sure to get going soon because we don't know how far we are going," Fution added more seriously.

"Then let's go," Starpig said, nodding to Fution and Orion.

Starpig walked off with Fution toward where the horses were tied.

"Bye, THB!" Jojo said, waving before walking off to join them.

THB replied, "farewell!"

"See you around, THB," Cicer said.

ArcticCat said his farewells and also left, leaving Orion alone with THB.

"I'm afraid this is where our paths will part ways," TheHappyBranch said kindly.

"Goodbye, THB. I hope we will meet again someday. Watch over the city ruins and the AquaCrafters staying there," Orion said.

"I will! Bye," THB responded, and waved.

Orion left and went to join the others.

Orion, the original AquaCrafters, AngelOfDeath, and five others had saddled up horses, and they set out along the river, following it upstream into the unknown. They traveled for many days. During that time, they passed through great valleys, lush forests, and peaceful marshes. Still, the river continued. They needed to travel for another significant distance before Orion would be satisfied that the Heart of the Sea was far enough from the Trident. Besides, many of these places weren't suitable to build a new city. It wasn't bad in the daytime, but in the night, dozens of monsters would roam the countryside. The farther they went into AquaCraft, the wilder it seemed to become. They needed to find a place with relative peace and safety from the monsters and unknown wild creatures that might lurk in these mysterious forests. On the peaceful marshes, the ground was all soggy and wet. Definitely not the best place to build something.

As the week passed, Orion began to notice the season change. It grew warmer, and the flowers disappeared. They were replaced with lush leaves on the trees and shrubs. It was almost summer. They had been moving through AquaCraft for just over three months. As they were walking across the land—at this moment they were resting the horses—Orion noticed ArcticCat writing something in a book.

Orion looked over and asked, "What's that?"

"Oh, this?" ArcticCat replied. "Well, you know, after all we have been through, I thought it might be a good idea to record all that has happened these last few months. It might be helpful if we have a recorded history of AquaCraft."

"Hmm, not a bad idea," Orion commented.

"Yeah, I thought not. But the only thing I can't figure out is where to start the book. I could start when we all arrived in AquaCraft, but that wouldn't explain why we came here in the first place," ArcticCat explained.

Orion looked thoughtful for a second, then said, "Start with Evenglade. We could always add the reasons for coming later. Cause everyone has come to AquaCraft for different reasons."

"Good idea," ArcticCat replied.

As they traveled on, Orion began to notice a faint blue line in the distance. As they neared, he began to see more clearly what was in front of them.

Then Fution exclaimed, "Water ahead!"

As they moved closer, a giant lake appeared out of the landscape ahead of them. That was what was feeding the river in the first place! Walking on, they came to the shore and stopped.

"Now what?" Cicer asked.

"I'm not sure. The lake seems too long to go around," Orion said.

"Hey, I think I see something," Starpig said, pointing to the center of the lake, "I think it's an island."

"You're right! And it would be perfect to defend from," Jojo agreed.

"Let's go out and check it out," Fution suggested.

"I hate leaving the horses behind though," ArcticCat said.

"That's OK, I will stay behind and watch them," AngelOfDeath volunteered.

"Thanks," Orion said, staring at AngelOfDeath for a moment. He turned his attention to the rest of the AquaCrafters. "Well, everyone? Are you ready to go check out that island?"

Everyone nodded. Then they gathered some wood from a few trees nearby and crafted up some boats that could be used to row them across the lake. Everyone except for AngelOfDeath got into the boats, two people per boat. Then they began the tiring row across the lake. Each stroke brought them a little bit closer to the island. It took some time, but they finally managed to reach the shore. There they realized that this wasn't an ordinary island. It was a mushroom island. These special islands were so special because no hostile monsters could spawn on them. They were practically the safest places in the world. They were exceedingly rare, and rare animals also lived on the island. Red-and-white looking creatures that looked a lot like cows lived on the island. They were called mooshrooms in Minecraft terminology. They were peaceful creatures, but if struck by lightning, they would turn into a brown mooshroom which could give special potion effects to a person nearby. A special kind of purple soil called mycelium covered the island.

The AquaCrafters slowly got out and began to climb onto the island. Orion however, hesitated as if unsure whether it was safe to touch the mycelium.

"What's wrong, Orion?" Starpig asked curiously.

"It's nothing really," Orion began, "It's just...I really don't like mushrooms."

"Oh, is that what this is about?" ArcticCat laughed. "Come on Orion, we can always get rid of it later."

"Fine, but I don't want to stay here any longer than I have to," Orion complained.

As they explored the island, they realized it was fairly large. In fact, it was large enough to build a small city on top of it. Not only that, but it was safe enough because of the special nature of these islands. It was, in fact, the perfect place for a city.

Jojo turned to Orion. "This would be perfect! Just imagine walkways running through the island connecting different buildings of the city. It's perfect!"

"Well, not perfect..." Orion muttered, lifting up his feet carefully.

"Hey, we can always remove the mycelium," Jojo suggested. "I prefer grass, too."

"OK, then. I'm convinced. Let's get AngelOfDeath and gather the others. We need to begin plans for this city," Orion replied.

The AquaCrafters gathered around and began to talk excitedly. Each of them had ideas for building plans. To start with they would build a structure made of quartz from off the coast of the island. They would use their remaining materials to build a grand staircase up to a magnificent piece of architecture that would soon become the new center of AquaCraft. They planned large pillars to come down to support the platform. Decorative spires would lead upwards to make it seem larger than it actually was. Here would be the new meeting place of the AquaCrafters, at least until a more permanent structure could be built.

They set up camp nearby. For the next few days, they would explore the surrounding area and map it out. Of course, they still had to gather resources for the construction of the new city. But that was only one of the many new challenges they would face in order to create a new society.

Now Orion sat on a pier watching the sun set. They were in a completely new place, far from anyone else, far from the old city. And now they were about to begin anew. He wondered how TheHappyBranch and the other AquaCrafters were faring in the old city. He wondered how they would rebuild the city. But most of all, he wondered what the future would hold. More adventures? More battles? More wars? Or would they finally find peace? Orion sighed; only time would tell. He watched as the sun finally went down below the horizon, then got up, and walked back to camp.

And so, the AquaCrafters had made it to a new home, deeper in the vast realm of AquaCraft. A new city would rise up from the ground, and a new society would begin. There they would hopefully find peace and prosperity. At least for a while... For a new age had begun. A new season, the season of summer, in the land of AquaCraft...